I0655010

SOULS OF VIRIDIAN

Ayin Weaver

NovelWeaver Press

ISBN 0974233986
ISBN 978-0974233987
Library of Congress Control Number: 2018953539

Cover Art: painting by N. Reimer, NovelWeaver Press
Photography: Leiah Bowden
Interior & Cover Design: Jo-Anne H. Rosen

Souls of Viridian is a work of fiction. All characters, names, places, events
are fictional and/or are used fictitiously; resemblance to real persons,
locales and/or events is coincidental.

Source notes: Chants, songs, musical references/titles used fictitiously in this work are not
subject to this book's copyright and/or may be in the public domain.

Author note: Source information, page 265

NovelWeaver Press
Sebastopol, California

www.novelweaverpress.com
1st edition, 2019
Printed in the United States of America.

Available on amazon.com and at local bookstores.

FOR MY FAMILY

Books by Ayin Weaver

Bleed Through, a novel
Blackberries for Oly, poems

Acknowledgments

Souls of Viridian, my second novel, could not have been written without the exuberant encouragement and support of my friends, family and creative colleagues. In particular, I wish to acknowledge my writing group partner, Leiah Bowden, whose keen eye, intellect, lightness of heart, and great cooking, enabled me to embrace the writing discipline as we met Friday afternoons for two and a half years. She listened to every first draft reading of each chapter, through the growing pains, and ah-ha moments—empathizing with my struggles, celebrating my successes and assisting with editing and photography. She was and is a true inspiration. Also, great appreciation to my friends, Claire Etienne and J. Longfellow for their friendship, camaraderie, eager support and expertise in editing and assisting in the navigation of historical maps and language translations. Much thanks and gratitude to my other writing pals, Batja Cates and Korie Shokmalli for their attentive insight, editing and/or proofreading; to professional storyteller, Olive Hackett-Shaughessy for her enduring friendship and wisdom, as well as her supportive enthusiasm and that of the FW storytelling group. To the many professional writers and workshop directors at the International Women's Writing Guild, especially Linda Bergman, Jan Phillips, Eunice Scarfe, Alice Orr, Dorothy Randall Gray and Vickie McIntyre—thank you for bolstering my spirit and encouraging me as a writer.

Special thanks to Redwood Writers, especially Robbi Sommers Bryant, for her editing expertise; much appreciation to designer Jo-Anne H. Rosen for her artistry in the book's interior design and adaptation of a painting by my alter ego, to create the book cover.

Last, but not least, to my immediate family whose love and devotion means the world to me. And to my extended family of supportive and creative friends, especially Lucy, Roberta, Abby, Danielle, Barbara, Sharona, Jean, Skyheart sisters and my life-long pals, Diana, Stephen, Marilyn and Paula—much appreciation for inspiring me with your talent and courage. Thank you for always being supportive of my creative spirit.

The Families

Rachel Rita Goldberg
Born 1956, Queens, New York;
1975, marries Joseph Padini, becoming;
Rachel Rita Padini

Michael – brother
Gary – Michael's partner
Nakisha – Gary's neice
Theresa & Kevin – daughter & son-in-law,

The Strega's Daughter, Maria
Born 1405, Po Valley, Italy
Adopted 1415 by Chaim and Bella di Moise Katzav, becoming:
Davina
The Strega's Daughter

Francesca – mother
Chaim & Bella – adoptive parents
Lupe & Bianca – cousins
Sarah – midwife

Mademoiselle Nicolette Marchand
Born 1754, Paris, France
Married 1779 to The Baron, Pierre Etienne L'ecuyer, becoming:
Nicolette L'ecuyer
Jean Paul Marchand – father
Claude Jacques Gustav – friend
Pierre Etienne L'ecuyer – husband
Cherise – handmaid
Claudine – servant

Rita Kerner
Born 1947, Brooklyn, NY

Cleo – Rita's partner
Noah – Rita's son
Donna & Sharon – friends
Marla – Rita's friend
Irene & Gregory – Rita's sister & brother-in-law
Kelly – Cleo's cousin

Professor Emari
AllSouls College, Pleiades

Graduating Class

SOULS OF VIRIDIAN

CHAPTER I

The Strega's Daughter

July 1415, Po Valley, Italy

Francesca took two clay jars from the herb shelf. She held each jar while her nine-year old child, Maria, scooped out dried knapweed and comfrey onto the counter. Mother and daughter took turns grinding one after the other with mortar and pestle. Francesca brushed dark strands of hair from her forehead as she looked down to observe the finished texture. Satisfied, she measured out specific amounts of each in a stoneware bowl, adding just enough oil to make a healing poultice for their precious cow's wound. The animal's infection had grown worse since the attack three days ago. Her torn hide, her flesh had been cleaned, but the puncture wound made by the wolf's teeth was deep. It had been a miracle that the old girl had survived at all.

"It is important to measure just the right amount, so the herbs will heal," Francesca explained. "Then we'll put clay from the river bed on cheese cloth and have a different poultice overnight. One day herbs, then one night clay. Then repeat," Francesca explained to her daughter, while she mixed the knapweed and comfrey with a spoonful of olive oil. Maria watched her mother warm the mixture in a pot over the hearth, adding a scoop full of bee's wax to make a healing salve. "Now we will let it cool." Francesca said, pouring the mixture into a wide-neck bottle.

Maria poured a little cool well-water from their pitcher into another bowl and placed the bottle in it as Francesca instructed, then set it on the shady windowsill.

"Here, Maria." Francesca handed Maria the remaining remnants in the jars of comfrey and knapweed. "Blend what we have left of these together with the pestle and mortar. After we're done, you can go down to the meadow and gather some more herbs for tomorrow." Francesca scoured the contents of her herb shelf to see what else she might need. "Ah," she said holding a few empty jars. "I will also need some yarrow and borage if you find any, my dear. The jar of valerian root is also empty." She opened her handmade plant book. Its worn, yellowed pages made mostly from shaved, soaked and dried tree bark made a crinkling sound when she turned the fragile pages.

Francesca had drawings of all the plants she'd found in the meadow and forest, and those she had cultivated herself. Using a mixture of charcoal and melted beeswax, she had fashioned suitable writing implements with which she was able to draw symbols of her inventory, measures for concoctions and cures, keeping records preserved. She had managed to color some of the drawings of plants with tinctures made from beets, crushed green leaves, marigold and indigo flowers. Maria loved looking over her mother's shoulder at Francesca's designs.

"Can I go to the river to get the clay too, Mama?"

Francesca paused and looked at her only child. Maria was growing up fast, though she remained small-boned and petite, much like Francesca. With her big brown eyes and a braid of thick hair, Maria stood only four feet tall. Francesca was not worried though. She herself had not reached her full height of five feet until she turned fifteen years old.

Maria was precocious—smarter than her years it often seemed to her mother. Francesca was proud of her daughter, grateful for her good nature, especially since her husband's death, when Maria was seven years old. Wife and daughter had both suffered his loss. Maria had rebounded learning to survive by watching her mother's resilience, her strength.

Perhaps one day when things were not so dangerous, Francesca thought, they would find a way to move to the city beyond the mountains, so her child's future would be blessed with a husband and children of her own.

"Tomorrow, if you promise to be very careful and not stay too long," Francesca said.

"Oh yes, Mama, I promise." Maria eyes twinkled.

"Very well, let's have dinner and get some rest," Francesca handed Maria the half loaf of bread that was left in the cupboard. From the still hot pot hanging over the hearth she ladled savory vegetable soup into two bowls, while Maria set the plates and spoons on the table, not forgetting the jug of wine.

Before they sat down Francesca walked across the room and reached under the bed for a covered woven basket. As she did every evening, she took two candles from it, along with a small wooden box that contained a piece of white cloth with blue letters stitched along the edge and a six-pointed star in the middle. "Your father brought us here from another land, before you were born. This piece of cloth is all I have left of that life, of my parents, your grandparents." Francesca had repeated the story so many times since Maria's father had died, that it had become part of their evening ritual.

Setting the candles on the table, Francesca placed the cloth on her head while Maria brought a burning twig from the hearth and lit the candles. Then Maria stood by her mother's side as Francesca began to pray. Maria closed her eyes listening and swaying to the melodic chanting of Francesca's prayer.

When Francesca was done, she smothered the candles, squirreling them away along with the cloth into its box, the basket and safely under the bed. It was only after this clandestine ceremony that they could happily eat their meal. She had never uttered the word "Jew" in front of Maria. It was best the child did not know, she thought.

The next day after chores Maria waited for instructions, eager to prove herself responsible enough to go down to the river for clay.

"Just scoop up enough wet clay in this bucket and come back promptly," Francesca reminded, handing Maria a cloth bag containing shears for cutting plants and a small shovel for scooping clay.

Grinning, Maria took the bucket from under the table. It was the first time she would venture out alone to the river beyond the meadow. She felt all grown up. But she did notice a sudden shadow of fear that swept over Francesca's face. "Don't worry, I will be careful, Mama. I promise."

"I know you will, my dear one." She patted her child's head of dark hair. Francesca did not want to scare her daughter. Maria was still too young to be told of the rumors—of women being kidnapped and killed, even burned as witches for the simple act of healing. "You go now, child. Just pick the plants, scoop the clay and come right back. If anyone sees you and asks what you're doing, you tell them we need clay for bricks and the wildflowers are a present for your mother—do you understand?"

"Why, Mother? Are our poultice recipes a secret?"

"Yes, dear, that they are. They are just for healing illness, like those for the women who come to me sometimes for their children, and the kind of wounds our dear cow has. Our secret recipe of herbs and clay poultices will help our dear cow, so in a few days she will be well enough to give clean milk again."

Francesca fingered the small wooden cross that hung from a chord around her neck, one that had protected her from persecution years ago. Then she took her daughter's hand and they walked down the short path to the edge of a narrow woods. She hugged Maria before the child continued on alone into the trees and out of sight. Francesca mouthed a silent prayer, putting dark thoughts out of her mind. It was no crime to pick wildflowers and scoop clay from river-beds, she thought as she went to attend to their sick animal.

Unafraid, Maria looked back only once, before she meandered along the path through the woods. She stayed alert as her mother had taught her, but was not concerned about wolves from the mountains this early in the day. She luxuriated in the smell of pine, the sound of birds and the occasional sight of scampering squirrels chasing each other.

Before long, she reached the edge of the woods where an expansive meadow rolled its way down to the river. The meadow's blooming red poppies, yellow dandelions, and white lace dotted the landscape of tall green grasses growing knee high, waving in the soft breeze. Maria could see that recent summer rains had widened the river's course at the natural lull of the land and the current was stronger than usual. Diamonds of sunlight danced on its turbulent surface.

Skipping with the delight of freedom, blue skies and sunshine, Maria scanned the hillside for yarrow, knapweed and comfrey plants. On a rocky ledge at the top of the meadow, she spotted the airy leaves, white buds and flowers of yarrow. Halfway down the hill in the shade beneath a large old oak tree, comfrey grew wild and plentiful. She pulled the shears from her satchel, snipping the stalks and white flowers of yarrow, and blue-violet flowers, spiny-leaves of knapweed. By the tree, she cut furry comfrey leaves with their purple buds and tucked them into her bag. She pulled dandelions and wild scallions from the rich soil as well. Wouldn't her mother be pleased, Maria thought. She carefully put her shears away, then scanned the ground for some old acorns from which to make flour and bits of oak bark for her mother's little book.

Maria continued down the hill to the river, her satchel of natural treasures slung over her shoulder, her bucket and shovel in her hands ready to dig the soft clay.

When she reached the river, she found a nook perfect for digging out some clay without going too deep into the water. Seeing how fast the river moved, she dared not venture too far. Maria plunged her shovel into the moist clay and lifted her first small glob, slipping it into her bucket with ease. More confident, she took another bigger scoop. She had not dug for long before she thought she heard something—people's voices she realized. They were men's voices.

She looked up to see four men in the distance trudging along the river bank, headed toward her. Maria threw her shovel into the pail. She would grab her satchel laying on the shore and leave before they saw her. But her feet were stuck in the soft clay and water pooled around them. With great effort she pulled one booted foot at a time out of the muck. But she was not fast enough. As she reached her satchel, the men approached.

Maria stopped and looked at them. They were soldiers. Two of them were half dragging a third. The fourth soldier carried their meager gear and weapons. Marie could see that the injured soldier had a large festering wound on his right thigh. Dried blood coated his dirty, tattered uniform. At first, they did not appear to notice Maria, even though they stopped only yards from where she stood in her clay-caked boots, her smock soaked along the hem.

The two soldiers lay the third wounded soldier down in the grass and sat down near him. The last one set down his weapons and gear, and rummaged for what meager rations they had. He brought the injured man some water from the river in a metal cup. Only then did they notice Maria standing like a statue nearby.

"You, there—girl," one of them yelled to her. "Come here. What do you have in that satchel?"

Maria's heart pounded. Frightened, she obeyed, moving a little closer. "I have wildflowers for my mother," she said meekly.

"Let's see." The tallest one stood up and walked toward her. He grabbed her satchel and examined the contents, taking the scallions.

"No other food? Where do you live? Where's your family? We need to get food and help. One of our soldiers is hurt."

Maria's mind raced. She instinctively knew she could not take them back to her mother. They might take everything or hurt them.

"I can tend to him," she said. Her words came without forethought.

"You?" the tall one laughed, an arrogant demeaning laugh. The soldier holding the injured one's head up on his lap, snorted.

"I can." Maria eagerly pulled some plants from her satchel. "All he needs is a poultice to draw out the infection. I know how to do that," she said.

The men looked at her wide-eyed and mumbled among themselves. "You sure you can help him? You some kind of *strega*, a witch, are you?"

Maria had never heard the word *witch*. She hesitated. "No, we have a sick cow and my mother uses these plants to make her better." Maria's innocence was apparent. Not understanding the consequence of exposing her secret, she held out a handful of comfrey leaves.

Once agreed that she could make a poultice for the injured soldier, Maria set about mashing the flowers and leaves with her fingers and adding water. She held the wad of mashed plants in her palm, massaging it into a ball. Instead of oil she added clay to her mixture to hold it together and make it a strong enough concoction to draw the oozing puss from the infected wound. She set the mixture of clay and herbs down in the grass for a moment. Tearing the wet end of her smock, she maneuvered the poultice into the strip of the torn threadbare fabric. With trepidation, she approached the injured soldier and placed it on his open flesh. The smell of his wound and putrid clothing repulsed her, but she kept her hands steady.

The man grimaced and groaned as Maria wrapped the clay and herb-packed fabric securely in place like she had learned to do. Done, she stood up quickly and walked back to her pail and satchel. "Leave it on for a day and it will help it heal." she said. Maria wasn't sure if that would be long enough. Nevertheless, she had done her best. She backed up very slowly, hoping the men would not notice her movements. Satisfied they were no longer paying attention to her, she turned and climbed the hill as fast as she could go. As she ran back through the forest, dry clay flaked off her boots imprinting her path home.

Francesca paced back and forth. Her only child had not come home yet and it was getting late. Maria had been gone too long. The sun was at the top of the mountain, soon to set beyond its peak. Too distraught to sit still, Francesca put on her shawl and headed toward the woods. Just as she got to the edge of the forest, she saw Maria tramping through the trees.

"Maria!" she called out. Then she noticed her child's wet torn dress, the clay and dirt on her face, her hands, in her hair. Francesca's heart jumped into her throat. She reached for her daughter. "Maria, what has happened? Are you hurt?"

"Oh, Mama! I am so sorry. I am late. I didn't get all the plants...I mean I did, but I had to use them and the clay on the injured soldier. I did what you said, but they wanted to come here and take our food and..." Maria tried to catch her breath. "What is a witch, Mama?"

Francesca's eyes were wild. She checked her daughter for injuries. "Did they hurt you?"

"No, Mama. I fixed the soldier and ran home."

Francesca looked around like a hyper-vigilant animal trapped by prey. "Hush now, come we must hurry, Maria." Wrapping her own shawl around her child, she quickly ushered her daughter into their house. She washed Maria with warm water from the hearth's kettle and changed her into warm dry garments. Then, she took her own satchel and placed a few more dry garments inside, while Maria warmed herself by the fireplace. "Here Maria, soup and bread—eat this now. You will need your strength."

"Why, Mama? What is happening?"

"You must be very brave now, my daughter." Francesca's eyes filled with tears.

"Are you crying, Mama?"

"I love you Maria, but I must send you away my child. Those soldiers will come back. They will come here looking for us."

"Where will we go, Mama?" Maria cried.

"We can't go together, child." Francesca hugged her daughter and smoothed her hair to calm her distress. "Maria, you will go first, by yourself. When you get to the town beyond the mountains, find the church— a building with big doors and a cross on the roof. Ask for food and shelter—do you understand?"

"But Mama..." Tears dripped down Maria's cheeks. "Please Mama, don't be mad at me. I helped the soldier. They will not come here. Don't send me away," she sobbed.

Francesca held Maria close and kissed her face. "Don't cry my little one. I am sending you so you will be safe. I will be here if they come. This way I can keep them from finding you."

"Why can't we go together, Mama?"

Francesca knew she could not save both of them, if the soldiers found them together. They would not look for the child, if they could have her. "I will come afterward, Maria. I will take the animals to a safe place and then follow you, understand? Come now, we must go into the woods and follow the path to the fishing raft your father, God rest his soul, made on the old dock. It can still hold you without sinking."

"But that is far, Mama. It's getting dark and cold out. Can't we go in the morning?"

"It is safer now. Soon, the moonlight will help us." Francesca wrapped the rest of the bread and some hard cheese in a cloth and added it to the bundle. She took the small cross she wore around her neck and placed it on her beloved child with a silent prayer. Taking her skinning knife from the shelf, she wrapped it in her apron. "Come, hurry my little one."

October 1415
Outskirts of Padua, Italy, Home of Chaim & Bella di Moise Katzav

"If you wish to be my helper you must watch me carefully when I bake. Do you understand?" The old woman shook her head, looking at the girl, a waif, orphaned by tragedy. She felt sorry for her. Plucked from the river like a soggy rag doll, the half-drowned child had been filthy and malnourished, incoherent. The child screamed in her sleep. Nightmares about her mother who'd been left behind making remedies to heal her cow and images of soldiers coming to kill them filtered through her dream time. Dreams of drowning tortured the young one's rest. She'd wake gasping for air and crying inconsolably for her mother.

Bella remembered when Chaim had brought her home—only four months ago. He had laboriously carried into the house, wet and bedraggled, what could have been a sack of potatoes or a stray lamb wrapped in his overcoat, the coat he always wore when he went outdoors no matter the weather.

"What is that?" she had exclaimed, holding her hand to her heart when she could see perfectly well it was a child that he had painstakingly laid on the table. "My God, what have you done?" she gasped, running for blankets to cover this wet, shaking, half-dead little girl.

"I was walking along the river's edge as I always do at dawn, and I saw her floating just beneath the surface." Chaim wiped the child's face. "She was not breathing when I plucked her from the current. I was sure she was dead," he explained, wiping his own face and gray beard, while Bella removed the child's wet garments and bundled her in blankets.

The girl's teeth chattered, but she did not open her eyes. "I pushed on her back, turned her upside down, and she sputtered water and coughed," he continued. "She finally breathed. I was relieved she was alive." Chaim put his hand on her neck checking her pulse and listening to her breath. "She has a fever. I will prepare a tonic."

"Some warm broth, right away," Bella added.

They moved her to the bedroom that had been their son's before he died and laid her on the bed, tucking pillows under her head and around her, lest she fall off.

"We can't keep her here, Chaim. Where did she come from? She might be a gypsy or a Christian child. Her people might be looking for her right now. If the authorities find out...oh, God in heaven, Chaim! Jews kidnapping a Christian child is what they will think, Chaim!" Bella's voice raised an octave. "We must tell the authorities you found her in the river. They can take her to a convent, an orphan child." Perspiration trickled down Bella's forehead. She had suffered with bouts of anxiety ever since their son, Benjamin, had died unexpectedly at sixteen—ten years ago.

"I will pour you some wine, my dearest, to calm your nerves," Chaim offered.

"Please, Chaim. Tell the Rabbi, tell the church authorities. They will not find fault with you for a good deed, a mitzvah. You saved a life! Tell them!"

But Chaim had not listened to Bella. He'd cared for the child day after day. As she got stronger, he seemed more intent on keeping her. "Bella," Chaim instructed, "when someone comes to inquire for me, tell them I am away visiting a sick cousin in Vicenza. We will tell people this is the child of my sickly cousin who can no longer care for her. We have taken her in."

Bella shook her head. She resigned herself to Chaim's stubborn refusal to listen to reason. Gradually though, she came to understand him. With all his great skills as a scholar and healer, he had been unable to save his own son. Now he had a chance to redeem himself, to help this child.

"She is a miracle given to us from God, Bella. A chance to have a child again," Chaim exclaimed.

Chaim's plan had worked. Bella and Chaim's friends and relatives were none the wiser. In time, they had given their blessing and the girl, although exceptionally quiet during her waking hours, had been accepted as one of the community.

Bella kneaded the bread and spoke again to the child, who stood watching her new mother's every move. "My family have always been bakers," Bella continued. "My mother and grandmother made bread and confections for the community when we came to Italy many years ago. Now, I make baked goods from fresh ingredients. She pointed to her table. Here is goat's milk, eggs, butter, flour, salt, and honey. We add raisins when the grapes ripen, to sell at the market." She looked at the pale child. "Your past is not to be discussed with anyone. Do you understand?" Bella paused. "Here physicians and midwives do the healing and birthing. Your new father is looked up to by many of our community for his wisdom. He is a scholar."

"Yes." The child mumbled, looking down at her feet. "I made a terrible mistake," she whispered. "I'll never see my mother again." Tears streamed down her cheeks.

"It's not your fault child." Bella's voice softened. "There are bad people in the world. But you are not one of them." She put her hand on the child's shoulder until the little one stopped sobbing. "There now," Bella said, giving the girl a soft cloth to wipe her tears. "Watch as I knead the bread and you can add the magic ingredient." She handed the child a jar of golden liquid.

"When I was a little girl we lived in the mountains. Spring was a special time," Bella continued. "On the full moon in June, the women would go up the mountain to sing and call to the bees. They would sing and dance until a great swarm of bees came over the mountains from the South, from warmer lands to pollinate our plants, to help us so that all our crops and fruit trees would grow, to bring the magic of golden honey to us." Bella reminisced as she mixed the dough. "Every year I was so excited to see my grandmother and great aunts dress in costumes of reds and yellows, bright blues and green, and trek up into the hills with drums and tambourines. Then when the bees came, the whole village would have a great feast. Oh, how I remember those days! Praise the bees, our wonderful bees, and the honey of those warm summer days." Bella smiled.

"Now child, you add the honey and I will mix," she said warmly.

Soon the first batch of rolls and loaves of bread were finished baking. "Now, go upstairs to Papa Chaim's room. Here." The stout woman gave the child a full basket. "Take this warm bread to your new father. And here is some butter and extra honey for you too." The child followed instructions taking the basket of warm bread wrapped in muslin, a dish of butter and jar of honey from this stern, yet kind woman.

"Grazie," she said to her new mother, one old enough to be her grandmother.

White-haired Chaim sat hunched over his books at his small wooden desk in the musty attic study, his wiry beard looked longer than usual hanging down to the middle of his chest. His worn muslin shirt, stained with spots of last evening's dinner, smelled of sour goat milk. The long fingers of his weathered hands roamed over wrinkled paper, as if they alone could hold the memory of the letters written on the pages. He squinted, reading and mouthing silent incantations, rocking slightly back and forth. Morning sunlight poured through the small window over his shoulder and onto his studies. He didn't see the little one come up the ladder steps, until she stood before him. Distracted by the aroma of just-baked bread that hid in her basket, he looked up to find her young face staring at him. Maria remained silent. She waited.

"You remembered the butter, yes?" the old man asked, at once hearing the harshness in his own voice. He had not meant to sound accusatory. He was no longer used to speaking to a child. It seemed longer than ten years since his only child had died, leaving him and Bella bereft. "Come, sit here, little one." Chaim smiled and patted the low stool next to him. "We will have some bread and butter together."

The child sat obediently and handed the basket to Chaim. He pushed his books and papers aside and placed the basket in front of him. Then he broke up some bread and buttered it, handing his new daughter a piece and repeating the process for himself. "What name have you decided upon, my daughter?" he asked between bites. "Will it be Davina or maybe, Esther?"

"Tell me why I need a new name again, father?"

"Ah, yes it is confusing." Chaim paused. "You are safe now here with us. You have a new life in a new place, with a new family. So a new name would be a good thing." Chaim couldn't explain the wrath of the Church or his own community if they knew the child he'd found almost drowned in the river, almost dead, was a Christian child. He had dragged her from the water and saved her life. But he had taken off a small wooden cross still around her neck, before bringing her home to his Bella. To him, it was a miracle finding this child. He remembered the look of horror on Bella's face when he'd brought her home. He hoped, in time, his wife would feel how blessed they were to have received this secret gift from God. Together, they could help the child become part of their family, their community.

I like the name *Davina*, Father," Maria said hesitantly. "Can I be called Davina?" Her dark eyes sparkled for the first time in anticipation of trying on a new name.

"Davina it is then!" Chaim handed her another piece of buttered bread with some honey. "I think Mama Bella will like that one too." He poured some wine from his pitcher into a stoneware cup. *God has plans that people can't understand,* he thought, as he took a sip of the sweet nectar. God brought them this miracle, after all. And no one had ever come looking for her.

"Papa Chaim? Can I ask you what you do with the pages? Are you making a recipe?" Davina asked after she had swallowed her last bit of bread. "Mama Bella says we are bakers. Are you making a bread recipe?"

Chaim smiled. It was the first time he'd heard the child speak more than a few words. He had not expected her curiosity. Except for her nightmares, she had been so quiet for months. "Ah, yes it is kind of a recipe. I am just trying to figure out some numbers."

Davina laughed for the first time. Chaim was delighted. "Ah, you are recovering! Laughter is a good sign!"

"Those are funny numbers, Papa. They look like letters on the page, not numbers."

Chaim suddenly looked serious.

"You need to measure for recipes," Davina continued not noticing his demeanor.

"My mother, she…" Davina caught herself, but it was too late. A vivid picture flashed before her eyes of her mother Francesca rocking back and forth, with a white handkerchief embroidered with blue letters inside a six-pointed star shape, covering her head. Then the image vanished, filling Davina's eyes with tears. "I mean, I thought bread had measures," she whispered, lowering her head.

Chaim dismissed his initial concern. How ridiculous, he thought, for him to have taken the child's confusion of numbers and letters as recognition of his esoteric writings in Hebrew. "All is as it should be, Davina. It will take time, little one. It's good you are remembering. It hurts to lose the ones we love." He paused, his own son's face appearing in his mind for an instant.

"It takes time to heal," he whispered. "Remembering that your mother loved you and wanted to protect you is important." Chaim knew hurt so deep that remembering was often too much to bear. He understood the child's tears, the weight of her perceived guilt.

"Knowing how to hold inside what must be held inside for your own safety, and ours, is very brave." Chaim's deep blue eyes looked directly into hers. "And yes, bread does have measures and you will make a fine baker like your new mama."

He handed Davina the empty bread basket and drew his books toward him trying to cover the pages from the eyes of this precocious child. But he wasn't quick enough. A rogue wind suddenly raced through the open window blowing his papers askew, off his desk and onto the floor. A few flew into Davina's lap.

Before Chaim could gather them back, Davina picked up one and held it up to the light. The dark letters were large and bold, the black ink twirled into intricate shapes. Davina was breathless. She felt each letter on the page vibrate and glow like the lightning bugs she had caught in front of her home on warm summer evenings. The letters beckoned her to touch them, to run her fingers over them, stroke them. Before Chaim could stop her, her small fingers caressed them. To Davina's amazement, the letters danced on the page. They changed color from black to red to gold, then to violet, green, and blue. They merged and flipped in all directions, changing into numbers and back to letters again. Davina giggled with delight. "Oh, Papa I see! It's a game. You're playing a game with letters and numbers for your recipe to see how it will come out!" She was gleeful.

Chaim could not speak. He held his breath. For one split second a premonition, a vision of the past and future, the vast cosmos itself had unfolded before his eyes. A knowledge so profound that it had taken forty years of study of *Sefer Yetzirah* and commentary to bring him closer to uncovering a great mystery that this child had recognized without effort, in just moments.

Air poured back into his lungs in a gasping breath. He exhaled, making great effort to quiet his breathing, allowing his heart rate to return to normal. He looked at his new daughter, a child he had pulled out of the river just months ago, half-drowned, half-dead. "How can this be?" he murmured in disbelief.

Before he had time to ponder the child's gift further, Davina looked down at the page of letters she had rearranged and then stared into her father's eyes. She murmured some words that were almost familiar, but ones he could not place. She chanted the words over and over, her child's voice deepening into a melodic low tone.

Chaim couldn't move. Feeling Davina's intense gaze, hearing her chant created a buzzing sound in his ears, then a tingling, burning sensation at the top of his head. Before he could register what was happening, he found himself standing in a place he didn't recognize. He was no longer at his desk in his attic study poring over his books, eating bread and honey with Davina. Chaim was standing in the blazing hot sun in a foreign, barren landscape.

He coughed the dry air and turned around and around seeing nothing but sand and sky that seemed to go on forever. Then, as if in a dream, his hands searched unfamiliar clothes, feeling his body beneath the cotton fabric. But it was not a body he knew, nor hands he recognized. They were black hands, black skin. At that very moment, he heard Davina's voice chanting, this time like a sweet distant lullaby. Automatically he began chanting too, following her lead, hearing her words, and seeing letters and symbols appear before his eyes in the air itself. Suddenly, everything went silent. He felt perfectly calm, perfectly transformed.

He looked again at the landscape of sand and tumbleweeds out beyond his immediate stance, to a road and a building far in the distance. He could see a lone figure, a woman with a dog walking about in the desert, looking for something. With extraordinary vision and fathomless depth of perception, information poured into his ethereal consciousness. He could feel her panic. He could read her thoughts. She had lost something important while walking her dog. As soon as the image appeared in his mind, he felt a cold metal key in the palm of his hand.

Seconds later, he was standing next to her, holding out his hand. He watched her take the key. He felt elated and as light as a feather. A sudden gush of wind blew him toward a large, wheeled vehicle. Then suddenly, Chaim was back in his study sitting next to Davina.

The child was beaming. "I like this game Papa," she said. She put the paper with the large black letters back on the desk and picked up the others from the floor. Just then, she heard Mama Bella calling her. "Here, Papa." She handed him the strewn papers and took the empty bread-basket. "Can I come do more letter and number games tomorrow, Papa?"

CHAPTER 2

Rachel Rita Padini

June 2004, The Berkshires, Western Massachusetts

Mrs. Rita Padini, as she was known, awoke on Saturday morning feeling displaced despite the cocoon of her familiar cottage in the Berkshires. Her things from the big house were still in storage, the sale of her and her recently deceased husband's home on Long Island finalized only weeks ago. She looked around at the pictures on her bedroom walls as a familiar anxiety of aftershocks rumbled in the pit of her stomach. "No," she said aloud. "No fear, no wallowing. It's a beautiful summer day."

Rita glanced at the clock on the nightstand. It was 9:00 am. Suddenly remembering that it was a special day, her nervousness vanished. She climbed out of bed smiling. Her brother Michael would be arriving from Arizona today to visit her. She washed up quickly, combed her auburn hair and grabbed her white terry cloth robe from the hook on the bathroom door. She could smell the coffee brewing in her automatic coffeemaker.

She headed for the kitchen with the image of her tall, handsome brother in her mind's eye. Joy spread over Rita like a warm security blanket. Michael was her hero, her protector—always had been. Even when they were kids and he had called her by her given first name, Rachel, he had watched out for her in his quiet way. Now, with Joseph gone and her daughter Theresa and son-in-law, Kevin, returning to their new home in England, there was only Michael to lean on.

But it wasn't completely clear how their relationship might unfold now that she was untethered, alone. She'd had misgivings when she'd spoken with Michael by phone yesterday. He wanted her to consider moving to Arizona, a choice that had never entered her mind. She was a New Yorker, an East coast girl through and through. Arizona was exotic, a desert, foreign. Granted she had never been there, even after Michael and his partner Gary had relocated some years back.

Her late husband Joseph had not been a fan of her gay brother Michael. He had made it clear he disapproved of her and the children, Theresa and Giovanni, spending time with Michael. His religious, macho attitude toward her gay brother had always been a bone of contention in their marriage and Rita grew to resent Joseph because of it. She would call Michael regularly in spite of Joseph's small-mindedness.

With hindsight, Rita also grew more understanding of her parents' consternation, when at nineteen she had revealed her pregnancy, and announced her intent to keep the baby and marry Joseph Padini. Blinded by love and hormones, she had agreed to convert to marry her handsome dark-haired lover. Keeping her pregnancy a secret from his family, they married in a Catholic church against her parents', the Goldbergs, wishes. She began using her more assimilated sounding middle name, Rita, rather than her first given name, Rachel—becoming Mrs. Rita Padini to his family's approval and the Goldberg's concern.

"Arizona is different, but it's not what you think," Michael assured her. "Really Rachel, it's changed—it's a 'go to' destination for snow-birds, hip retirees. It's cosmopolitan with an international staff at the university," he boasted. "It's not the *wild west* anymore, at least not as much. We have a symphony, theaters, galleries, art festivals, up-scale restaurants, golf courses. Sis, it's really a cool place. You can start a new life, Rachel—get away from those cold winters."

"That's quite a sales job," Rita said. Michael was the only person who still called her Rachel.

She reflected, conflicted. She had moved into her and Joseph's summer vacation home in the Berkshires when the warm spring breezes had chased away the snow. She'd sold their big house in Port Washington thinking she would find a smaller place—maybe a townhouse or condo by late autumn. She needed time to rethink her life, to figure out who she was now. She had lost so much of herself it seemed, never envisioning herself a widow at forty-eight. In some ways it was a relief, even if the glimmer of freedom brought guilt.

But Arizona was not on her radar. It seemed too far away from everything she knew. Joseph and her little Giovanni were buried at St. John's cemetery in Brooklyn. How could she leave them? On the other hand, Michael was alive and would be there for her. Perhaps that would be enough.

Mulling over Michael's description of Tucson, she toasted a bagel and drank her first cup of coffee. If she moved far away, it should be some place romantic, a little mysterious, she thought, like Venice or Madrid—maybe Paris.

After breakfast, Rita checked the computer for Michael's plane flight into Bradley Airport. With hours to spare, she could drive to Springfield with time to do a bit of shopping at her favorite boutiques in Northampton. Disgusted with her clothing choices of late, she needed a change. She wanted a more modern style to match her new short haircut, dyed to a rich red auburn that covered the recent gray strands, and her slimmer figure, from weight lost during the emotional turmoil of the last few months. She picked a light green blouse and gray slacks from her wardrobe. Finishing her outfit with a gold chain and earrings, Rita took a last glance in the mirror before leaving.

Turning off the Mass Pike exit onto I-91, it wasn't long before she arrived in Northampton's quaint town center. Rita parked and decided to window shop for a while. Strolling down Main Street, she came across a small clothing shop she'd not been in before.

"This place is new, isn't it? When did you open?" she asked the young, blond-haired girl behind the counter at Sally's Boutique.

"Yes, about three months ago," the young woman replied looking up from her magazine. "Can I help you find something?"

"I'm looking for a new jacket mostly, something rather casual for summer evenings in the mountains," Rita said, spying a few white jeans jackets. "Oh, these are very nice." She looked at the labels until she found one in size twelve. She tried it on thinking how strange it was to no longer know what size she wore. Gazing in the fitting room mirror, she thought it looked perfect.

Next, Rita looked through the fashionable scarves to dress it up. When she got to the checkout counter, she purchased the jacket, but could not decide on a scarf. She handed the salesgirl her credit card. "Maybe I'll come back, later. I can't make up my mind yet on a scarf," she shrugged.

Rita stepped out into the sunshine. Funny, she thought, buying a hip white jacket was not at all something she would have done when Joseph was alive. It made her feel young and suddenly free. Rita checked her watch. She still had an hour left before she'd have to head out to the airport, enough time to grab a bite. Meandering to the closest cafe, she ordered a decaf and a salad. It was warm enough to sit outside at one of the sidewalk tables, so Rita settled down to enjoy her coffee and people watch. She had come to Northampton over the years on her own, on the pretext of doing a little shopping without Joseph. She loved its quaintness and diversity of people, especially the young women who frequented the town from nearby women's colleges.

In more recent years, the women seemed older, walking arm and arm was a common site. Lesbians didn't make her uncomfortable, actually the opposite. Watching the mature women strolling together had an oddly calming effect on her. In fact, she had talked to Michael when she heard about Massachusetts same-sex marriage ruling earlier in the year. She supported the ruling whole-heartedly with her brother. Maybe gay people could have some peace, she thought.

Rita finished her salad and took the last sip of coffee. Then, she rummaged through her purse finding the pad she carried to write grocery lists and notes. As of late, she had taken to writing descriptions of people and impressions of places to keep her mind occupied. She had begun to keep her own private journal at the suggestion of a therapist she had seen briefly. Between pages of her inner-most thoughts, she found herself dabbling in poetry, moody and depressing sometimes, but poetry nevertheless. Today, she took out her pad to record her impressions of shopping for something new and unusual, but ended up watching a couple of women walking arm in arm down the street, until they were out of sight.

She turned her attention to her dilemma of moving and memories of her brother. Before long, she found herself writing a poem.

If I could turn myself inside out
Let go and leave it all behind
What might I find? A new life?
To be a goddess, not someone's wife
A flamboyant artist living by the sea
Follow my dreams and just be free.
Perhaps a magician with vision too?
Maybe I can be something new
Not collecting dust upon a shelf
Can I break through and be myself?

Rita stopped writing and checked her watch again. Time to go, she thought. A feeling of excitement overwhelmed her, then a fleeting sense of dread. What if she could not bring herself to change? What if she could not become a new person with a new life? She imagined the old Italian widows like her mother-in-law had been, dressed all in black, withering away their lives, praying to Mother Mary, waiting to die.

Rita shook off the image and the notion. She put away her pad, and then checked her lipstick in her compact mirror. Taking the new jeans jacket out of the boutique bag, she removed the tags and put it on. She loved the crisp feel, the figure-hugging fit. After leaving a tip for the waitress, she walked up Main Street, an unfamiliar but glad confidence in her step.

As she passed Sally's Boutique, she looked at her reflection in the window. Testing her resolve, she entered the shop again.

"Hello," said the mature Black woman at the counter. "Can I help you with something? Are you looking for something special?"

"Oh, hello," said Rita, "I was in just a while ago and I spoke to another—a younger woman..."

"Ah, yes. Kathy's on lunch break. I'm Sally, the new owner. Are you local?"

"No, not really. I come into town in the summers sometimes. I have a place near Lenox."

"Oh, yes the Berkshires are beautiful. Were you looking for something special?" Sally inquired again, noticing how similar the woman's white jacket looked to ones she had for sale.

"Actually I bought this jeans jacket here just a little while ago."

"Ah, I thought I recognized it," Sally smiled.

"Your salesgirl, Kathy, showed me some nice scarves and I've come back to purchase one," Rita said, closing in on the scarf rack and a particular viridian green one with thin gold threads running through it. "Here's one I really like," she said, running her hands over its silky texture. "I'll take this one."

"I like a customer who knows her mind. Good choice. Green is a good color for you. It looks stunning with the white jacket and your hair's red highlights." Sally took Rita's credit card and finalized her purchase. "Enjoy it." Sally smiled handing Rita back her card and receipt to sign.

"I will, thank you," Rita replied. She walked out of the shop and headed straight for her silver Toyota. She would park in short-term parking and meet Michael in the airport terminal, she thought, turning onto I-91 south to Springfield.

Rita was excited and nervous at the same time, waiting for her brother's face to appear among the throngs of people rushing toward baggage claim from the escalator. Then, suddenly there he was. Tall and tan, his sun-bleached hair thinner, but his body still robust. Rita waved.

Michael's hazel eyes lit up, a smile spreading wide across his clean-shaven face when he saw her. "Sis, Rachel!" He dropped his carry-on bag and scooped her up in his arms, giving her one of his famous bear hugs. "Oh, Sis it's so good to see you! You look fabulous. I'm so happy to see you looking so...different, I mean younger." He held her at arm's length. "I've been worried about you, but it looks like you have really taken good care of yourself. Love the jacket and the hair, darling."

"Oh Michael, you look so good too. Tucson agrees with you, I can see that. How's Gary? How are the two of you doing?"

"Good, we're good. He sends his love. He's on the Cape visiting his niece. She just got into Yale graduate school for September so the family is celebrating. I'll meet him there after our time together," Michael said putting his arm around his sister's shoulder.

Rita gave him a squeeze too. "C'mon, let's get your luggage. We have so much to catch up on. Are you hungry? Want to go to your favorite—the Red Lion Inn in Stockbridge?"

"Oh Rachel, you're the best. That sounds great! I'm famished."

Before too long, they had Michael's luggage and were on their way. They pulled into a parking space next to the inn as dusk turned a warm day into a cool summer evening.

"So really, Rachel, how are you?" Michael looked directly at his sister, leaning slightly over the table with its clean white tablecloth, their stuffed mushroom appetizers and glasses of Pinot Noir between them.

"Well, some days I feel sad, you know. But mostly I feel strange, like a rubber-band that has broken. I still have parts of me that feel the same, but everything is different. Everything is not held tightly in its place." Rachel sighed and sipped her wine. "After Giovanni died, well you remember. It took years for me to wrap myself around life again. If it hadn't been for Theresa and you..." She paused. "I expected to feel like that again, now that Joseph is gone. But I don't." She looked at Michael. "I feel oddly...free," Rachel whispered.

"But too guilty to let yourself feel okay with that?" Michael added.

"You know me pretty well, my dear brother." Rachel's eyes softened.

"I guess it's the sense I have of abandoning them, especially Giovanni," Rachel eyes watered. "I can't imagine not being close enough to be able to place flowers on his grave."

Michael was quiet. His little nephew's face appeared to him. He had seen him rarely, but the child had been the epitome of a cherub, with his rosy cheeks and big brown eyes. A smart, joyful child, his tragic death from meningitis had been so hard to bear for everyone.

Devastated, Rachel had lost not only her beloved young son, but her husband as well after that. Joseph became sullen. His drinking escalated, as did his reactionary behavior and angry bouts of irrational jealousy. Had Rachel agreed to let Michael come for her and Theresa, he would have whisked them away to his apartment in Los Angeles. But she'd been in no condition to make such a choice. Now, perhaps she could make a new choice, maybe with a little encouragement.

"Sis," he said very softly. "You know Giovanni's spirit is with you, right? Not only at his graveside. "He reached across the table and took her hand. "And no matter where you live, you can always come back each year—on his birthday, Christmas, whenever you want to visit." He paused watching Rachel's teary eyes fill with hope. "Joseph's sisters and their families can care for his grave, bring flowers. They go regularly now to Joseph's graveside next to Giovanni's at the cemetery, don't they?"

"His sister, Lucia will think it's awful for me not to honor Joseph's memory, not go every week." Rachel said. "She and I have grown closer over the years. Her oldest girl, Connie and our Theresa grew close, like sisters after Giovanni..." Rachel shook her head. "I guess it's all so new to me. It's like being in a movie or a dream that just suddenly ends. You look back and it feels like someone else's life. I feel removed and yet sad at the same time." She stopped abruptly, and finished the wine in her glass. "Oh listen to me, I sound crazy."

"Not at all, Sis. It makes sense."

"Well, that's because it's genetic—you're a little nuts too!" Rachel laughed.

"Funny." Michael filled both their glasses again. "*L'chaim!*" He raised his glass to toast his favorite sister.

"*L'chaim! Saluti!*" Rachel responded smiling. Her mood lifted. So did Michael's as the waiter set the prime rib, seafood Newburg and buttered noodles before them.

After dinner, Rachel and Michael drove by the Stockbridge Cemetery, their parents' final resting place. Joseph had arranged for the plots at Rachel's request when their father had passed.

Michael looked out at the carpet of green grass. He'd only been there a few times since their mother had joined her husband— heart failure after a long illness. "We can come place some flowers and stones on the graves tomorrow." Rachel noticed his distant gaze.

"I'd like that, Sis. Thanks for taking care of them all these years." Michael sighed.

"It's okay," Now it was Rachel's turn for comforting. "We all did the best we could, you know." So much history passed between them in a split second—their youth playing hide-and-seek and stick ball on their street in Brooklyn, trips to Aunt Helen's in the country on warm summer weekends where the river cooled them, where they learned to fish and pick wild berries. Winter snow falls wrapped in snowsuits, Hanukkah candles burning bright and the smell of lat-kes frying in Grandma Sophie's kitchen—the carefree days before the harshness of failure, before their parents' disappointment in them took over their lives—before Rachel's pregnancy and marriage, before Michael's choosing a boyfriend, not a girlfriend.

"You know they really tried. They were good grandparents. And they accepted you and Gary toward the end, especially Mom," Rachel added. "It was a different time, for them. The America they dreamed of, the plans they had for who we would be. We just didn't fit. It was a big adjustment."

"I know," Michael said." I've made peace with it. There is just so much left unsaid. I wish I could have told them..." his voice trailed off.

"Yeah, me too."

"I'm glad you went to celebrate the Jewish holidays with them most of the time with Theresa," Michael added. "I know it meant a lot to them after you married Joseph and converted."

"You managed to go when I couldn't. We both did that. It did mean something, you know," she whispered.

Rachel turned the car off Main Street and drove along the lake road. Michael opened his window and breathed in the lushness of the woods, the sweetness of freshly cut grass, of honeysuckle and jasmine. Soon, they pulled into the driveway of Rachel's summer house, a Cape Cod cottage with white shutters adorning light gray wood shingles. In front of the wrap-around porch, a rose garden bloomed in shades of red and pink. What had been a small vegetable garden in happier times lined the side of the house, its tomato supports still entrenched in the soil awaiting plants. Several brightly colored birdhouses placed along a small fence between two birch trees separated the garden from a wide swath of berry bushes, beyond which a creek ran.

"This is such an idyllic setting. I hope you're not thinking of giving this place up too. Are you, Sis?"

"I was. It has a lot of memories for me." She paused, turning off the engine and gathering her purse and jacket. "I've thought of redecorating instead of giving it up. But, I wouldn't want to live here full-time, at least I don't think so. I guess I haven't made up my mind, yet."

"If you need the money, I could..."

"No, it's not that, but thank you, Michael. It's paid for and I have enough from the sale of our house on Long Island. I guess I am just conflicted about next steps."

They walked toward the porch arm in arm. Dusk triggered timed lights along the front porch. "C'mon, let's get in before the mosquitoes realize we're here. We can sit on the screened patio out back—have some tea."

Michael set his things down on the full-sized bed in the guest room. Except for a small cross next to the mirror above the dresser, the only other wall décor was a large seascape painting on the pale blue wall, above the brass bed frame. A matching gold-framed photo of his niece, Theresa, and her husband sat on the nightstand alongside a milk-glass lamp. Michael picked up the photo and shook his head. It had been four years since he'd seen her. Since her wedding only sporadic emails between birthday and holiday cards had kept them connected. They'd spoken by phone after Joseph died, but Michael had been down with the flu, unable to attend Joseph's funeral in January.

In the kitchen, Rachel turned on the electric kettle. "What kind of tea would you like?" she called.

Michael walked into the granite-countered kitchen. "Something herbal, caffeine-free, I guess, although I doubt if even caffeine will keep me from a good night sleep tonight," he smiled. "Speaking of hitting the hay, I saw the picture of Theresa and Kevin by the bed. How is Theresa doing? I miss her," he said, wandering toward the next room.

The kitchen opened into a family room where a stone fireplace took up the whole of an angular wall. It boasted an oak mantle adorned with small animal statues, mostly elephants. Some were carved in wood, others made of clay, porcelain or blown glass. In the middle, stood a small copper elephant tarnished a green-blue color that Michael recognized as one from

India. He picked it up.

Rachel brought a tray with tea and cookies into the room. "Theresa's doing great. She just got a job at the London Jewelry Exchange, not far from where Kevin works. She and Kevin are planning a trip to the states for the holidays." Rachel's eyes lit up. "Maybe we can have a family reunion here. You think you and Gary might be able to come?"

"Maybe, Rachel, if I can persuade Gary. He wants to visit his grandmother in Louisiana. But I would come if it means seeing Theresa!"

Michael was still holding the Indian elephant. "Where did you get this one? It's a *Ganesh*, the elephant-man God from India."

"Yes, you know I adore elephants. Joseph was always opposed to my giving to elephant protection charities, but once he was no longer able to protest, I put a little aside each month for that."

"I never knew you to be political, Sis—good for you!"

"I'm not too political really, but when it comes to elephants, I think ivory should be boycotted," Rita said firmly, taking a sip of her tea. "The killing of elephants is a travesty, like genocide as far as I am concerned. Another twenty years like this and you'll only see elephants in a zoo."

"You're right," Michael agreed. "So many precious animals and for what? Money? Greed? It's such a lack of respect for nature, for the earth."

"Elephants are mistreated all over Asia, although most of the poaching for Ivory is in Africa, these days." Rachel added. "Theresa told me the demand from Asia drives the market. I don't think one can blame the poorest of Africans who take advantage of the money to support their families.

"They're coerced by middle men who are getting rich." Michael said.

Rachel took the Ganesh from her brother, feeling the cool weight of brass in her palm. "I found this one at an antique shop. I know it's not really an elephant figurine—yes, it's a Ganesh, but

I really liked it, especially the color of the tarnish. You know, I am always fond of anything green.

"Oh yeah! I remember when you were ten you found the words *Viridian Green* on a can of paint Dad had and decided you wanted to be called, Viridian." Michael laughed. "Mom would call you *Vivian* and you would keep trying to correct her."

"Well, everyone has their quirks I guess." Rachel laughed too. "That Ganesh came with a little card I liked also." Rachel reached over to the mantle and handed the card to her brother. Michael read the card aloud.

"In Hindu teachings, Ganesh is known as the God of wisdom, prosperity, spirituality and compassion. He is revered as the destroyer of obstacles and brings challenges when needed for growth, as well as healing and protection.

Om Gama Gamapataye Namaha
I bow to Ganesh who is capable of removing all obstacles.
I pray for blessings & protection."

"Sounds perfectly fitting for a time of healing." Michael winked at Rachel. He followed her through the sliding door onto the screened patio. Lightening bugs and crickets were already putting on a show. Rachel lit a few candles and set the tea pot, cups and cookies on a low table between two deck chairs.

"The little elephant statues and the Ganesh are not what I would have chosen when Joseph was well. But by the time he got ill, well, you know, we had grown apart." Rachel looked at the floor for a moment as the image of Joseph, bedridden and depressed, flashed before her.

"When I took that job at the museum after Theresa got married," she said looking up directly at Michael, "I found myself in a whole new world. He couldn't appreciate my excitement over the art and culture I was experiencing. He didn't like that I was going into Manhattan three times a week." Rachel shook her head. "I mean, I appreciated Joseph's support and care, his family's closeness and my ties to his sister. But I knew I needed more. After Theresa got married…well, I'm just so glad you encouraged me to expand my horizons." Rachel smiled. "That job really opened my eyes to how small my world had become." She sipped her tea.

"But enough of that! I'm a free woman now. Why, I can even imagine traveling to India, not just buying things made there." Rachel waved her arm in the air.

"So what about expanding again and traveling? Maybe come out West for a visit? You'd like the new house Gary and I bought—see how we're renovating it."

Rachel settled into the ease of being with Michael again. "Okay, Brother. You've got yourself a deal. I will come for a visit to Tucson around Thanksgiving, if you promise to come for a family reunion when Theresa and Kevin come for the Christmas holidays—how's that?"

"It's a deal!" Michael grinned.

They finished the cookies and tea and sat back listening to the crickets and the faint sound of an owl hooting into the warm night air.

"I put fresh towels for you in the bathroom," Rachel said, breaking their silent retreat. "Tomorrow I want to hear all about your new house. We can go down to the lake for a picnic."

The next morning, Rachel arose early for her usual morning walk. She set the coffee maker on brew and took a small bucket for blackberries she'd pick on her way back.

Michael got up at ten, washed and put on his swim trunks and T-shirt. "Good morning, Sis. Something smells good," he said peeking into the oven. "Um-mm, muffins!"

"I baked them with the berries I picked. Thought I'd pack them for our picnic." She poured Michael a cup of coffee. "I have deviled eggs, potato salad, fried chicken and sliced oranges. We'll have brunch!" She poured the remaining hot coffee into a thermos.

"Ah, sounds fabulous. I'll have to swim *before* a meal like that!"

At the lake, only a few people had arrived for a day of sun. "It's a little early, so we can get a good spot." Rachel picked out a half-sunny, half-shady spot and put down their blanket and picnic basket. How many times had they picnicked at their Aunt Helen's on the Hudson when they were kids and swam in the shallows of the river? she thought.

Michael took in the scene and turned ten years old. He peeled off his T-shirt in one quick move. "Last one in," he laughed, heading for the water.

The lake was as wide as it was long. Catching the sunlight, its sparkling surface danced in the light breeze. Michael raced through the blue-green shallows and dove into its cooler depths, swimming under water out to the raft in one breath. He surfaced howling with delight like a teenager.

"C'mon Sis. It's fabulous!"

Rachel waved from shore. She took off her beach robe and adjusted the straps of her bathing suit, which were a little loose now that her weight had dropped. But something else didn't feel quite right. She noticed a knot in her stomach. Rubbing her midriff, she mentally retraced her morning routine—her regular cup of coffee and some berries with a little yogurt. Nothing unusual, she thought. Rachel shrugged off the physical annoyance and headed for the shore's edge.

She waded in up to her knees, then dove in, the cold water consuming her senses. She came up for air and swam a few yards, her brother in sight on the raft, waving. Rachel dove down again swallowed by the dark water. Too dark, she thought. Mind racing, she realized she had dived into a small forest of what appeared to be seaweed. Instinctively, she headed for the surface. But to no avail. Her legs were entangled in the web of underwater flora. The more she struggled to free herself, the worse it seemed to get. Panicking, she thrashed. Her lungs burned, her eyes throbbed in pain.

Then suddenly, she saw someone near her. It was an old man.

He was reaching for her. His wrinkled hands explored the water paddling faster and faster, while his head appeared several times bobbing up and down, in and out from the surface. His beard and scraggly coat sleeves waved back and forth in the green water, thrashing and scouring until he reached her. She felt her hair being pulled, and a hand under her jaw wrenching her upward, then her arms being gripped by large hands lifting her, as if she were a small rag doll. Before she knew it, someone was thumping on her back. Sunlight blazed in her eyes, air rushed into her lungs. She gasped, sputtered, and coughed all at once.

"Rachel, Rachel!" Michael's voice broke through. "Easy, take it easy. You're okay. Breathe." He patted her back as he held her up. "You can stand here. It's not too deep."

Rachel put her feet into the soft clay of the lake floor. "I'm okay, I'm okay, now." She reassured Michael and herself. She looked down at the clear water. There was no seaweed or plant growth to be seen.

"What just happened, Sis?"

"I honestly don't know," she whispered.

CHAPTER 3

Rita Kerner

June 2004, Northampton, Massachusetts

After brunch, Rita and Cleo walked arm in arm along Center Street inhaling the sweet aroma of blossoming roses wafting through the late spring breeze. Rita squeezed Cleo's arm, a squeeze laced with sentiment Cleo understood.

It meant how special it had been sharing their lives the last three years since moving in together. It meant how glad that they could tolerate each other's idiosyncrasies, share a common history of hard fought battles for equality, and parenthood. It meant a simple hand-holding stroll felt like well-earned freedom. The gesture of a squeeze said all this and—*I love you.*

Together the two turned onto Main Street for their usual Saturday ritual of window shopping at their familiar haunts for antiques, clothes and jewelry. Today though, they came upon a new store. The sign in gold letters announced *Sally's Boutique on Main.* "Looks like a great place to get your birthday gift, don't you think?" Cleo's green eyes twinkled. There was nothing she liked better than actually shopping.

Rita nudged Cleo playfully. "Okay, but let's keep it under thirty bucks, okay? We're saving for the move to California, remember? Besides, my birthday is a few weeks away," Rita added, while Cleo pushed open the shop's glass door. Brass wind chimes announced them, ethereal tones rippling through the still air.

"Oh, hi again!" exclaimed the young blond salesgirl at the counter. "Back for something else?"

Rita and Cleo both turned around to see to whom she was speaking. There was no one else there.

"Excuse me?" said Rita.

"Well, I just thought perhaps you were returning for that scarf you looked at, to go with the jacket you bought." The salesgirl shrugged.

"You must be confusing me with someone else," Rita smiled.

The salesgirl furled her brow. With a perplexed expression, she tried again. "You were just here about ten minutes ago, remember? You're Rita, right?"

"Uh...yes," Rita startled. "How did you know my name?"

"You just bought the white jeans jacket, size twelve. You gave me your credit card." The salesgirl opened the cash register and rummaged for the receipt. "I checked your ID, remember? Your name is Rita, right?" she repeated.

Cleo gave Rita a look of concern.

"Must be another woman with the same name," Rita smiled at the girl. "I've had people tell me they know me when they don't, all the time. Even on grocery lines, strangers will say hello to me like they know me," she paused. "Maybe I have one of those familiar-looking faces, I figure." Rita tried to allay the girl's obvious disturbance—and Cleo's.

"Well, that's weird, 'cause she looked just like you. I mean like she could be your identical twin. And her name was Rita too. Really..." The salesgirl tilted her head in disbelief. "What are the chances of that?" She scrutinized the previous customer's receipt. "Here it is! Rita R. Padini," she exclaimed, her blue eyes lighting with satisfaction.

Cleo and Rita sighed in unison. "That's not my last name," Rita said. "But it is quite a coincidence." She pulled out her driver's license to assuage the young woman's skepticism. "See, Rita *Kerner*—that's me. Not a very flattering picture, obviously." The picture was two years old and faded. Taken in the DMV's dull florescent light, her olive skin looked a sickly blue. Her hair had been brown and graying then, and she'd been heavier. Now Rita was svelte, tanned, her short hair dyed a rich auburn color.

Cleo walked over to the lingerie aisle and looked through the rack of delicate garments, glad she did not have to deal with more coincidences. Being with Rita was always an adventure—had been from the beginning. Cleo recalled their first winter a few years ago when Rita had come to visit, presumably to talk about the paintings that Cleo had purchased at Rita's gallery in Rhode Island.

Rita's paintings of two Native American women had captured Cleo's attention with a magnetic force she could not explain. Not until months after she and Rita were together, that is. One evening as they were falling asleep, Cleo was sure she heard the beating of drums. "Do you hear that?" She turned to Rita.

"Sounds like drums." Rita whispered half asleep. The beating drums seemed to come from under the bed, which of course they both knew was absurd. When the drums subsided, owls hooted, calling to them, or so it seemed, though the bedroom windows were closed in the dead of that snowy winter night. Rita was unafraid. She reached out and hugged Cleo. Suddenly, like a lightning flash in an autumn storm, Cleo found herself standing in an open plain along a rocky ridge with Rita at her side. They were both dressed like the people in the paintings hanging over Cleo's bed, on the plains of North Dakota.

That night was the first of many experiences with Rita that made being with her both exciting and unnerving for Cleo, never knowing what waited around the corner.

Meanwhile, Rita had preferred to think of people confusing her with someone else as just a case of mistaken identity. Now, trying to convince herself that there was still the possibility of coincidence was futile. Ignoring the situation was no longer an option. She knew from experience that it would stalk her like a repeating dream, until she got to the bottom of it.

"Geez, that was weird, huh?" Cleo turned to Rita as they headed home empty-handed.

Rita sensed Cleo's nervous anticipation. "Yeah, I think maybe I'll see if I can find someone named Padini on the Internet. Maybe she is listed somewhere. Wouldn't it be strange if she really does look like me—like a parallel universe thing?" Rita laughed.

"Two of you, oh no! I can barely keep up with one of you." Cleo winked.

They arrived at Cleo's flat on Cherry Street. Rita had moved in a year after their romance had bloomed, leaving Rhode Island for Massachusetts, only after her son, Noah, had left New York with his California girlfriend, Kate.

Rita shuddered remembering how close Noah had come to still living in Tribeca, so close to the horror, the tragedy that engulfed New York that terrible day in September. But he was safe now, she thought. Rita breathed away the images of a friend's daughter starting her new job that morning and early to work in the North Tower. Rita said a silent prayer, focusing on the rose bushes lining the path to Cleo's building. She pushed her face into a big yellow rose, its soft velvet petals wrapped her senses in sweet fragrance, temporarily smothering the still painful images.

Cleo picked through the mail from the hallway mailbox, then opened the door to their apartment. Oliver, Rita's small shepherd mix, jumped up and ran toward them, tail wagging, smacking against half-packed boxes that lined the walls of the foyer. More boxes sprawled along the edges of the main room that served as both a living and dining room. Rita gave Oliver a tussle. "Who's a good dog?" she chortled. She had gotten him for Noah when he was in high school to soothe the loss of their older pooch. Now, eight years later Oliver remained with her, devoted to the one that fed him.

"Can't we finish packing at least some of these boxes, so we don't have to live in this mess?" Cleo complained, exasperated.

"Moving is messy business," Rita followed behind Cleo scanning the room. She was an expert at moving, having done it so much in her life that she could practically pack in her sleep. "Okay, why don't we try to finish two or three boxes a day and a few more on the weekend? How does that sound?" she said, appeasement being her best defense against Cleo's irritability. Better to agree with her neat-freak girlfriend, she thought, than ruin a perfectly nice day. Besides, if she kept the main living area somewhat under control, Cleo might bug her less about packing up her painting studio.

Although Rita maintained her connection to her craft by teaching art at local school programs, she hadn't painted much since she'd closed the gallery and moved in with Cleo. But keeping her paints and brushes out and at the ready made her feel like she could dive in any time the muse beckoned.

"If you take Oliver out for his walk, I'll get started on these," Rita bargained pointing to a stack of books.

"You got it!" Cleo agreed, quickly tying her light brown hair back into a ponytail and grabbing the dog's leash from its hook in the hall. "There's a letter for you on the hall table too, from Nakisha Williams."

Rita opened what turned out to be an early birthday card from a young college student, Nakisha Williams, whom she'd met some years ago. Rita sat down near the bookshelf in the main room and read the note inside.

Dear Rita,

I just wanted to wish you a Happy Birthday and say thank you for encouraging me. I've been so appreciative of the opportunity to be accepted into graduate school at Yale. My undergraduate classes at NYU in women's studies and cultural anthropology led me to research in botanical entomology. I have decided to pursue study in environmental science at Yale. Maybe we can talk soon. Have a great birthday! Nakisha

Rita smiled. She closed the card with its whimsical cat cartoon on the front. Then she noticed Aries, Cleo's cat, curled up inside

the half-filled crate where Rita had started packing books last evening in her attempt to sort those she no longer needed from those
she would never read, if she hadn't already. "Look Aries," she said
scooping up the cat, and showing him the card just for fun. "This
cat looks like you." Aries whined his displeasure at being moved
from his hide-out.

Better get down to business, Rita thought, refocusing on the
task at hand. Though some of her books had pages yellowed with
age, Rita had unloaded everything into the bookcase when she'd
moved in with Cleo and had never really bothered to go through
them for purging. But California was a long way. It would be
costly to take anything they didn't absolutely need.

"We're not going to a deserted island," Cleo announced,
returning from her outing. She observed Rita' s dark eyes scrutinizing her collection of reading matter. "They have bookstores in
California, I've heard. You can start a new collection."

"Very funny," Rita quipped back. "Some of these are out of
print. They are my treasures. They are memories—like old records.
She pulled out a ragged copy of *Chariots of the Gods* by Erich von
Däniken. "Do you know where I read this one?"

"Uh," Cleo held a hand to her forehead. "Wait...the great Mer-
lin is telling me."

"I read this in Venice, Italy," Rita said.

"When were you in Venice?" Cleo laughed, "Oh wait, you
mean in another lifetime? Or as Rita Padini?"

"You're on a roll today, huh?" Rita chuckled. "No, actually
it was when my grandfather died, at the end of my first year at
Hunter. He left my sisters and me each six hundred bucks. Wasn't
much, but he was wasn't a rich man. To me it was a huge wind-
fall, you know?" Rita's eyes twinkled. "I decided to go to France
for the summer with a college friend, Marla Remy, and then to
Italy by myself to see the great ones—you know, Michelangelo,
Da Vinci, Donatello." Rita gazed into the past. "I was taking art
history in school."

Aries climbed onto Cleo's lap. She pet his thick orange fur, then looked at Rita. "You never told me about that. For real?"

"It was the summer of '69. Six hundred dollars meant I could travel cheaply for the whole summer. I was in love with my friend Marla, only I didn't really let myself know it until we parted ways," Rita confided. "I went to France for a week with her and then I went to Italy by myself for a month staying in youth hostels mostly." Rita ran her hand over the book's worn-out cover. "This book was given to me by another American student traveling in Italy, who I ended up hitch-hiking with, part of the way from Florence to Venice. Being in Venice was otherworldly in a way, like being at the edge of the world with all that water. It gave me such an odd feeling—this book seemed to fit."

"I've never had the desire to go to Venice. Now, Rome or Florence—that's a different story. You've never shown me pictures of your trip."

"No, I lost my camera about halfway through the trip." Rita shrugged. "This is really all I have left of that journey. Florence, Rome, Perugia, even Naples were all so beautiful. I loved Italy." Rita's dream face glowed. "When I hold this book in my hand, I remember everything. Like magic, it brings me right back to the time, the places, the memories of the people I met on that journey—farmers in vineyards where only oxen and carts traveled—how they laughed about us hitch-hiking back to Rome." Rita sighed. "Like the Mom and Pop who owned the *penseone* in Rome where I stayed. Each morning they climbed four flights of marble stairs to carry water from the fountains on the street where the open-air market was filled with flowers, and cheese and fresh fish. Every evening they made Sangria and sang Italian folk songs to all of us, their guests." A broad smile lit up Rita's face.

"Oh, and the places! The Trevi Fountain, the Sistine Chapel, the Colosseum, the art in Florence and Rome, remains of Pompei, the art schools in Perugia, seeing the works of Michelangelo, Donatello, Giotto with my own eyes." Rita was transported. "Oh, and the food! The pasta, the wine and chocolate!" She licked her lips. "It's how I felt on that trip going to the bathhouses for a steamy soak, swaddled dry in clean muslin sheets, swimming half-naked in the Mediterranean's blue water, eating real Italian ices from paper cones." Rita eyes shone. "Ah, it's like another lifetime, you know?"

Cleo walked over to Rita and kissed her gently on the lips. "Yeah, I get it." she said. "That's a part of your life I didn't know about." She wiped wisps of auburn hair from Rita's forehead. "I have books that remind me of things too. But not so many—it's my CD collection I hoard, it's the music that brings back fond memories."

Rita pulled out several more books from the shelf and tossed them in the give-away box. "Okay, I'm purging," she said. Then she came across a small leather bound book with faded gold embossed letters. She opened it to the title page and gasped. "*The Little Old Bookshop,*" she read in a whisper. "Oh my God! How do I have this? I was supposed to give this book to Noah after my father died. It was my Dad's wish that Noah have it." Tears welled up in Rita's eyes. "I must have forgotten." She wiped her eyes with her sleeve, sniffling. "Well, I am not going to throw this one away, that's for sure."

"Hey, not this one either." Cleo came over to sit next to Rita. Going down memory lane was best done together, she finally decided. Cleo pulled a book from Rita's shelf. "Remember this one?" Cleo smiled holding the book, *Intuition and Creativity; The Art of Marla Cherise Woods.* "I showed you this one the night you first came to visit me, the night of our first kiss," she winked. "I see you liked it enough to put it on your shelf."

"I do remember that." Rita's lips found Cleo's. She dropped her books and leaned into Cleo's embrace, one that would make the end of their nice day together perfect.

The next morning woke softly. Spring had given birth to the warmer air of summer. Swainson thrushes trilled in birch trees outside the bedroom window, welcoming the sunrise's hazy pink and yellow rays that illuminated the sky. Cleo stroked Rita's bare back, waking her gently. "Good morning, lover," she whispered. Rita rolled over and hugged Cleo. She kissed her neck. "So nice," she said. Just then Oliver came bounding into the room and was up on the bed in a flash, refusing to be left out of the cuddling.

Pet chores then began an otherwise lazy morning with the *Sunday New York Times,* steaming mugs of coffee, toasted bagels with cream cheese, and the soft crooning of k.d. lang filtering though the apartment. Rita and Cleo relaxed before planning a full day of packing. The only interruption was the phone. Cleo picked it up on the third ring.

"Hello? No, this is Cleo. Just a minute, I'll get her. What did you say your name was?" Cleo walked over to Rita. "Someone named Geraldine. Says she knows you from college?"

"College?" Rita whispered, a look of astonishment on her face. "Hello, this is Rita," she answered. "Oh, yes, I remember. Wow, yes. Geraldine! Well, how are you? God, what has it been, like thirty years?" Rita sat up animated now. "So you're married, how nice. And what about Marla? She went off to Philadelphia to marry that accountant boyfriend she had in college, right? I remember he used to join us for dinner on Fridays. How's Marla doing?" Rita looked over at Cleo and held up her index finger— one minute.

"Oh, she didn't marry him?" Rita listened remembering how guilty she felt not calling Marla to say goodbye when she left to marry that guy, too afraid to tell Marla that she was a lesbian, too scared to let her know she had fallen in love with her. "Really she's been looking for me? Sure, you can give her my number. Yes, great to hear from you, too."

Rita hung up the phone. Pensive, she stared out the window, her mind drifting to a small sunny room with a double bed covered by a white, cotton eyelet bedspread. Marla stood half undressed in her bra and a slip in front of a bureau mirror brushing her long dark hair. Her breasts pushed up against her dresser while she leaned forward, peering into the mirror to apply her creamy lipstick.

"Is that the friend Marla you had a crush on? The one you went to France with for a week when you were in college?" Cleo said stroking Rita's arm.

Rita turned toward Cleo's voice, suddenly realizing where she was. "Oh, honey," she said automatically. "Yes, the girl I knew in college when I was in New York. I was just coming to terms with who I was. I couldn't tell her, or anyone else back then. I couldn't even say the word." Rita shrugged. "Funny isn't it—that we were just talking about her yesterday?"

Cleo knew Rita. Something had been awakened. "So you didn't see her? Sleep with her?" Cleo turned and looked into Rita eyes, those deep eyes she knew could read.

Most days Rita loved that Cleo was intuitive, almost psychic. But today she wasn't sure. "Yes, I had a crush on her. That's when I knew that I couldn't deny I was gay anymore. But I had a hard time coming out. I couldn't risk her hating me, thinking it was, you know—a horrible thing." Rita sighed. "It was a very long time ago." Rita grabbed Cleo around the waist and pulled her close. She kissed Cleo. "*You* have nothing to worry about, woman."

But there was a knot in the pit of Rita's stomach that Cleo couldn't detect. A visceral memory of the anguish she experienced after she assumed Marla had departed. In Rita's heartbreak, Marla had appeared to her in dreams calling to her, looking for her. Intermittently and for many years thereafter, Rita thought she'd seen Marla—on a bus, in the subway, just walking up ahead of her on a crowded city street. She had actually run up to women, who resembled Marla from a distance, with dark hair waving in the wind or her familiar profile that Rita thought she recognized, only to find a stranger's face giving her a frosty expression.

"Well, if you're sure. Are you going to be in touch with her?" Cleo asked.

"If she calls me, I guess. Geraldine said Marla married another man and has two kids in college." Rita brushed off Cleo's insecurity.

She did not mention that Geraldine had said Marla had looked for Rita for years. That she'd gone back to France to pursue her art and traveled to India, before marrying. Now, the fact that Marla was still thinking of her pulled on Rita's heartstrings. But she didn't say another word about it. Better to let sleeping dogs lie, she decided.

"Why don't we take a break from packing and go out for a long walk with Oliver? It's such a nice day," Rita offered. "Enough reminiscing for one day. Let's live in the present. How about we go for ice cream?" Wasn't that the next best thing to sex for a mood elevator, she thought. After all, they were two hot-flashing women with an unending craving for cool sweets.

"Okay," Cleo agreed. "Now you're talking! But no more running into any other look-a-likes named Rita! Can we just have a normal day?"

"Normal? Really? How boring!" Rita laughed.

August, 2004

Dear Noah,

How are you honey? How are you liking California? Please send Kate my regards. How are things going with her parents? I can't wait to hear more about your new job. I will be seeing you very soon.

Cleo and I are almost done packing and should be leaving tomorrow or the next day for the cross-country trip—very exciting. I haven't traveled this beautiful land since I was your age—yes, centuries ago! It should take us about two weeks, since we'll be stopping to see Aunt Irene in Santa Fe and Donna and Sharon in Arizona. Did I tell you they bought a house in Tucson?

Let me know if you need anything. Call me anytime. I'll check in with you along the way.

Big Hugs, Mom

Rita folded a check for one hundred dollars into the note and sealed the envelope. She put Oliver on his leash and walked to the post office. Everything was ready to go, she thought. She had gone over her checklist at least a dozen times. Now all she had to do was wait for Cleo to return with the car and small U-Tug they'd arranged to pick up in Springfield. Bright and early the next morning their grand adventure would begin.

Rita stopped at the market after posting her letter. She left her sunglasses on in the store, hoping her disguise might thwart more "coincidental" encounters. But it didn't help. Bob and Harriet Wolkee from Indiana were visiting Smith with their daughter. They were sure they knew Rita, accosting her the checkout counter.

"Oh yes, sure we have met. You look so familiar too. Must have been at that, uh, college orientation for the kids." Rita decided to just go along with it. She thought about her standard line—"I'm an old soul and I know everyone!" But she didn't think Mr. and Mrs. Middle America might like that one. Then again, maybe with a daughter interested in Smith.

"That will be twenty-two, sixty," the clerk interrupted. The bag boy plopped the turkey sandwiches, chips, apples, soda and cookies into a brown paper bag.

"Oh, I forgot the gum." Rita reached for some peppermint and spearmint flavored gum. "Can't have too much chewing gum for a road trip!" she laughed, in spite of the clerk's annoyance at having to add her last minute items. She hurried out to Oliver who she'd left tied to a railing as usual for market runs. A teenage boy was kneeling and petting him. The kid looked up at Rita.

"This your dog?" he asked. "I knew he looked familiar."

Oh no, now my dog looks familiar too? Rita thought. Surveying the boy's face, she suddenly brightened. "Oh yeah," she said. "You're the Super's nephew—Tim, right? Here visiting for the summer?"

Rita was happy to let him carry her bag back to the apartment. Cleo was just coming up the walkway when she arrived at the front door. "Hi Babe, what's the good news?" she asked hoping for a positive outcome despite the frustration telegraphed on Cleo's face.

"The guy said he can't meet us with the car..."

"What does that mean? We have to go to Vermont to pick up the car?" Rita interrupted, her high-pitched voice reverberated through the apartment hallway. Cleo could almost see the smoke coming from Rita's ears.

"Yes, but he has..."

No longer listening, Rita made a bee line for the kitchen phone and dialed Edward 's number, the same number in the ad offering five-hundred dollars plus gas to drive his Chevy to LA.

"What's wrong with the car?" she asked as soon as Edward picked up the phone. "Oh, I see." Rita's tone softened, her shoulders drooped. "Well, yes, I guess we can come up to Brattleboro then." Rita paused and scribbled down directions on the back of an old envelope. "Okay, I have it. We'll be there tomorrow. Yes, about 1pm. Thanks, see you then."

Rita looked sheepishly at Cleo.

"Did he tell you he broke his arm?" Cleo asked. She took the two remaining glasses not yet packed from the dishwasher and poured some lemonade.

"Yeah, did he tell you that, too?" Rita replied.

"Yes, you didn't give me a chance to tell you. But it was good you arranged tomorrow. I couldn't get him to commit to a time for us to get the car."

Rita frowned. "Sorry," she apologized, accepting her glass of lemonade. "What a hassle. That means we won't be able to leave until at least Tuesday or Wednesday. We'll have to ask Sarah if she can watch Oliver and Aries, and go to U-Tug movers on Monday."

"Well, let's just enjoy Vermont. Maybe stay over at a little B&B and take a leisurely way home, stop at some farm stands, see the scenery." Cleo put her arms around Rita. "Could be romantic." She kissed Rita's neck.

"Okay, I guess so." Rita tried to relax, hugging Cleo back. Driving a stranger's car all the way to California was financially practical, but nerve-wracking. Rita took a deep breath, resigning herself to the inevitable. But what other complications were in store for them, she wondered.

"I only got this one key," Edward said, when Rita and Cleo arrived in Brattleboro to pick up the car. He held up the one ignition key to the old Chevy. My mom in California, she's got the only other one. She told me to tell you all that she forgot to send it in time. She said to go to Dave's Garage in town and maybe get another one." He adjusted his overall straps with his uninjured arm. "I think the engine needs oil too."

"Great," said Rita sarcastically.

"You'd better give us your mom's phone number, so we can contact her in case of any problems," Cleo said. She checked the glove compartment for the registration, insurance card, and manual, refusing to be distracted by the young man's stoned-out demeanor.

Deciding to drive halfway home to find an actual Chevy dealer on Monday, they opted for a chain motel and ate dinner at the adjacent small diner. Neither the food nor accommodations encouraged romance. They just downed some antacids and went to bed early.

The next day did not prove much better. The Chevy dealer could not reproduce a key on order for two to four weeks. "We'll have to go with the key we have. I don't want to wait longer," Cleo shrugged. "I'm pissed, but I'm done. I called Edward's mom. She apologized for not letting us know about the key situation. But, she said she'll pay us for any unplanned expenses we have along the way—hopefully we won't have any of those." Cleo brightened. "The good news is I had the car all checked out—tires, brakes, fluids. We can pick up the U-Tug trailer this afternoon and we're good to go! We'll just have to be really careful not to lose the key or lock it in the car, that's all." She rolled her eyes for effect. Then Cleo put her arm around Rita's shoulder and gave her a squeeze. "C'mon, Babe, let's get some pizza."

CHAPTER 4

The Strega's Daughter

Summer 1417, Outskirts of Padua, Italy

Davina finished milking the goats and wiped her brow with her kerchief. The heat of the day had begun to dissipate, but she was drenched with sweat nevertheless. Her wavy dark hair clung to the back of her neck as she carried the bucket of milk to the old stone house. Her mother was cleaning out the cold storage of remaining root vegetables when Davina placed the bucket down on the kitchen floor. She turned around and smiled.

"Good milk today from our sweet old goats, yes?" Bella asked, peering into the milking bucket.

"Better than last time, Mama," Davina said. "There is even enough cream today to make butter."

"Do you want to make it yourself?" Bella asked acting like it was a normal occurrence. Her spontaneity took Davina by surprise.

"Really? Could I?" Davina bubbled.

"You are old enough now. You can do it I am sure." Bella smiled, aware of how the child was blossoming. "Besides, I have to go to the bathhouse, so that will be very helpful. Soon you will be a woman and can go with me for our ritual baths," she added with a smile.

"Oh, thank you Mama." Davina was proud. At twelve, she felt all grown up. Now, she would prove her skills in the kitchen. She would make both bread and butter for her family. Wouldn't Papa be surprised when he came home, she thought as she took the flour and a large bowl from the cupboard. She gathered the rest of her ingredients, mixing then kneading as the dough took shape. Davina reached for the bucket of milk and a ladle, scooping the top layer of cream into a bowl to taste.

Suddenly, she was back in her mother Francesca's kitchen. The memory of her cow's sweet milk, of drying plants, the aroma of spices, herbs, and oils, ingredients for poultices surrounded her. The vision was so vivid it was as if no time had passed. She noticed the shelf where Francesca kept all the herbs in ceramic jars each labeled with numbers and symbols. She saw the book of old yellow parchment in which her mother wrote notes and drew pictures of every plant she found in the forest. Davina remembered waking up at night, finding her mother creating mixtures and tonics—new remedies for the women who came to their humble home seeking cures for the ailments of their children, elders and animals.

Like waves in a stormy sea, memories came flooding back. Memories of watching the stars come into view against the night sky, her mother pointing out all the constellations they could see. She memorized each by name along with the stories Francesca would tell of their origin. Davina remembered learning about the cycles of the moon, and planting their garden according to the seasons—seeds in spring and bulbs in fall.

Without as much as a second thought, Davina took an empty muslin sack and a piece of charcoal from the cold hearth and began drawing from her memory. The impulse was so strong, she lost track of her task of baking. Minutes ticked by. When she had finished drawing several plants, she stopped and observed her handiwork. It was not as she wanted it. She would need different materials. "Paper," she said aloud.

Suddenly, Davina knew what she must do. Forgetting the milk and flour she climbed the ladder up to Papa Chaim's attic room. Hot and stuffy from the heat of the day, the room seemed smaller than usual. Davina wiped her brow and scanned the desk and shelves. Papa would be home soon, so she needed to move quickly. She rummaged through her father's papers and some books looking for any parchment she could find that might have a clear portion with few letters or symbols. Some of the papers were tattered at the edges, so it would not be hard to find small scraps of parchment, ones that wouldn't be missed.

Shortly, with a few choice scraps stuffed in her apron pocket she descended the ladder, returning to the kitchen. She noticed the cream had formed a layer of skin and the flour seemed damp. Quickly, she skimmed all the cream off the top of the milk, poured it into the butter churner and began to mix. But her mind was elsewhere. Pictures of plants and tonic mixtures danced in her head. Davina felt elated. "I will make a book," she whispered. She would write and draw everything she could remember that she'd once been taught.

With big plans swimming in her head, she turned back to her chores of baking and making butter practically skipping through the remaining steps until the bread was baking and the butter had been sufficiently salted and molded to preserve it. The remaining milk had curdled and would soon ferment into buttermilk, Papa's favorite.

For many weeks that followed, Davina gathered scraps of parchment, cotton and muslin from anywhere she could—from rag peddlers to fish mongers. From potato sacks to scraps of worm out clothes and shoes from her mother's friend's children, she squirreled away bits of anything from which she could make paper. To prevent being discovered, she would wait until she was alone at home to make concoctions of mush, experimenting with a combination of materials by mixing tiny torn and hand-shredded pieces in a bowl with water until a gray soggy mush formed. Then she would drain and squeeze the remaining liquid out of the mixture. She'd pour the mush on a wood board covered with cloth, press it down with cotton cloth, then pound it gently into a flat rectangular shape. She placed each embryonic page outside beyond the chicken coop in a secret spot in direct sunlight to dry. It was an imperfect, slow and tedious process, but she was determined. Each day she would wait until her mother and father were away from home to repeat the process until late into the summer.

As the vineyards and fruit trees morphed from lush green to blazing yellow and reds with the turn of the season, Davina managed to produce her first twelve pages of what she thought would be paper. Each was slightly different in texture, some a little thicker and coarser than she would have liked, but workable nevertheless. She had persuaded Chaim to teach her to craft a quill pen for him, so she could later make one for herself. She managed to get some ink from the local cobbler. Creating her own colors from plants, flowers, and berries, Davina even experimented with a mixture of copper tarnish shavings.

But after all her hard work, it was not to be. The paper crumbled easily and was too porous to hold the ink, which bled until the words and images became amorphous pools of color, indistinguishable one from the other. Davina was heart-broken. She could barely get through her chores the next few days and didn't feel like eating.

"Davina, are you feeling unwell?" Bella worried. She made her daughter some beet soup with garlic, in case she was getting sick.

One day shortly thereafter, Davina wandered up to Chaim's study. Forlorn, she just wanted to be near him. Her father was bent over his books in deep concentration. "Papa?" she whispered. "Papa?"

Chaim looked up at her. "What is it Davina? Do you need something?"

"I need paper, Papa," she blurted out. She amazed herself at her bluntness. She waited for a negative reaction.

"What do you need paper for, my dear?"

"I wish to make a recipe book, Papa—write down some recipes."

Chaim squinted, looking hard at Davina. Skepticism laced his response. "I hardly think you need cooking recipes, Davina. You have a good memory. Parchment is expensive."

"I know Papa, I tried to make my own paper. Can I show you?" Davina went back to her room and fetched the paper she had made. When she showed it to Chaim, he was more than impressed with her effort.

"This is very good, Davina. You did this by yourself?"

Davina nodded and smiled for the first time in days. "Please Papa, see how it crumbles. The ink and colors don't hold. You see how they bleed across the page?"

Chaim looked carefully at Davina's handiwork. He walked over to a small cupboard near his desk and reached under some manuscripts. He pulled out a package wrapped in muslin and tied with twine. He opened it carefully. Davina's eyes gleamed. There in the folds of the fabric were sheets of new parchment.

"These are made in part with calf hide and take ink very well. Some of the pages are thicker than others because they are each individually made." He pulled out one sheet of parchment for Davina to touch. She did so like she was touching gold. Chaim saw a golden light with tinges of light green and pink appear around her. She was glowing.

It was not the first time Chaim realized that Davina was no ordinary child. "I will give you some of this parchment provided you do not tell anyone what you are doing with it. Do you understand?" Chaim wore a serious expression. "It's for you own protection, Davina."

"Oh, thank you Papa! It will be a secret, I promise." She hugged her father for the first time.

A few months later

It did not take long for Bella to notice a change in her daughter's appetite and see her energy return. "Davina has become so helpful again." Davina overheard Bella talking to her neighbors.

"She helps tend the garden, run errands and bakes. She even comes to help me at the market with the bread stall," Bella boasted. "She never complains about too much to do."

Davina, of course, managed to take extra time to do her chores, squeezing in an hour of writing and drawing whenever she could. Each evening before going to sleep, she would reach under her bed and pull out the pages of her small book, wrapped in a cloth. She'd inspect the pages to make sure the most recent of her ink drawings were still in pristine condition. Before she could sleep, she'd tuck them safely back in their hiding spot.

Davina dreamed of potions. Sometimes an image of Francesca came to her in her dreams to assist her with her drawings. Other times she dreamed of a stranger, a odd female figure with green skin, draped in a cape of dark green velvet and gold. The magical woman came to her in a scene—a forest near a lake, flooded with the light of a full moon. She instructed Davina much like her mother did in the preparation of tonics, but unlike Francesca's potions for healing humans and animals, the stranger's instructions were mostly about water. Oddly, she showed Davina what the finished page would look like. The writing was neither in Davina's native language, nor a language that was recognizable to her. But Davina remembered her vivid dreams and although she did not understand them, she copied them into her book exactly how they appeared to her in her dream. Then one day in late fall, Davina's life changed.

"Mother!" Davina cried. Tears welled in her eyes.

"What is wrong, child?" Bella saw Davina come in from the outhouse.

"I am sick. There is blood, Mama."

Bella's eyes opened wide. She had been waiting for this day now that Davina had begun to mature.

"Ah," she said. "You are a woman, now. Come." Davina followed her mother into her private alcove where a small ornate wood dresser stood, filled with Bella's clothes and linens. From the bottom drawer Bella pulled a red undergarment and satchel of clean square pieces of cotton cloth.

"You will have blood once a month until you are with child, someday when you are married," she added. "So now you will know what to do, my dear daughter. You will fold one cloth at a time and place it inside this undergarment, then put it on." She demonstrated. "When it absorbs the blood you will bring it outside to the stream to clean. I will show you how. Then you will take a clean, dry one to replace it." Bella held up the red underskirt. "This goes under your dress in case of any leaks, understand? We will also have cousin Lupe, make some new dark skirts for you, yes?" She smiled and kissed Davina on the forehead. "Now, it's time for you to join the women in our ritual baths! We will go when menses ends in a few days. In the meantime," she patted her daughter's tummy, "I will make some green nettle broth for you, like my grandmother made for me when I became a woman."

Davina was overwhelmed. She was happy and sad at the same time. Suddenly, she was part of a secret society of women who all shared the bleeding ritual that ushered in motherhood. She was excited to go to the ritual baths, *mikvah*—to finally be included with her mother, aunts and female cousins. But she didn't want a husband or a baby. Would her body force her into such a predicament? Chaim would receive a dowry for her when she was of age, a marriage ceremony would follow shortly thereafter. Her sixteenth birthday was only a few years away. Davina shuddered at the thought of leaving home to live with a strange old man like her cousin Lupe, betrothed at seventeen. She went to her room and put away her new womanly belongings. Soon she heard Bella calling her for soup.

A week passed before she stepped into the warm waters at the women's bathhouse. The water was murky but smelled sweet, brimming with essence of lavender, mint and olive oil. After her initial shyness, Davina relaxed into the warmth and camaraderie of the women and girls she knew. Most were family friends or relatives. They were all glad to see her, congratulating her on her entrance into womanhood as if she had planned the event.

With the advent of her change in status, Davina's dreams became more vivid. The "green woman," as she called her night visitor, instructed almost all of her writing about her drawings depicting her experiences in the bathing ritual. Davina felt there was some connection between the potions, healing herbs and the constant flow of water in her drawings, but she could not figure out what it was until one day when she noticed a rash on her arms. It itched and burned.

"Mother, I think I have accidentally brushed against some stinging nettles." Davina rolled up her sleeves to show her mother.

"Why it's funny you should have done so, Davina. I think I have done the same. I have burning and itching on my arms and my legs too." Bella rolled up her sleeves. Their rashes appeared the same, red and irritated from scratching. "I will get some mud for this rash," said Bella.

"Clay," said Davina.

Bella looked at Davina suspiciously. "Clay?"

"Clay from the river bed will soothe the rash, if it's nettle." Davina added looking directly at Bella, unafraid of her mother's mistrust.

By the next day, the rash and itching had spread. Bella's cousin Lupe, came by to complain of an itchy rash as did Bella's neighbor. Soon many women found themselves itching. "The only thing we have all done is bathe together, Mama. Maybe the murky water in the bathhouse is causing it," Davina blurted out.

Bella stared at her daughter. The thought would never have occurred to her, but somehow she felt Davina might be right. Now that she considered it, the water at the women's bathhouse, in spite of it's aromatics, had seemed much darker and murkier of late. She had attributed it to the late summer rains which naturally churned up the river waters. But maybe something else had made it unsafe. People used the river water for bathing, not drinking. There was plenty of fresh spring water for cooking and consumption. "What might have gotten into the river water?" she pondered aloud. "Are the men, the children getting rashes?" Although Chaim had not complained of any problems, she would ask him and her other relatives and friends.

"It is only in the women's bathhouse," Lupe whined. The women had gathered in the market square to discuss the crisis. "We will have to have a thorough cleaning of all the channels, walls and floors," they agreed. They would work in groups with help from their husbands to block the water channels until the job was done.

In the meantime, Davina dove deeper into her book. She drew the bathhouse over and over with combinations of ways to divert water, purify water with clay, rocks, plant concoctions, and combinations of tinctures and potions.

One night, the green lady came to her in a dream with mesmerizing chants, wands of golden light and luminous crystal balls, beckoning her into the forest to learn the secrets of healing water. Davina awoke that morning to find herself in a strange land of grasslands and bluffs. Forested mountains appeared in the distance. A small group of horses grazed along a small creek where brown-skinned children with long black hair splashed in the clear water. They were bare chested and yelled to each other in a strange tongue. Suddenly, a dark cloud appeared in the sky and the horses and children disappeared. A belching, metal object appeared digging into the earth until a black oily substance sprang up from the earth spilling out over the land and into the water. The clear water of the creek turned black, a slick oily substance floated on its surface, along with dead fish.

Davina heard the green lady chanting. She closed her eyes and listened intently. Images of letters that looked like the ones in Chaim's books appeared in her mind's eye. She tried to memorize their shape and connect them to the chant. Suddenly, she realized that she knew this chant. It was one she had heard in her dreams since she was very young. One she had heard the first day she had served bread to her father in his study too.

Davina opened her eyes. To her surprise she found herself in her own bed, still in her night clothes. She could hear Bella preparing the morning porridge. She could hear Chaim greeting the rag peddler. She waited until all was quiet. Then she dressed and climbed up the steep steps to the attic, finding Chaim in his study.

"Papa, can I speak with you?" Davina tiptoed.

"Yes," he said looking up from his papers.

"Papa, what makes water turn black?" Davina asked.

"You mean running water, river's fresh water, or ocean? Why?"

"I had a dream about an oily black substance coming into a river and making it thick and black. It lay upon the water's surface reflecting a sickly glow of colors. The ducks and fish died."

Chaim sat up now paying attention to Davina. He knew she was seeing into a future scenario of he knew not what, certainly not the bathhouse. "I know only that what is making the water impure in the bathhouse may be fixed by cleaning it," he offered.

"Just soap and clean water?" Davina asked, even though she knew this was not so. She didn't dare mention the problem that the green lady had imparted. "And the rash, Papa. What about the rash and itching?"

Chaim stroked his beard and squinted. "The alcohol—the wine will alleviate some of the problem." He looked down at his notes. "Perhaps mixed with some herbs," he mumbled.

"Alcohol," she whispered. "And purple cornflower."

Rita Kerner

Summer 2004, Across-Country USA

The next morning, Rita and Cleo headed out leaving city traffic behind them. Trailing the small U-Tug with all their worldly belongings, they were finally on their way to a new life on the West coast. They hadn't driven for long when the air-conditioner stopped blowing cool air. The temperature was bearable at first, but climbed into the humid nineties as they drove south. They kept themselves and the dog cool with ice water and the fan, stopping at night in air-conditioned motels. By the time they turned onto I-44 near Tulsa, Oklahoma though, it was over ninety-eight degrees. "Maybe it's just out of freon? We can go to Tulsa and have it checked." Rita suggested, filling their travel mugs and Oliver's water dish with more ice.

"Okay, we should stop for the night, anyway. I think any decent gas station with a mechanic can check it," Cleo agreed.

Early the next morning, they pulled into the first full-service station they found.

"You ladies traveling alone?" The attendant at the gas station smiled a toothy grin. The name Brad was embroidered on his breast pocket.

No, we're together, Rita and Cleo both thought of the same lyrics in an old Holly Near song. "Well Brad, you see, my sister and I seem to have an air-conditioning problem. Any chance you could see if we need freon?" Cleo inquired instead.

Brad eyed Oliver in the back seat. "Well, Dirk's out there in the garage doin' an oil change. Should be able to look into your gals' problem in a short while. You all from New York City?"

Rita thought that might be code for "You all are Jews?" But she tried to dismiss her negative thinking in spite of her insecurity about her Jewish looks and New York accent, one she had not managed to shake, in spite of leaving the city of her youth.

Cleo was quick to pick up the ball though. "No, we're headed out West from Massachusetts."

"Oh, yeah? I got a brother lives up there in Boston. Geez, you know I thought maybe you looked familiar when you come in," he said turning to Rita. "You been to Boston much? I was up to see old Billy last summer at one of his big old Red Sox shindigs. Maybe you know him—Billy Wilcox? Maybe I met you at his place?"

Rita almost choked on her ice water. Oliver barked.

"Could be," Cleo chimed. "Rita here is a big Red Sox fan! Aren't you, Sis?" Cleo gave Rita a firm smack between her shoulder blades and winked.

Rita's coughing suffocated her laughter. "Oh, yes, I do like my Red Sox, just like Billy and all of us in Boston," Rita managed.

"Looks like they be making the World Series this fall." He turned to face the car bays. "Hey, Dirk!" Brad yelled, walking toward the garage. "Will you take a break and check these girls' car right quick. Their air-conditioner ain't working—maybe just a quick look-see, will ya?"

He turned back to Rita and Cleo. "Don't you should have to wait too long in this heat, ladies." He paused looking at Oliver again. "Your dog friendly?" he asked.

"Shit!" Cleo said as they left the gas station and headed back onto the interstate with the still broken air-conditioner that old Dirk could not fix. "Half the day gone! I'm going to give Edward's mom a piece of my mind. We should stay in the most expensive places we can find with air-conditioning, pools, and room service, and give her the bill."

"Would be nice, but we have the dog. I have mapped out our route with the dog-friendly motels, hon," Rita coaxed. "They're air-conditioned at least." Cleo was silently glum.

"Hey gal, don't you know old Billy from them baseball shindigs? Why, he'd make you a big grinder for the Red Sox game!" Rita chortled. Cleo burst out laughing.

"Hey, watch it—those Red Sox are cool!" Cleo caught her breath. Then she turned up Janis' *"Me and Bobbie Magee"* as loud as the car's speakers would go. Singing along at the top of their voices, they both turned twenty-five years old again. Oliver stuck his head out the open back window smiling into the warm breeze.

The next day, Rita and Cleo took turns driving and watching the land change. Mostly flat, there were hills in the distance and the earth turned the color of orange honey. The late afternoon air was warm, and the barren landscape stretched before them in endless miles. The only sign of civilization was a faded sign along the road that featured a stereotypical 1950's housewife in an apron, holding a pie. The entire sign was in shades of light blue making her eerily pale. Like a program from the *Twilight Zone,* the sign kept appearing every few miles in various conditions of weathered wear and tear, with words that were partially worn off. The first one read "Mighty H," the second read "ty High." Like the "Jesus Saves You" signs of the Bible belt, they got the whole message at the last one. The words "Mighty High Pie" finally came into view, above the last worn-out housewife.

They both looked at each other. "Pie!" they drooled in unison. Nothing like sweets for curing exhaustion and hunger.

At the next exit they turned off to find a shimmering white building with royal blue awnings, a freshly surfaced parking lot with crisp white lines, and two trees on either end, flowers planted around their bases. It looked as if the whole place had just dropped from the ether, brand new and shiny in this otherwise desolate, dusty landscape.

Parking in the shade for the dog's sake, they walked into the cafe. The cool air-conditioned room lowered their blood pressure instantaneously. Twenty meringue pies, each nine inches high, covered an antique mahogany bar. The mighty white clouds of meringue reflected ten-fold in the enormous mirror behind the bar, creating a dizzying illusion of endless sugary delight. The site almost brought Rita and Cleo to tears.

A waitress appeared immediately beside them to soothe their joyful shock. "Would you like to have lunch or just pie?" she asked. She was obviously ready for the almost incoherent stuttering of weary travelers entering pie heaven.

Embarrassed by their gluttonous rapture, Rita looked at Cleo. "We should have some real food first, shouldn't we?" They wolfed down a shared chicken-salad sandwich with lust for pie in their hearts.

"We'll have one slice of banana, one lemon, and one chocolate, to go please." Cleo ordered, her mouth watering. The waitress brought a box containing their pie slices and soon they were on their way, stuffing themselves happily with forkfuls of sweet dreams. Rita was sure even Oliver grinned after his first mouthful of banana meringue pie.

The following day Rita, Cleo, and Oliver reached Santa Fe. Rita's sister, Irene, and her husband, Gregory, lived just inside the city limit in a small house they had moved into after Irene's breast cancer surgery. In remission a few years, Irene looked healthy and tanned as she came out to meet them in the driveway.

"Wow, Sis, you look really good." Rita hugged her younger sister. "You've gained back some weight. And look at your hair, grown long again!"

"And look at you too. Wow, you look younger than when I saw you last. How do you do that?" Irene turned to Cleo. "And you too. You both look like you're enjoying your adventure. C'mon in and have some iced tea. Gregory's out back on the deck."

Rita took Oliver's leash, giving him a tussle on his head. "Good dog. Come see Gregory."

A well-deserved rest followed for two days with visits to restaurants and shopping sprees to buy some turquoise and silver jewelry made by local Native American artists at an open air market. Rita noticed how different the light and air felt. The expansiveness of New Mexico was like nothing she had ever experienced. Her heart felt suddenly connected to the earth. Rita hugged Irene. "This place is good for you, Sis. I can see why you are happy here." She understood now why they'd moved here after Irene's surgery. It was a healing place—one Rita promised herself to come back to again.

"Maybe we can try to get the kids to come for the holidays, maybe one year here and the next in California. Cleo will have her kids up for Christmas, so it would just be us and our kids, if we can get them to join us."

"Great idea, Sis. We can certainly try to plan something, if not this year maybe next, after you're more settled. I have a feeling you two will like California. The weather is so much nicer than back East. Glad you're missing the awful heat wave they're having back there." Irene shook her head.

"How people can deny global warming with all the tornadoes and heat, is beyond me," Cleo agreed.

"Hey, we will certainly be more than happy to come see you in California, even if you all will have another actor for a governor!" Irene winked. "Besides, Gregory loves San Francisco. He has fond memories from his time at UC, you know." Irene finished packing a few goodies she had prepared for the next leg of Rita and Cleo's trip, adding some extra carrots for Oliver. "Now you drive really carefully through the desert, okay? And call me when you get settled." Irene waved as Cleo and Rita pulled out of the driveway.

As the day went by, the desert grew hotter than Rita and Cleo imagined it could be. By the time they crossed into Arizona, it was one hundred degrees. To make matters worse, they found they had misjudged their gas mileage, not realizing the infrequency of gas stations on the interstate. Scouring their maps, they estimated they were two hundred miles from the nearest town. With nothing but desert ahead and behind of them and the gas tank running low, they were worried.

Luckily, they soon came to what was advertised as a trading post. It was a run-down shack with a soda machine and two gas pumps that unfortunately hadn't functioned in years. They pulled off the highway hoping for gas, but all that was available aside from soda was Native and Mexican pottery, rugs, hats, small cactus plants, and postcards. Some candy bars that had seen better days were sold at the counter. The saving grace was the old couple that ran the place. Sweet as peaches, they spoke enough English to communicate with Rita, while Cleo understood enough Spanish to discover that there was a gas station twenty miles west, on the other side of the highway.

It was a modern gas station with a little mart. A big picture of frozen strawberry smoothies hung in the window. Rita pulled up alongside a gas pump in the shade of its overhang. There were no other vehicles in the station except for one eighteen-wheel truck with red, white and blue pictures of icy Pepsi bottles painted on its sides, parked in front of a pump to the right. Cleo and Rita looked at each other and began breathing again. "I'll go get some smoothies and pay for the gas," Cleo offered.

"Okay." Rita released her seatbelt. "I'll walk Oliver and pump the gas afterward."

Cleo walked to the mart while Rita took the key from the ignition and carefully put it in her breast pocket. Oliver was anxious to get out and walk. Even in the extreme heat he pulled her along into the desert. They had not walked for too long before the dog relieved himself. Glad to get out of the blistering heat, Rita made a bee-line back to the shaded car.

Reaching into her breast pocket, she felt for the car key. At first, her mind did not compute that her pocket was empty. Patting herself down, panic rose from the pit of her stomach. She checked every pocket over and over. From a distance her frantic movements might have been mistaken for a seizure.

Finally, Rita just stood still. She tried to focus and breathe to calm herself, go over her steps, out into the sand where she had walked with the dog. But to no avail. Back at the car again, she noticed Oliver staring out at the desert and wagging his tail. Rita squinted, peering out to the steaming empty landscape. Suddenly, she saw something moving. From the hazy horizon, it seemed to be a person coming out of nowhere. She looked harder. It was a man. He was far away, but walking toward her. Oddly, in a matter of seconds he was close enough for her to see him clearly. His ebony skin and white dreadlocks stood out against the sun-bleached sand.

Rita just stared, suspended in disbelief. The old man approached her. He looked deep into Rita eyes and smiled. His dark green eyes shown with an intense radiant light unlike any Rita had ever seen. She was transfixed, barely noticing that he held out his left hand, palm up. She didn't see his lips move either, but she was sure she heard him ask, "Is this what you are looking for?" Rita looked down to see her car key shining in his wrinkled hand. Before she could comprehend what had happened, she held the key in her own hand and watched as the man simply walked away, behind the big Pepsi truck and out of sight. Out of the corner of her eye, Rita saw Cleo walking toward the truck also, carrying two large frozen smoothies.

As if waking from a dream, Rita opened the car door and settled the dog in the back seat. She had just sat down when Cleo handed her a frozen drink.

"Who was that man I saw you talking to?" Cleo asked.

"I don't know," Rita's whispered, startled and relieved at the same time that Cleo had also seen him, that she hadn't imagined the whole incident. "Didn't you see him when you walked behind the truck? You must have passed him."

"There was nobody behind the truck," Cleo said. "I saw you talking to an old Black man here for a moment next to the car. Didn't I?"

"Uh, yes." Rita did not know what to say. Should she tell Cleo she had lost the key? "You won't believe this maybe, but I think he was...well, you know—an angel." Rita waited for Cleo's ridicule.

"You think so?" Cleo said nonchalantly sipping her icy drink.

Now it was Rita who looked awry at Cleo. The heat must have fried some of her brain cells, Rita thought. "Who the hell are you and what have you done with Cleo?"

They both laughed as they drank their cold strawberry smoothies. Then Rita got out of the car and pumped the gas. With the tank full she retreated to the driver's seat.

"Want me to drive, Louise?" Cleo asked.

"Maybe later, Thelma." Rita smiled. She turned the precious key in the ignition, then steered the old Chevy back onto the hot pavement of the interstate and headed west toward the setting sun, music blaring.

CHAPTER 6

Professor Emari's Class

AllSouls College, Pleiades

"Good Day, class. Welcome to the Orientation." Professor Emari stood tall, her ten-foot frame draped in turquoise and gold, bright colors highlighting her dark skin, black eyes, and hair. A silver breastplate and an ornate head-dress partially covering her forehead completed her adornment.

Emari momentarily held up a large golden disk which hung from a chord and struck it with a soft-tipped rod. The tone rolled through the air in waves, capturing her students' attention.

"Please take notes if you wish. You will find your recorders already enhanced. So let's begin." She waited until all her students had settled into their seats and looked up to her at the podium.

"The thing you need to understand about the incarnated human species at this stage of development on Gaia I, Blue Sector in D minor is that they, as well as the planet itself, are going through a shift again." Emari pressed her silver breastplate and forehead. A hologram of the Earth appeared in the center of the room. The students' excited whispers laced the air.

Professor Emari continued. "The shift is on many levels and dimensions at once, but most of the human species is not at a point in the seventh evolutionary cycle of this period to comprehend its complexity. Each being made a choice to incarnate, just as you are about to do, knowing they would be programmed to live in a three-dimensional world."

Images projected onto a large clear wall to the right of Emari, depicted scenes of life on earth through many centuries—humans living and working in towns, cities, and rural countrysides.

"Most do not comprehend their programming and still live on a survival level with instinctual fears, negative thought patterns and hallucinatory perceptions guiding their actions." Emari pointed to images of war, riots and poverty. "They live driven by territorial manifestations and fear of death."

Then an image projected a twentieth century city and close ups of scenes of abundance. "About half the human species have the perception that they have conquered imminent danger of starvation and disease through systems of finances and trade, construction, agriculture and energy, to live out their earthly life-span, some with perceived relative comfort. Regardless, the majority are unable to transcend their contracts or understand the bigger picture related to energy, thought, the time-space continuum, or ancestral origins." For a moment, the professor looked distracted.

"Ah," she continued, focusing again on her students. "But this is understandable you see, because of the outmoded program. In other words, the old standard involves suspending belief in, or understanding of the duality of the natural world and forgetting the multi-dimensional universes that we all take for granted here. The physicality, slower vibration and extreme gravity of Earth enhance this manifestation. Your group will have easier access to over-ride this programming." Professor Emari paused for effect. A few students raised their hands.

"I will take questions and make clarifications shortly as needed," she advised them. "First some background. Some humans understand that they have a duel operating system, that is an instinctual animal brain some call the reptilian brain, and a more highly developed brain which incidentally is programmed more like their planetary ancestors—the genetic material incorporated into an earlier evolution. So there is the ability for transmutation, but it has diminished greatly.

There are a few incarnated groups whose DNA has been adjusted during what humans refer to as the last few centuries—a century being a time-based equation that is an approximate length of what humans believe to be a generous life-span, but it's really only a fraction of what it once was. It may have been an oversight in the original DNA sequence. We have been enhancing the program since then with the help of our advanced team and you are about to enter that new phase. I am pleased to tell you this." Professor Emari smiled ever so slightly, but it was not in her nature to do so. She quickly reverted to her more somber persona.

"So there are a few humans and by that I mean a relative handful, who grasp what they call quantum physics—those who understand that there is no such thing as time, space or solidity, as it appears to them in the third dimension. There are those who are aware that fear has a dense frequency and solidifies matter. It has become necessary to dissolve and break though their thought-based status in order to expedite the passage for them, as well as all others, to the next level. We have enhanced a portion of the genetic code in some of their species to accommodate the cooperative spirit, a higher frequency we call *Eviray*, which is similar, if there is a comparison to be made at all—to their aptly named *Apis mellifera Linnaeus Order: Hymenoptera*—or honey bee."

By the nods and musings of her students, Professor Emari knew her telepathic lecture had been grasped by the majority so far. But she also knew that while the information would be understood in theory, the experience was monumental. Nothing her students, at least the new incarnates, could comprehend intellectually or intuitively would totally prepare them for the moment of impact. Even for the seasoned students, the moment of incarnation into a world where the expansiveness to which they had become accustomed would be suddenly compromised, confined, condensed by the claustrophobic nature of physicality. The disappearance of soul identity and a tidal wave of emotions would be overwhelming. The diminishing of color and luminosity that was everything here, would only be part of the shock. Incomprehensible sensations and fear of death would be altogether unfamiliar, but were inherent in the process.

But there was nothing Emari could do to prevent it. They had answered the call to serve. It was their choice. They could jump or not. It was up to each one to make that decision. She knew, though, which of her pupils would not hesitate when the opportunity arrived to do the work imperative to advancing the whole.

"Now, we are going to regroup—literally. No one will be going alone to any dimension. You will be going together in groups. There will be several entities appearing here, as I complete this portion of the lesson, whom you will recognize. They will have significant questions to ask each of you to determine your call, motivation and goals. They will assist you in placement and groupings, so you will be fully prepared even though memory and identity, as you know it, will be initially forgotten on impact. Any retention of former knowledge will be seen as delusion by the majority of humans around you. Nevertheless, your DNA will be altered appropriately, so you will each have the enhanced memory paths and resources to quicken your ability to operate multi-dimensionally, beyond the confines of your new environment."

Emari looked around at her pupils. "Before we proceed further, are there any questions?"

"Yes, Professor, I have one," Indigo initiated. "Can you explain the physical nature of fear or fear of death? What happens to the human organism?"

"Yes, good question, Indigo." Emari cleared her aura. Her eyes glowed. She pressed her middle eye with a finger of her hand, then momentarily touched her breastplate to produce a hologram of a human body lit from within. The image replaced the one of the earth in the middle of the room.

"Intuit the coagulation of energy solidifying with your essence inside of a body like this one. Meditate on the positive aspect of its chakras." Rainbows of luminescent color swirled above them freely. Then suddenly, all the color and light appeared to be sucked into a large dark hole. With a wave of Emari's hand the whole room was devoid of light.

Their was a audible groan from her students.

"The absence of light, is a negative aspect like fear. It produces a dramatic effect—a sense of loss of connection," Emari offered.

Emari waved her arms and light returned to the room. In holographic clarity above her students, a picture of two light-skinned female humans appeared in an earth-like desert landscape near a highway. One entered a small building. The other stood near a car and appeared to be looking for something. Her face was suddenly distorted. The students zoomed in on the image. "This is fear, a face of panic." Emari noted. "Now watch the desert landscape."

Her students observed as another human male form arose from the desert floor and walked toward the female standing by a vehicle. He handed her a small metal object. Then he walked away, his molecules disintegrating again into a hot dry breeze.

"Among many species, trans-mutative resources are available utilizing the multi-dimensional frequencies we all experience here." The professor enlarged the hologram of the dark-skinned, human male figure emerging from the desert wind. "However, it's not so for most humans at this stage, for whom persistent confinement is the thought or belief that they cannot be separated from solidity of form."

Emari continued. "Interpretation, which is actually *thought* or *belief,* stimulates the emotional reaction called *fear,* which in turn produces an automatic biochemical response within the cells. In other words, the instinctual brain automatically interprets when the physical vessel is in danger of perishing—or in the case of the woman in a desert, of being stranded."

The hologram shifted again to the woman standing by a vehicle looking bewildered and scared. "The organism's heart races, skin sweats, breath becomes hard. Even when given a glimpse, a portal to an alternate dimension of reality, belief in the finality and solidity of confinement persists. Then again, in this case there is movement—she's making progress."

Professor Emari checked the monitor to see if the dignitaries had arrived and she would have to end the lesson. With no one apparent, she continued. "Furthermore, in all species in general, there is a fight or flight reaction from perceived imminent danger, which you will learn further in the biochemical session of your anatomy and physiology class. The human animal like the non-human animal incarnating on this planet, will either run from whatever will destroy it or will attack, defend or attempt to destroy the perceived threat. However, the human brain comprehending that the physical entity is fragile and can perish, can misinterpret non-lethal threats as total destruction of the entity's essence. Regardless, even in cases of destruction of the body, most humans misunderstand the nature of '*Mutable Essence*,' although the species has a word for it."

The word 'soul' in 4,500 earth-based languages flashed across the breadth of the hologram.

"Fear manifested from thought is one of the heaviest and powerful forces we know." Professor Emari continued. "In order to shift, the lightness of being must be of greater value and hue. Fear is in direct opposition and impedes access, so to speak, to the light frequency of *Mutable Essence*." Emari paused, watching some of her students take notes.

"More often than not, the human animal fights back when confronted with what it perceives to be a threat to it's physical well-being," she continued. "But what is more serious is the effect that belief-based fear reactions are having on universal expansion and the stability of the earth herself." Emari waited to see if she could sustain her students' attention for one last point.

"Lastly, fear's side effect is heat, as I mentioned. The organism sweats, gets hot. So does the vibrational energy, the atmosphere, the elements. The very planet heats up. The complete illusion of threats—those generated from negative thoughts and emotions create heat and accelerate an actual attack. Whether on an individual basis or a mass scale. Arguments, disagreements we would consider insignificant or delusional can culminate in a mass delusion, whereby humans attack and destroy their physical bodies en masse and the environment of the earth herself."

Chartreuse raised her hand. "Do you mean that humans do not comprehend the planet as a living entity?" she asked.

"Correct, for most. At this point of evolution, the cause and effect of heat on electromagnetic energy, for example—the very energy that protects Gaia is only partially understood. We have engineered some changes in programming to promote greater understanding of the Gaia's electromagnetic field and the nature of environmental systems."

A murmur arose from her students. The professor knew that there were a few older students who were not new incarnates. If they had done their homework, replayed their programs, their own incarnations to earth would have exposed their own participation in a myriad of destructive energies.

But there was no contradiction. They could choose any part in any scenario to enhance evolutionary consciousness, be it an old pattern or new. "As I mentioned, your group will have a new program. There is no good or bad. Each one of you will play an important role. All contracts are universal and binding—treated with respect and esteem. Equal love and appreciation is shown to all incarnating or re-entering souls, with the exception of Oversouls and avatars. Whether benevolent or tyrannical, they are the divine providence of the higher councils and held to different standards of experience and capacity. Their exemplary compassion means a shift is imminent for Gaia." Emari looked over to a green-skinned figure standing in the back of the room, and smiled a rare smile.

CHAPTER 7

Rita Kerner

August 2004, *Tucson, Arizona*

Sharp peaks rose out of the flat desert floor like relics, skeletal spines of giant prehistoric animals. The jagged landscape seemed foreign and foreboding to Rita, but alluringly exotic at the same time. The sky was bluer than she ever remembered seeing it. The air, cleaner. But it was the light that was different. It was as if everything vibrated at a higher frequency, shimmering golden orange, giving the landscape a surrealistic glow.

Rita remembered having flown over the Southwest on her first trip to the West Coast years ago. Observing the desert from the air, she'd had the distinct impression of a huge ocean floor, the bed of some ancient sea. Now seeing it at eye level, it made sense. This land was a million years old. It was not just an American desert. It was planet Earth, a planet like Mars or the moon. Rita suddenly realized that it was not the place that was foreign, but she who was foreign, different, and out of place. It was her human existence that was a momentary blip on the radar, a microscopic spec in the vastness of the wind-swept sands. It was a feeling she'd had for as long as she could remember, like looking up at the Milky Way at night and feeling such an infinitesimal part of the great beyond. How is it we humans are here, such recent trespassers on this particular molten rock spinning in the middle of a vast universe?

Rita stared out the window of the car at the solid lava rocks of Picacho Peak and the giant Saguaro cactus with hundred-year-old arms reaching upward, as she and Cleo neared Tucson.

"Earth to Rita..." Cleo's voice broke through Rita's existential contemplation.

"We're getting close to Tucson. Can you check the directions, honey?" Donna said to get off at the Ina Road exit. She and Sharon said that they live on the Northeast near the Catalina Mountains. Do you see any of that on the map?" Rita checked the map.

Within an hour, they drove into Donna and Sharon's driveway. The majestic Catalina's loomed almost within reach it seemed, a powerful backdrop to the sandy backyard complete with pool and patio. "This is amazing!" Rita exclaimed, hugging her old friends.

"Come in, we'll show you around," Sharon said. She pet Oliver. "Then you can get settled, have a drink, go for a swim."

"Ah, I can't wait—wow!" Cleo was almost speechless.

"It's so great to see you both in this beautiful place. A far cry from Manhattan life, huh?" Rita laughed.

"Do you think?" Donna smiled. "Some days I can't believe how lucky we are to have found this place. And wait 'til you see the community of women here and all the incredible places to paint. It's an artist's paradise. Speaking of which," she winked, "there are some great art galleries not far from here. We thought you might like to go see an art exhibit with us on Saturday evening. You will be staying until then, right?"

As if needing any more enticement, Donna, who was not one to boast, smoothed back a wisp of blond hair and opened the glass sliding doors to the patio with a grand gesture. A plethora of colorful flowers, and stone sculptures of Kuan Yin and Buddah sat nestled into white-pebble rock gardens. Prickly pear cactus, fuchsia oleander, and orange and lemon trees, grew near the slate path that led to the bar and pool with its adjacent blue pool house. Two large palms towered at the edge of the yard providing shade and a natural place for a double-sized hammock. Rita and Cleo walked dreamily through paradise. Oliver followed, sniffing all the new smells.

"Hey, you two," Sharon grinned. She was in her element. Short brown hair with wisps of gray at the temples framed her round olive-skinned face, tanned from the desert sun. She had happily shed a business suit permanently two years ago for more retiring apparel—Hawaiian shirts, shorts, and sandals. "What are you two drinking?"

"I'll have lemonade," Cleo replied, following Sharon to the poolside bar. "Incredible set-up you have out here." Cleo tried to hide her envy. "So this is how the *other half* lives, eh?" she teased.

Sharon nodded. "We are fortunate. We have had some dynamite parties with a full-moon, music, dancing, barbecues, midnight swims. It's pretty magical."

Rita and Donna meandered toward the bar past the Spanish-tiled pool. Its cool water beckoned Rita. Even with the sun heading toward the horizon, the air was still a balmy 93 degrees.

"And you, Rita? A cold beer?"

"With a twist of lime—sounds great." Rita took a deep breath. "Ah, this is the life." She looked at Cleo longingly. Maybe we should settle here instead, she thought. But she knew it was not something Cleo would ever consider—too hot for her hot-blooded gal, who longed for the cool ocean breezes of the Pacific.

"Here's to friendship!" Sharon handed Donna her icy coke and raised her own beer glass. "We're so happy you're here."

Later that evening, they sat down to home-made chicken enchiladas and beef tacos, catching up on lost time. "So how's Noah? Still seeing that girl from California? Do you have any recent pictures? God, I don't think we've seen him since his college graduation, right Sharon?"

"Yeah, he's pretty grown up," Rita said. "I do have some pictures in my suitcase. I can show you tomorrow. I told him I was coming to visit you—I'm sure he'd like to see you too."

"How are your kids, Cleo? Are they happy you're moving to California?" Sharon asked.

"I think they're looking forward to not having to fly across country for school breaks. They're happy about it, even if they don't say it in so many words."

"What are your plans when you get settled. Are you still going to paint, Rita?" Donna inquired. "I think your work would do well in California."

"Oh, yes I plan to paint, and also teach. It would be nice to paint here, too. The light is really different. The cactus plants are beautiful." She eyed Cleo.

"Why don't you? I can take you to Tohono Chul Park, a great place to paint." Donna turned to Sharon. "You want to join us or show Cleo the Sonoran Desert Museum, while we go paint. Whada ya say? Oliver can stay here in the air-conditioning."

"Hmm, that sounds like fun." Cleo perked up. She liked spending time with Sharon. She was easy going and direct—no surprises, no innuendo, just down to earth.

The next morning Rita and Donna headed out to Tohono Chul. They walked along the sandy paths to the little museum gift shop with its cool courtyard surrounded by flowering prickly pear cactus, acacia, and mesquite trees in the shadow of the Catalina Mountains. There, Rita set up her easel, canvas and paints next to an old wooden bench, while Donna pulled out the zoom lens for her camera.

"I haven't painted in a while," Rita admitted.

Donna could hear remorse in her voice. "Why is that?" Donna broached the subject cautiously. Why would Rita squelch her own creativity?

"It's just that I kept painting two portraits that kind of haunted me. I could not figure out who they were. One was a petite French woman and her maid, like from the eighteenth century and the other a modern-day woman in jeans and a sports jacket." Rita laughed. "It sound silly, pretty innocent, I guess, but they each made me feel nervous and sad. I had upsetting dreams." Rita shook off the image. "Mostly I stopped because I thought whatever I was painting was causing something I didn't understand, beside the dreams, I mean." Rita paused and leaned toward Donna as if revealing a secret. "Everywhere I go people seem to confuse me for someone else." Rita stopped talking, thinking she must sound nuts.

She looked at the idyllic scene in front of them—flowering cactus against a backdrop of orange and purple mountains, a turquoise sky. "It's not important, now. I'm here with my dear friend, painting *plein air* in this enchanted setting."

Donna, being the inquisitive type, was about to question Rita further when the door to the nearby park gift shop swung open. A man and woman came out into the courtyard, hugged and parted. The man turned. "Hi, how are you?" He waved to Donna and walked toward them.

"Oh, hey, Gary! Nice to see you! You still working here?" Donna greeted the tall handsome Black man dressed in a crisp white T shirt and jeans. "How's Michael?"

"He's better, thanks. Turned out to be just an allergy—thank goodness. I'm just here part-time to train the new docent."

"Oh, excuse me," Donna said. "This is my friend, Rita. She and her girlfriend are moving to California from the East coast and are visiting. She's an artist."

Rita smiled and shook Gary's out-stretched hand. "Nice to meet you," she said.

"Same here. Wow, you look really familiar," he said squinting at Rita.

"I get that a lot," Rita said, glad Cleo was not with them to hear the refrain.

"No, really. I know I've seen you before." Gary couldn't place where he'd seen her face. He strained his memory. "I got it! I think you look like my partner's sister, Rachel. Where on the East Coast are you from?"

"I'm from New York originally, but we're moving from Massachusetts," Rita said.

"My partner Michael and I both have family in Massachusetts—small world. Mine's in Boston mostly." Gary smiled. "You do look a lot like Michael's sister. So, you're an artist, huh? Can't go wrong in the desert. Wonderful light here."

"Yes, it's the first thing I noticed." Rita consciously relaxed a little. "Do you paint too?"

"Gary's a culinary artist!" Donna chimed in.

"I'm an art lover, girlfriend," he said with flair.

"Well, where would we painters be without you?" Rita laughed.

"It was nice to meet you, Rita. I look forward to seeing your art one day." He turned to Donna. "Don't be a stranger, girl. Say hello to Sharon for me. I hope you two are coming to our party after the film festival," he reminded.

"We wouldn't miss it, Gary. Love to Michael." Donna returned his hug. Meanwhile, Rita busied herself picking out a few brushes and tubes of paint from her bag, trying to put aside the resemblance issue that plagued her.

"Gary and Michael are a great couple—and they do buy art," Donna added putting her arm around Rita's shoulder, noticing her pensive mood. "It's probably just coincidental you know, you reminding people of someone they know. Maybe painting landscapes for a while will help chase away those blues and nightmares, huh? What you need is subject matter that is pure nature!" She demonstrated, holding up her hands, her fingers creating a frame around the distant mountains ablaze in the mid-morning sun. Then she picked up her camera took a shot of the mountains, and another of a large prickly pear cactus boasting fuchsia flowers.

Rita squeezed out an assortment of bright colored paints onto her palette. Mixing each with small amounts of water, she brushed the paint in all directions on her canvas and watched swirls of color mimic the same light and shadows she observed in the desert flora. Her mountains came to life in majestic purples and orange hues against an azure sky, while cactus flaunted viridian green, chartreuse and turquoise. Mesquite and acacia wore crimson and yellow ocher. Lost in the shapes and colors of desert sands and sky, Rita melted into creative meditation. All thought, all worry, time itself ceased. There were only colors, warm breezes and the sweet scent of desert flowers.

When the sun began its descent toward the Tucson Mountains in the West, Rita put the finishing touches on her new painting. "Voila!" She stood back and admired it. "Not bad, if I do say so myself."

"Not bad?" Donna exhaled. "It's fabulous. Can I buy it?"

"Oh, c'mon. Really?" Rita was surprised and pleased, but she could not sell this to her friend. "I wouldn't think of it. You can have it as my gift to you and Sharon."

"You can't go giving away your work, my friend. Besides, I can afford it, and I'm sure you could use the money toward the expenses of relocating. Right?"

"Well, I'll think about it." Rita said, her sentence cut short by Donna's ringing cell phone.

"Really? The casino? Okay, hold on," Donna smirked. "Our sweeties want to stop off at the new casino. They have a buffet of meats galore. Do you want to meet them or dine here? The menu here is more, uh—upscale."

"It would be nice to have more time here," Rita replied, preferring quiet time with Donna. Some fine dining and wine would make it a perfect end to the day.

As nightfall descended, the two friends drove back along Ina Road winding close to the Catalina foothills. Coyotes howled in the distance. Rita breathed in the cool evening air. Adjusting her seat to lean back, she looked up into the silent night sky. A sliver of moonlight and a blanket of stars twinkled in the vast deep blue universe. "Magical," Rita whispered.

Two more days in the desert flew by for Rita and Cleo. "I'm sorry you can't stay longer." Donna said to Rita as they prepared a final breakfast in the kitchen. "I think it would be healing here for you. Maybe get to a place where whatever transition is happening can feel okay," she offered. "There are so many spiritual people here—artists and healers from different cultural backgrounds. After you get settled you can come back for a visit, maybe Thanksgiving. You think Cleo would like that too?"

Donna suddenly remembered a note on her calendar. "Oh!" Her eyes lit up. "There is a wonderful show by a unique artist I just discovered last year—Marla C. Woods. She is scheduled for a one-woman show at Aphrodite's Gallery in Tubac, opening Thanksgiving weekend. I have a post card somewhere showing one of her pieces." Donna rummaged in her handbag for a gallery announcement.

"Marla C. Woods, the sculptor?' Rita asked. "Amazing! I mean, I have a book of her work that Cleo gave me." Rita had goosebumps.

"Oh, then you must come! You and Cleo would love this place around the holidays. It's a wonderland." Donna smiled. "And you have to come to the gem and mineral show here in early February. It's like nothing you've ever seen! Magical really."

"That seems to be the theme here in the desert," Rita laughed, the knot in her stomach finally dissolving.

After breakfast, Sharon got some maps from the glove compartment of the convertible and handed them to Rita and Cleo. "By the way, this is the clearest map I have of the West including Arizona and California. Route 10 to California is probably best," she said laying the map down and drawing a route with red pen. "If you want to miss the traffic in LA, take 210 after Ontario to the 5 to 126, then head north on 101. Noah lives in Santa Cruz, right?" She drew the spot on the map.

"Thanks." Rita smiled. She was looking forward to seeing Noah. But the allure of the desert had done something to her. She was someone else here. It was as if some part of her was melting away.

Two days later, Santa Cruz, California

"This is his apartment building." Rita read the number again to make sure. Cleo drove into the parking lot and took a visitor's spot. "Looks pretty nice with all the Bougainvillea in bloom everywhere. California is something, isn't it?" Rita smiled and dialed Noah's number. "Hi honey, we're here. Yes, down in the parking lot. Want us to come up? Okay, apartment 4B, got it." She hooked Oliver's leash on him.

Cleo grabbed Noah and Kate's presents, then followed Rita up the flight of cement stairs after a short walk with Oliver.

"Hi, Mom," Noah greeted them with a smile and hugged his mother. Oliver jumped up licking his pal. "Hey, Buddy." Noah hugged the dog. "Okay down, boy." Then he turned to Rita. "What's all this, Mom?" he asked eyeing the gifts.

"Just a little something we bought you in New Mexico when we were with your Aunt Irene. This one's for you and this is for Kate. Where is Kate?" Rita asked.

"Uh, she isn't here right now. She's visiting her folks." Noah opened his package. "Nice!" he said, feeling the woven blanket. Rita sensed something was wrong.

"I ordered a pizza about 20 minutes ago when you called to say you were close to Santa Cruz. It should be here soon. Figured you'd be hungry. I know I am. I didn't have much before work this morning."

"Sounds great." Cleo smiled and patted Noah on the back. "Thanks, we didn't stop since breakfast. The ride to the coast was mesmerizing—breathtaking."

"You work on Saturday?" Rita tried to sound nonchalant.

"They called me in for a few hours to help with an issue in the mainframe. No, not usually," Noah seemed uneasy. "Look, Mom, things are okay, but Kate and I have been going through some stuff. I'm not sure she will be visiting while you're here." His dark eyes were sad behind the bravado.

"Oh, honey, I'm so sorry," Rita said. She had dismissed her doubts about Kate after first meeting her, since the two had seemed happily in love.

"Yeah, well, you know. It's mostly her family. I don't think they like me much."

"What's not to like?" Rita raised her voice. "You're a great guy—good looking, smart, employed and nice, to boot. And you adore her, right?"

"Yeah, thanks, Mom. I think it's the New York Jewish thing though."

Rita looked wide-eyed at Noah, then to Cleo and back to Noah. "They're anti-Semitic?"

"Not blatantly. They're polite to me when we visit, but there is this undercurrent, a feeling like I'm not what they want for their daughter, like she could do better." He fidgeted with some utensils and napkins for the anticipated lunch. "You know, like they want her to marry her own kind, own class, have blond, blue-eyed grandchildren, I guess. It's been uncomfortable since the Christmas holiday. I'd had a little too much wine and made a joke about Christmas celebrating the birth of a Jewish guy like me." He laughed nervously.

Rita shot Cleo a knowing glance remembering the kick she'd gotten from Cleo under the table at one Christmas dinner when Rita had reminded Cleo's minister brother and his wife of the same thing. "Yeah, some Christians don't appreciate that detail. But I'm so sorry, honey. It's awful."

Rita had always tried to protect him from anti-Semitism once they had moved from New York. Now, she could only support him. She knew the complex feelings and pain he was going through. Rita's first lover had left her for a zealot, before the born-again movement even existed. Rita remembered the letters she started to receive after they broke up, telling her that she might save her Jewish soul if she found Jesus. It was hurtful at the time, but Rita dismissed it eventually, sending back a final letter that read: *I have no worries about my soul. If you wish to believe that the Rabbi of Nazareth is the son of God—you're entitled. Best wishes to you. Shalom.* Rita sighed. The apple didn't fall far from the tree, she thought.

"Have you and Kate had any luck talking about it?"

"No, not really." Noah paused. "She's very close to her family and they have money. I don't think she wants to rock the boat." He sounded discouraged. "Maybe I just need to move on."

"Well, you can always talk to me about it." Rita put an arm around his shoulder just as the doorbell rang. "I know talking to your Mom is not the thing you want to be doing, but I'm here for you," she added. "Let me pay for the pizza. How much is it?"

"My treat." Noah was already at the door with cash in hand.

He set the pizza on the counter in the kitchenette and then pulled out some plates and glasses. He looked around at the small clutters of books, magazines and papers on the dining room table. "Let's eat on the porch. Not a lot of room," he apologized, "but it's got chairs and a clean table at least."

After lunch, Noah suggested he take them on a little tour of Santa Cruz and a walk by the beach with Oliver. It was a warm, clear dusk when they reached the boardwalk. The sun had turned the sky a misty pink. The smell of the sea relaxed them. "Anyone want to go on the Ferris wheel?" Rita laughed.

"Not me." Cleo said. "You two can go. Me and Oliver are happy with our paws on the ground. I'll go play some games, win you a big old teddy bear," she winked.

"It's that Capricorn energy of yours." Rita nudged Cleo. Then she turned to Noah. "Speaking of which, have you thought about getting an astrological reading? It could be helpful, honey."

"Ma, really?" He rolled his eyes. "Remember when you got me a reading for my eighteenth birthday with your friend, Jane? I think that was enough."

"Your chart is in motion like the universe. Things change, you know. Besides, you're not a teenager anymore. Maybe it would help to get some insights."

"I'll think about it, okay?"

"Okay." Rita knew when to drop the subject. "Hey, I almost forgot. I brought you a book that your grandfather wanted you to have. He said it was his favorite when he was a young man."

"Oh, yeah? I could use a good book to read. What's it about?" he asked glad to change the subject.

"It's called *The Little Old Bookshop.*" Rita approached sharing her intuition on the matter slowly. "I think he wanted you to have it because it reminded him of you—your love of music. There is a character in the story…well, you can see for yourself."

"Okay, sounds good." Maybe he'd read it and maybe not, he thought. Noah could sense when his mother had ulterior motives. "It's not about astrology, is it?"

"No," Rita answered.

"C'mon Mom…I know you. Why would Grandpa leave me this book? When did he give it to you, anyway? "

"He was rereading it before he died and he asked me to give it to you. I didn't know why until I read a bit of it, the first chapter. I think it's a story of a past life he had."

Noah's eyes widened. "Geez…really, Mom? Grandpa was not like you, you know. He was—normal."

"Thanks, dear."

"No, I didn't mean that. You know what I mean. He wasn't into past lives and all that lala-land stuff." Noah tried to appease Rita.

"We live in lala-land now in case you haven't noticed, hon." Rita smiled. Then her tone turned serious, "No really, I think there is something important he wanted you to know somehow. I realize it is out of character, but he gave it to me on his death bed to give to you, so it was important to him. I had somehow overlooked it when I moved in with Cleo. I came across it when I was packing to come to California." Rita explained.

"Well, I will…" Noah interrupted.

"Wait, hon, let me finish," Rita said. "Sometimes people have a different sense of the world as they are in transition to death, like glimmers of things, visions of things. Even if he did not consciously realize it, there is a story here." Rita paused. "You know how my father and I did not really get along. You were witness to our fights when you were growing up, remember?"

Noah nodded. "Yeah, he did not treat you very nicely, I remember that."

"But, he did adore *you*, you know. I think it was through you that we managed to make amends finally." Rita tried to tie the loose ends together. "I think this book is a story of a past life he and I and you shared, one of love and caring—a deeper connection. I think I have had other lifetimes with my father, your grandfather and you. I believe this story is one of them, somehow. And somehow he knew that too." Rita could see Noah's attention waning. "I know it sounds way out there, but I think he left it for you because he wanted you to know, say how sorry he was." Rita's eyes watered.

"Okay, Mom easy does it." Noah put his arm around his mom's shoulder this time. "I'll read it, okay?"

Rita wiped away a tear. Suddenly, a vision of the painting she had begun appeared in her mind's eye—the picture of a little French woman. "Why, of course!" Rita said aloud.

Noah looked puzzled.

"I think that it's Nicolette from *The Little Old Bookshop*." Rita announced.

"You okay, Mom? Maybe we should get home. You want some water?" Noah was worried.

"Oh, son, I'm fine." She turned and yelled to Cleo who was busy trying to win the teddy bear at the toss-a-ring-bottle game. "Cleo, Cleo! I figured out who the painting of the French lady is," Rita hollered. People stared at Rita as she made a beeline to Cleo.

"Is she making sense?" Noah caught up and gave Cleo a look of embarrassed concern.

Cleo tossed her last ring, missing the bottle she was aiming for. She reluctantly took a little plastic monkey from the game vendor, grumbling about not getting the teddy bear. She turned to Noah. "It's about your mom's paintings, you know. She did one a while ago of a French woman and she's been trying to figure out who it is," she told Noah. Cleo turned to Rita. "So you figured it out? What's the verdict? Who is she?"

A big smile spread across Rita's face. "It's Nicolette—from the *The Little Old Bookshop.*"

Cleo looked at Noah and they both burst out laughing. Rita didn't see what was quite so funny. Cleo and Noah's laughter sputtered to coughing.

"Let's go get a beer!" Cleo suggested, putting an arm around Noah's shoulder. "This is one for the books." She paused digesting her own pun. "For the books! Get it?" she chortled.

"You know, the last time I saw Mom, we went out for lunch," Noah said, his eyes twinkling. "Right in the middle of our fish and chips, she told me she'd had a past life as a gorilla!"

This time they howled. Even Rita, who had learned to laugh at herself once in a while, chuckled. It was easier to do when seeing herself through the amused eyes of her son.

"Let's have some seafood with our beer, my treat," Cleo laughed.

"I know just the place." Noah grinned.

Before long they had devoured a dinner of shrimp scampi, stuffed lobster tails and spinach salad. After dessert of fresh strawberries and cream they drove Noah home.

"Let's stay in touch, hon. As soon as we get settled you'll come and visit, stay for a weekend. It's not far." Rita gave Noah a hug. "I love you, son. Things will be okay. Just believe in yourself."

Noah hugged them both and pet Oliver. "Drive safe." He turned to Rita "Love you, Mom. Don't worry, okay?"

"Well, that comes with being a mom—but I'm getting better." Rita smiled.

CHAPTER 8

Nicolette Marchand

Early October 1778, Paris, France

Nicolette combed and braided her dark wavy hair, securing the ends neatly up on her head with the tortoiseshell combs that had belonged to her mother, Violette. She had few objects of remembrance, making the combs a precious treasure. As a child of seven, Nicolette remembered holding them up to the sunlight and squinting, watching prisms of refracted light cast rainbows through the shiny translucent shells. She would lose herself in the play of color, as her mother waited patiently for Nicolette to hand her the combs.

Nicolette's memories were semi-sweet. The deep void only her mother's love could fill, lingered. Although seventeen years had passed, Nicolette placed the combs in her own hair each day, feeling for just an instant the sensation of that special bond that once embraced her.

Finished pinning up her hair, she heard the water kettle boil over, hissing on the stove. Her father was already sitting at the breakfast table in their tiny flat above the noisy city street's open market He poured over his account books with his spectacles sitting low on the bridge of his nose, when she entered the kitchen to prepare their consommé and rolls. He looked older to Nicolette today. "Bonjour, Papa. You're up extra early. Didn't you sleep well?"

"Good morning, daughter. I slept well enough. I am preparing for the new shipment of rare sheet music you found, calculating its price should we have a buyer, soon. Once Marcel hears about it, well, it's as good as sold."

Papa's getting old, Nicolette thought again. She placed a plate of warm rolls and butter in front of him. Jean-Paul Marchand was elderly at sixty-five and his memory was fading rapidly. He did not remember that his old friend, Marcel had passed away last winter.

Jean-Paul had once been a hardy man appearing younger than his age. At forty, he had met and married Nicolette's beautiful mother, twenty years younger than himself. They'd been happy, soon conceiving their only child, Nicolette, and opening the little bookshop. He'd been utterly forlorn when Violette died only nine years into their marriage. Too distraught to care for his young daughter, Jean-Paul had sent Nicolette to live with her Aunt Juliet in the countryside just west of Paris.

There, in a small cottage next to the village bakery, her aunt had cared for her. She taught Nicolette the duties and responsibilities of womanhood—cooking, cleaning, caring for the chickens and milking the goats. Nicolette liked to cook, but especially loved to bake. She soon learned some simple recipes. Cinnamon bread pudding was her favorite, and she prepared it often for her father when finally she persuaded her aunt to let her return to Paris, on her tenth birthday. Jean-Paul had not taken another wife and did the best he could to raise his only offspring. Nicolette became a loyal daughter, devoting all her time to him and his beloved books and sheet music.

She was happy to be home. The familiarity of the old bookshop where she had played as a small child, comforted her. The musty rare books and sheets of classical music became the foundation of her education. She read every book that her father bought. She taught herself to read musical notes and learned compositions by some of the great master composers that had flourished in Europe for over a century. Writing every chance she got, Nicolette kept her own thoughts, poems, and favorite quotes, filling a dozen journals as the years went by. Her vocabulary grew impressive, even by her father's high standards. Her French was impeccable, her German and Italian, excellent.

Now, Jean-Paul relied on his daughter's sharp memory and business skills. He leaned on her for the details of running the shop, selling, and stocking. He trusted her experience and intellectual expertise to locate rare manuscripts that would keep the gold flowing, keep their finances in order. While Nicolette took over the organization of the small shop, her father spent more time in their personal reading corner close to the shelves that held his most precious treasures. Old leather-bound volumes of Homer's *Iliad* and *Odyssey*, works of Vivaldi, Handel and Bach, as well as his rare copies of *Harmonice Musices Odhecaton,* Petrucci's 1502 *Canti B,* and a valuable fourteenth century Bible of Matteo di Planisio were all close to his heart.

Smoking his pipe and reading by low gaslight, Jean-Paul sat in his large, over-stuffed chair with its worn, red velvet upholstery next to a wooden side table that held his pipes, sweet tobacco, and crystal ashtray. An Italian tapestry hung on the stone wall behind Jean-Paul's chair, while a tattered-edged Persian rug lay under his feet providing warmth and comfort. Nicolette's chair, positioned directly across from her father's, was covered in heavy silk brocade. A faded pink tinge remained from its original rose color, after years of use. On the adjacent wall, a fire lit in the small stone fireplace warmed them on chilly winter days, its mantel crowded with porcelain figurines, a fine wood clock, a gilded mirror and two candelabras. In the soft lit ambiance of their personal alcove, father and daughter became best friends over volumes of Voltaire, Jean de La Fontaine's *Aesop* and *Phaedrus* inspired fables, poems of Jean Racine and Nicolas Boileau-Despréaux, Shakespeare's *Hamlet* and *Romeo and Juliet.*

When Nicolette was absorbed with orders, customers, or shipments, Jean-Paul would sit reading by himself, dozing off occasionally. Routinely, he'd take out his gold pocket watch to adjust the time, matching it by the minute to the hourly chimes of the mantle clock, or check the time when a customer came into the shop. Now, Nicolette noticed, he hardly got up anymore to greet anyone, unless it was an old friend or a regular customer.

Jean-Paul appreciated loyal customers, but he had no more interest in small talk or idle gossip, no time for the occasional curiosity seekers who wandered in by accident, who had no idea what they wanted, or money to buy anything. He stopped remarking about the daily weather. "It's sunny, it's rainy, it's hot, it's cold. I'm not a farmer, so I don't need to discuss it," he'd say sardonically. "If the weather's bad, this too shall pass. *C'est rien*," he recounted when the subject arose, even though he still grumbled when it grew too hot or cold.

His demeanor was different with Nicolette, though. He would talk to his daughter about almost anything. He appreciated her exuberant curiosity. Answering all her questions had drawn him from the depths of a widower's despair, back into life. He took great pleasure in being her mentor. Conscious that she exceeded him in her knowledge of art, music, history, and language, he felt great pride in his protégé. Of late, however, Jean-Paul had begun to worry about Nicolette. He needed her, but her prospects for a husband were getting slimmer with the years. Jean-Paul knew his own life would end soon. How many years could he have left? Who would care for his precious daughter?

So, it was a great relief when a handsome young man came into the shop one early October day, a few months before Nicolette's twenty-fifth birthday. He seemed at first glance a proper, well-dressed man, but with the creative flair of the younger generation. His light brown hair was a bit wilder than the fashion, his beard a bit scruffier. His eyes were a bright and brilliant blue.

Nicolette stood behind the polished wood counter near the glass-paned front door. A little bell rang when it opened.

"Bonjour, Mademoiselle," the gentleman said softly.

Nicolette, smiled. "Bonjour, Monsieur."

"I am Claude Jacques Gustav, from Strasbourg." He coughed suddenly, covering his mouth with his scarf. "Oh, pardon, Mademoiselle. I am a little hoarse from my long trip." He paused and gained his composure, clearing his throat. "I wonder if you can assist me. I am new in Paris. Actually, I am here at the request of Madame de Brionne, wife of Louis de Lorraine. She has invited me to play for her and her guests at the home of her brother, Charles Jules, Prince of Rochefort, in a few weeks. Unfortunately, on my travels, I seemed to have lost the sheet music I was to play and wondered if you might have a copy, or perhaps direct me to a source for obtaining Bach's *Prelude and Fugue in A minor,* and *Concerto in D major?*

"It's so nice to make your acquaintance, Monsieur Gustav," Nicolette said. "Why, I think we do have just what you are looking for." Nicolette was pleased she could help him—an obviously talented, and perhaps soon to be famous, musician. She liked him right away. He was not stuffy or arrogant like some of the musicians that came to the shop, but rather refreshingly charming.

Jean-Paul observed the encounter from his reading corner and put his pipe carefully in the ashtray. He marked his place in the manuscript he was reading. Then he rose from his chair and walked past the shelves of books to the front of the shop. "Bonjour, Monsieur Gustav," he said, holding out his hand. "I am the proprietor, Jean-Paul Marchand. This is my daughter, Mademoiselle Nicolette. *Bienvenue a Paris!*" Jean-Paul was almost gleeful.

Nicolette could see the wheels in her father's head turning. She knew exactly what he was thinking. She gave Jean-Paul a sideways glance. Then she turned back to the young man. "If you wait here just a few minutes, I can get the first of the two selections for you. We have those sheets on hand, right Father?"

"Yes, of course—excellent choices," Jean-Paul said buoyantly, turning to Claude Gustav.

"We can procure the other in just a few days if you can come back on Thursday, two days from now," Nicolette said. She smiled demurely, looking down at the young man's hands with his delicate long fingers and white, almost translucent skin. *Pale*, she thought. The word reverberated in her mind, although she did not know why. She looked briefly at him again, somehow sensing an intensity she had not noticed before. Then without another word, Nicolette went to fetch his sheet music.

"Oh! This is wonderful!" Claude Gustav smiled broadly and shook Jean-Paul's hand. "I thought I would lose so much practice time. Thank you so much. *Merci, beaucoup!*" Claude was jubilant. He cleared his throat again.

"Here it is." Nicolette appeared at the front counter again carrying a muslin wrapped bundle tied with twine. We had one complete set. It must have been waiting for you." She noticed a little twinkle in her father's eyes. "That will be three livre tournoi," she said writing down the amount and placing the number in the log.

"Actually, since you are a new customer, we can give you a better price. Two livre tournoi for this first order!" Jean-Paul slapped the young man's back gently. Nicolette now cleared her throat.

"Well then," she said, "You have caught my father in a good mood today."

"Thank you again," said Claude Gustav. "I will be back on Thursday afternoon. I think I am going to like Paris," he smiled. "Goodbye, for now, Mademoiselle Nicolette. Merci, Monsieur Marchand, Merci." Claude Gustav wrapped his wool scarf more securely around his neck. Holding his package under one arm, he opened the door of the shop. A gust of Paris' autumn air caught him. He held his hand over his mouth and coughed once. Then he closed the door behind him and hurried out into the bustling city street.

Early November, 1778

"Papa," Nicolette danced into the kitchen holding a letter. "Papa, I have received an invitation from Claude Jacques Gustav to hear him perform!"

"You are surprised that he likes you, my dear daughter? You have been so good to him these last few weeks, showing him around Paris and taking him under your wing. It is only fitting he should show you such favor," Jean-Paul reasoned. "Perhaps he has feelings for you." Jean-Paul could only hope for such an outcome.

"Oh Papa, he is so much younger than me," Nicolette said. "I highly doubt he has designs for me. I'm more like an older sister to him, I'm sure."

"Seven years is not a lifetime. Your mother and I were twenty years different in age."

Nicolette gave her father a furtive glance. "You are a man—naturally. I don't think a younger man wants an older woman."

"Older?" You are only twenty-five. You have so many years..." Jean-Paul stopped. Nicolette's mother had passed at age thirty. He did not want to think of his daughter having such a short time. To outlive his only child was more than he could contemplate.

"I want you to take one hundred livre from our account and go see Madame Francoise Courtier on Rue Saint-Honoré. She will make you a dress to match your beauty, to wear to such a prestigious event." Jean-Paul beamed.

"Oh, Papa. That is fashion for the nobility. I am in no need of such a fuss. I can wear my Christmas dress. It's almost perfect. And it's appropriate even if the weather gets colder."

"No, my dear. I want you to have something new. Please, allow me this pleasure to spoil you just this one time. You have worked so hard." Jean-Paul's voice cracked, his eyes watered.

"*Merci,* Papa. Thank you." She hugged her father noticing again how fragile he had become. Shorter and thinner, his body was shrinking, his vigor evaporating with the passing months. Nicolette knew he wanted to see her married before he died. Now it was Nicolette who grieved in silence. No husband could make up for the loss of her father and certainly not the young Claude Jacque Gustav, no matter his talent or imminent good fortune.

Nicolette took her father's wrinkled hand.

"I love you, Papa," she whispered. "Don't worry."

Nicolette finished clearing the books she had logged, while Jean-Paul made his way to his reading corner. He threw another log into the fireplace prodding the hot embers until it caught fire. Then he settled into his chair and lit his pipe. He watched his daughter count out one hundred livre for a proper dress, fit for such an occasion.

"I won't be too long, Papa. Madame Courtier is probably busy, but I will let her know I wish to order a new dress. I should be back soon." She waved to her father.

Making her way down Rue Haute Feuille, Nicolette turned onto Rue Saint Andre. At Rue Dauphine, she turned and continued her long walk to Rue Saint-Honoré where Madame Francoise Courtier and her sister Mademoiselle Amelia had a small dress shop. Their father and uncle before them, both tailors of some regard, had made clothes for many of the wealthier Paris residents. Now, a new gold-lettered sign hung from its stained glass trimmed window with the store's name prominently placed. As *Madame Courtier's Fine Clothing* designed current and in vogue fashions for the nobility, aristocratic and wealthy women of Paris, the merchant class did not commonly frequent the shop. Nicolette hesitated at the front door, unsure of herself. Then, summoning her courage, she entered.

Madame Francoise and Mademoiselle Amelia sat next to each other sewing an elaborate brocade cape.

"Bonjour," Nicolette said softly.

"Bonjour, Mademoiselle." Madame rose to greet the new customer. "May I help you?" she said scrutinizing the face of the young woman. "You look familiar to me. Do I know you?" she added.

"I am Nicolette Marchand, the daughter of Jean-Paul Marchand, owner of *Le Petite Vieux Librarie* on Rue Haute Feuille. We met some time ago when you accompanied your father to our shop in search of a rare book.

Madame Francoise squinted. "Oh yes, I know your father's shop. How nice to see you," she smiled demurely. "What can I do for you?"

"I am in need of a dress for a musical recital at the home of Charles Jules, Prince of Rochefort." Nicolette tried to sound confident.

"Oh, I see." Suddenly Madame Francoise' checks flushed, her eyes lit. "How lovely. And what is the occasion for this honor?" Her tone belied her doubt.

"I've been invited by the well-known musician Monsieur Clause Jacques Gustav of Strasbourg to accompany him. He has been invited to perform by Madame de Brionne."

"I see. That is quite exciting for a young woman like yourself." She motioned to Amelia. "Amelia will fit you for a suitable dress, my dear. The price will be two hundred livre, as a favor to your father."

Nicolette swallowed her surprise. The price was double the money that she'd brought.

"You can give us half now and half when we are finished." Madame Francoise advised. "When is the salon, so we are sure to have it ready in time?"

"It's in three weeks time. Is that enough time for you to make a dress for me?" Nicolette asked innocently.

"You understand it is not much time for me. I have orders ahead of yours. However, Amelia can do it in the time you need. She is very accomplished."

Amelia disappeared behind a curtain. After some time, she reappeared carrying three bolts of fabric, her measuring tape, scissors and a few drawings. She seemed an anxious wisp of a woman, but with intelligent eyes, Nicolette noticed.

"I have these patterns and fabric that might make just the appropriate dress for you," she said politely. Taking her cue from Madame Francoise, Amelia took a deep breath to relax and slow her movements. On the table, she laid out the deep turquoise velvet, white lace, and cream-colored silk with gold brocade. In graceful movements, she folded one fabric over the next.

Nicolette had never seen anything so beautiful. She could barely speak. Reaching out to touch the velvet, its soft luxurious texture almost made her weep. Finally, she found her voice.

"I could not imagine anything more beautiful, thank you," she sighed.

"I think this color would do perfectly for you and the occasion. Here is the design we will make." Amelia held a picture in front of Nicolette, pointing out the details. "The bodice and skirt in velvet, the neckline in silk brocade and sleeves trimmed in lace."

Amelia guided Nicolette to a small wooden box in front of a tall mirror. "Please stand here while I take your measurements. You will have to take your clothing off...just leave on your undergarments." Amelia was all business. Measuring and nervously writing notes on a log that sat on a table alongside the mirror. She meticulously measured every inch of Nicolette's body from toes to waist, from waist to chest to neck to chin, under and around breasts and arms. She did not miss a spot.

Meanwhile Nicolette tried not to blush. She had never been touched before like Amelia touched her. Feeling a woman so close to her, leaning into her neck, pushing up her small breasts, grasping her shoulders, squeezing her waist, hips and derrière. Nicolette tingled. Was it excitement of anticipation for the magnificent dress or from embarrassment at being touched so, she did not know.

"Voila!" said Amelia. "The measurements are complete. Now, I will create a beautiful gown for you to wear to this special affair."

"Merci, Mademoiselle Amelia. I am so grateful." Nicolette smiled politely. She was glad to climb down from her pedestal and put her outer garments on again. By the time she dressed and paid Madame Francoise, Amelia was already cutting the azure velvet and threading needles with matching strands of silk. To

Nicolette it all seemed like a dream.

By the time she stepped back into the street, the gas lanterns were being lit. Nightfall caught Nicolette by surprise. Jean-Paul would be worried she thought, as she hurried home.

Jean-Paul was anything but worried. He had made dinner for both of them, something he had not done in years. And a fine dinner it was. He had spared no expense to fetch fish from the market to simmer in butter, cream and white wine.

"What is the occasion, Papa?" Nicolette lifted the pan cover and smelled the sweet delicacy.

"Do we need an occasion to treat ourselves well once in a while? We have had a very good month at the shop, no?"

Nicolette knew this was not the reason that Jean-Paul was celebrating. So she said little. She could not spoil his reverie, his hopes and dreams for her. Let him have his fantasy, she thought. If it means he can be joyful, unworried about money, the shop, and the future—even for a little while, it was worth it.

As for Claude Gustav, he had been like a delighted child seeing the sights of Paris. She felt a bond with him, but more a sense of nurturing. He was easy to talk to, yet very intense, wanting to absorb every nuance of life all at once. He could delve into the deepest conversations on the nature of art, philosophy and politics and didn't think twice about sharing his most profound thoughts with her, as if she was a trusted old friend. But there was something else, something that Nicolette had noticed on the first day when he came to the shop, something she was hard pressed to ignore the more time she spent with him. She pictured him with his pale skin, his persistent cough.

"A toast!" Jean-Paul interrupted Nicolette's thoughts. "To you, my beautiful daughter and your future—*à votre santé*!" Jean-Paul held up a glass of rare wine. Nicolette smiled and hugged Jean-Paul.

"Merci, Papa for this delicious dinner, the dress, your blessings." Nicolette could not disappoint him.

That night Jean-Paul slept well. Nicolette woke often from

dreams she could not comprehend. In one, she held a baby boy with curly auburn hair and dark eyes. He looked at her adoringly, smiling and gurgling as she held him to her breast. Another woman dressed in white suddenly appeared in the dream, admiring the baby. "I will put Noah down for his nap, so you can both rest now," she said. The woman in white lifted the baby from her arms and placed him in what looked like a glass bassinet next to the bed. In her dream, Nicolette could see through the glass and watched as the baby slept. She felt both love and concern for the tiny child. Then suddenly, his little face grew larger and paler until she realized it was the face of Claude Gustav.

Nicolette awoke with a start. What did the dream mean? Why had the baby turned into Claude Gustav? Nicolette breathed slowly to calm her racing heart. The baby had seemed so real to her, to be her own child. But with whom would she have had a child? Nicolette tried to put the dream out of her mind. Slowly she fell back to sleep.

CHAPTER 9

Rachel Rita Padini

A Few Days Before Thanksgiving 2004, Tucson, Arizona

Rachel Rita Padini's plane landed right on schedule in Tucson. Her brother, Michael, met her at the end of the escalator near baggage claim with a big sign: *Welcome Rachel.* Rita laughed and waved when she saw it.

"How was your flight Sis?" Michael asked, hugging his sister and taking her carry-on.

"Fine, thank goodness. How are you?"

"Excited to see you here finally!" Michael beamed, heading with her to baggage claim.

As they left the airport, Rita felt the warm desert air hit her like a wave. It was much warmer than she thought it would be in November—a pleasant surprise. No snow for the holiday, she thought. But could she get used to the dryness and heat?

They drove out into the desert until the houses grew few and far apart, until they finally came across a shingled house with a three-domed roof.

"Here we are." Michael escorted his sister to the red front door. Colorful Mexican ceramic planters decorated each side. As they stepped into the air-conditioned foyer, Rita breathed a sigh of relief, the cool air revitalizing her. Michael set her luggage down.

"You made it! Welcome, Rachel!" Gary came out from the adjacent living room extending his hand to Rita. He hadn't changed much, she thought, although it had been five years since she'd seen him. He was still the handsome fellow with those dark smiling eyes that she remembered. Only his hair was different, cropped close to his head, his graying temples contrasted against rich coffee-colored skin.

"How was your flight? It's so nice to see you again, Rachel— shall I call you Rachel too, or do you prefer Rita?"

"Well," Rita hesitated. "I guess I'll have to get used to *Rachel* while I'm here." She smiled. "We'll keep it in the family," she added warmly. They all laughed.

"*Rachel* it is then." Michael smiled.

"Come, have something to drink. I made lemonade." Gary pointed the way. "If there's one thing you have to do here," he leaned toward Rachel, "it's keep hydrated, honey."

Rachel liked Gary. "Okay, will do," she smiled.

The foyer opened into a wide kitchen. Except for the white tiled counter tops and silver metallic appliances, the kitchen was a palette of colors, the walls splashed with brightly painted murals. "Atlantis under the sea, we call it," Michael offered. "We'll give you a full tour later. Let's get you settled and we'll have dinner out on the patio."

With the sun setting at the horizon. the sky had turned brilliant orange, with wisps of purple against a deep turquoise backdrop. The breeze and balmy eighty degrees made dinner on the patio perfect. "Your home is really different—I like it." Rita relaxed with a cool martini in her hand. "When the renovation is complete it's going to be very eclectic and beautiful with the landscaping of cactus and palm trees."

"We hope so," Gary said. "We got a fixer, so we could really make it our own, you know?"

"It has good bones, as they say, for a 1960's build in the desert. The biggest problem here is how the weather does a number on the houses, especially if they're built with cheap materials like a lot of the newer construction." Michael added. "Oddly enough, mold can be a issue."

"Really?" Rachael said.

"Yes, the monsoon season wreaks havoc," Gary explained.

"And the swamp coolers can really be problematic," Michael added.

Rita looked puzzled.

"They're a cheaper form of air-conditioning used a lot here—saves energy and costs much less. The house didn't have a swamp-cooler, which is unusual—no air-conditioning at all. But then again we are at higher elevation, so maybe the former owners just tolerated the heat." Gary rolled his eyes for effect.

"Don't worry though, Rachael. The first thing we did was put in central air," Michael laughed.

Gary changed the subject holding up his half-filled wine glass. "Rachael—here's to you. So glad you are visiting us."

Michael followed suit. "A toast! May you come to love the desert as much as we do, so we can have your company on a regular basis, Sis!"

"*La chaim! Saluti!*" Rachel raised her glass. "And to both of you. May your new home bring much happiness."

Gary went into the kitchen and returned only minutes later. "And here is the dinner requested by my beloved," Gary announced placing a lavish steaming stew in a white porcelain serving dish in the center of the deck table. "Voila!—Jambalaya!"

"Gary's been honoring his Creole roots and honing his culinary skills in our newly completed kitchen—he is making me a very happy camper!" Michael grinned.

"Yum, it smells so good!" Rachel breathed in the savory aroma. "I've never had Jambalaya. She looked at Gary in his crisp black chef's apron. "New Orleans, right?"

Gary nodded as he heaped portions of the chicken, sausage, and vegetables onto each of their plates along with some rice. "My French Creole grandmother taught me to make it. She lived near the French quarter." Gary finished serving. "It's traditionally a French and Spanish dish—but my people, honey, we have our own recipes. Hope you like spicy!"

Rachel closed her eyes at the first mouthful's sumptuous flavors. "Oh, so delicious," she swooned. "And spicy," she added.

"Oh, this is incredible! You outdid yourself, lover." Michael soon took a second helping.

After dinner and coffee they settled down in the living room, a long narrow room with windows and sliding glass doors at one end. The sofas arranged in a U-shape, faced the only unadorned wall. A hammer, screwdriver, and several as yet unwrapped boxes of various sizes were piled at its base. "We should be done putting up the TV screen here tomorrow, then get the room back in order—Oh, which reminds me. We have a special guest coming to meet you tomorrow, Rachel." Michael's eyes twinkled. "She's an artist. We're going to take you to see her show opening at the Aphrodite Gallery on Friday evening. We got a sneak preview of her show when she was setting up and invited her for lunch tomorrow. We were able to get some pictures of her latest work, which we thought we'd view on the big screen."

"We're big fans of hers. She's a marvelous sculptor," Gary added looking directly at Michael. "We're planning to buy a piece of her artwork, aren't we, Babe?" A hint of flirtation passed between them.

Michael turned toward Rachel. "I remembered that you enjoyed the job at the museum, how you loved seeing the art, so I thought you might like a gallery tour in Tubac. It's a great artists' community about an hour from here," Michael offered.

"That sounds great," Rachel perked up. "So who's this artist you invited?"

"Her name is Marla C. Woods—she studied in France," Gary replied, his dark eyes smiled. "This is her second show in the area. I'll show you the book she published some time ago of her early work," he said, walking across the room.

He opened a door Rachael had not noticed. The obscure door knob blended into the paneled wall. Gary turned it and flicked the light switch. Rachel could see into a small room, that appeared to be an alcove with no windows, just shelves from floor to ceiling lined with books. Michael followed his sister's gaze .

"Oh, it's our library," he said. "Tomorrow I will give you a proper tour of the house. We have some odd little nooks and crannies."

"Looks marvelous. How different," Rachel said leafing through the pages of Marla Wood's book, the one Gary had pulled from the library shelf. "I'm excited to meet her too," she added, feeling a bit overwhelmed by their exuberance over her visit, this mysterious artist, and quirky old house. Something felt amiss. Maybe I am just jet-lagged, she thought.

The next morning Rachel woke to the sound of hammering. She looked at her watch on the nightstand. "Oh, my gosh!" she said aloud. It was 11 am. She washed up quickly, put on her robe, then walked through the kitchen. Coffee brewed in the coffee maker. She poured herself a cup and followed the noise of men and tools.

In the living room she found her brother and Gary attempting to install a large movie screen they intended to pull down from the wall. The metal frame required drilling into the wall.

"Oh, good morning sleepy head." Michael stopped working. "Sorry we disturbed you. We wanted to let you sleep in, but we needed to get this done. Marla will be here soon." Michael walked over to Rachel and wrapped his arm around her shoulder. "Did you sleep well?"

"Like a rock." She rolled her eyes. "Wow, I don't remember the last time I slept so soundly, for so long."

"That bed is comfy, right?" Gary chimed in. Then embarrassed he had revealed some intimacy, a quarrel between lovers that found him sleeping in the guest room once, he quickly returned to looking at some instructions from one of the boxes.

Rachel and Michael walked back into the kitchen. The sun streamed through the window from the patio as Rachel reheated her coffee. Michael took cold water from the fridge. "Did you bring your bathing suit? You can take a dip in the pool if you want before lunch." He paused. "Oh, Sis I'm sorry. Are you feeling better since that incident at the lake? I can join you, but Gary's really hot to get this screen installed today."

"I'm okay. I'll swim later," Rachel replied. She didn't much relish the thought of being in deep water, though. Maybe just a dip in the shallow end to cool off. "I'll get dressed and join you—see if I can be of any assistance," she laughed. They both knew that mechanical things were not her forte.

Just then, they heard a car drive up to the house. Dust rose from the driveway as Marla C. Woods stopped her BMW short, in front of the carport. Michael got to the door before Marla rang the bell. He opened it wide, an equally broad smile of welcome spreading across his face. "Marla, darling, how are you? So glad you could come. Did you have any trouble finding us?"

Marla removed her sunglasses, shading her eyes from the day's glare. She was an attractive woman with porcelain-like skin, large brown eyes, and shoulder-length salt and pepper hair. Michael 's six-foot frame seemed to tower over her thin, yet shapely figure. "Hi," she said, smiling and shaking Michael's hand. "No, it wasn't hard to find. You gave good directions. This is a unique place tucked out here in the hills, so far west of town. I've never been out this way," she said peering into the foyer.

Gary appeared immediately by Michael's side. "Welcome, Marla. Come in, come in!" He gushed, leading the way.

"Marla, this is my sister, Rachel," Michael said.

Rachel held her robe closed with one hand and shook Marla's hand with the other. "Nice to meet you," Rachel smiled. "I'm a little late getting up today, still jet-lagged," she apologized.

Marla peered at Rachel with an expression of surprise. "How... do you do?" she said ever so slowly. "We know each other, don't we?"

"No...uh, I don't think so." Rachel looked equally surprised, while she tried to jar her memory.

"My sister's just come from the East coast to visit. I wanted her to meet you. We're all coming to your opening reception on Friday."

"Oh excuse me," replied Marla. "You look so much like a friend I had in college." She composed herself. "I'm glad you'll be here for my show."

"I'm looking forward to it," Rachel said politely, wondering if she was the only one feeling awkward. "Tell you what—while you get the house tour, Marla, I will go get dressed for lunch." Rachel excused herself.

By the time she returned, the guys were back in the living room explaining to Marla the difficulty they were having putting the screen in place. They had hoped to have it ready to show her art today and see the ball game that evening.

"There is a problem with this wall. It's hollow." Gary reported. He had already put in mullets and screwed a metal portion of what was to hold the screen on, with no success. "We're sorry it won't be ready today."

"No problem, really." Marla said calmly. "I can talk about my art just from the pictures you have on your camera, if you'd like."

"What is on the other side of the wall?" Rachel asked innocently.

Before Gary could answer, Rachel walked over to the wall, seeing a dime-sized hole at eye level he had made in his failed attempt. She peered through it. On one side she could see the library, but to the right only a darkened space. "Isn't that the library, in there?" she asked.

Gary looked like a deer caught in the headlights. He looked at Michael.

"Uh, no Sis," Michael answered. "That's another room we found on the blueprints. We never had the house inspected and no one who showed us the place seemed to know about it."

There was an awkward silence. Marla looked embarrassed, as if she'd walked in on a private family discussion.

"What do you mean?" Rachel's voice raised an octave. "There's a secret room in this house? Wouldn't you see it from the outside?

Rachel's suspicion of something odd going on was now heightened. Her skepticism and curiosity were only tempered by a knot
of anxiety in her stomach.

Ignoring their distinguished guest, Rachel pursued the issue.
"Have you ever been in it?"

"Well, yes," Michael said, looking at Gary momentarily. "We
found the space behind a shelf in the library, adjacent to a paneled wall. We've thought about taking it out, to expand the living
room, but can't bring ourselves to do it. There is something both
beautiful and mysterious about it." Michael looked a bit sheepish.

"It's a bit spooky, but it's also a wonderful attraction of the old
place," added Gary. "Clearly though, we can't count on this wall
to hang something as heavy as our new screen."

"You have a secret room behind a wall in the library and you're
concerned about your TV screen?" Rachel looked at Marla now.
Would another woman get the absurdity of this male obsession
with big screen TVs?

But Marla's face had changed drastically. Her eyes were alight
with excitement. An almost sly smile appeared at the edge of her
lips. She looked as if she were about to taste something delicious.

"Let's see it." Rachel said without hesitation, picking up some
visceral cue from Marla's expression.

"I don't know if that is a good idea." Michael said. "It's kind of
old and musty."

"What can it hurt?" Marla suddenly found her voice. "I love a
new adventure. We can look at my art afterwards."

Reluctantly, the guys walked into the library with Rachel and
Marla hot on their trail. Surrounded by three walls of books and
no windows even on the empty paneled wall, the room seemed
small. Michael moved slowly to the blank wall and pushed firmly
on it. The wall creaked and looked about to fall over when suddenly a door size panel opened. An old stained burlap panel
behind it automatically lifted from the bottom, curling upward
in a not so neat roll. Revealed was a room that appeared as if from

another time. A picture of a Madonna and child in a gilded frame hung on a wall beneath which an antique table stood. In the middle of the room a tall intricately carved, cherrywood chair stood on a pedestal, making it look bigger and taller than average.

Rachel stood transfixed. Her keen eyes scanned the room feeling a sense of its history. She noticed the red velvet curtains draped on a window that looked out on what appeared to be a flower garden. But it didn't register that this was impossible, since this side of the house was adjacent to the carport.

Rachel felt the rooms eerie quietness, just waiting to come alive somehow. She felt strangely disoriented, but not scared. At least not at first. She looked at the throne-like chair trying to sense its purpose. Who could have sat there holding counsel, commanding attention?

Just then, Michael looked to his right as if he heard something. Rachel followed suit. Just beyond a statue and a small cabinet was another set of burgundy velvet curtains. These were closed, unlike the ones adorning the window.

As if by mere suggestion of its viewers' curiosity, the curtains slowly parted exposing a hallway, not a window. Religious paintings hung along its walls. To the right, partially hidden by the curtain, Rachel saw a stairway.

She walked toward the hallway in a dream-like trance, drawn in by something moving on the staircase. Whatever it was cast a dark shadow onto the rug covered floor. Rachel stopped. The shadow grew bigger, bolder. It changed shape, looking like a wild fire with flames flickering upward, sideways, disappearing and reappearing bigger. Rachel felt something slither onto her path. She heard what sounded like people wailing. Suddenly something grabbed her ankles. Terrified, she managed to tear free and run for the opening in the wall.

Marla, Michael and Gary moved quickly, disturbed by the terror on Rachel's face, by her screams. They themselves had not seen or heard anything beyond the curtain. As they reached the panel exit, Rachel was sure she saw two more people with them. Oddly, each was not more than three feet tall. Both were little men dressed in clothes from the turn of the previous century. As incongruous as it seemed, one resembled the character of Sherlock Holmes and the other a laborer in overalls and a cap. But the two disappeared as soon as they crossed the threshold into the library.

Breathless, Rachel leaned all her weight against the door helping Gary and Michael to close it, until the library was to all appearances intact. "What just happened?" Michael looked at Rachel. "Are you okay?"

"Didn't you see it? The hallway, that fiery shadow thing?" Rachel asked, incredulous that they were not all on the same page.

Marla, Gary and Michael looked from one to the other.

"What hallway? It's just a room with some old furniture," Gary said. He looked at Michael, not sure he should say, what he was thinking. "Some people do have a gift for seeing things, though." He refrained from launching into the stories of his Aunt's gift in the Santeria traditions.

"Sis, really. What scared you in there?" Michael seemed genuinely concerned. First the incident at the lake, now this. What was troubling her, he wondered.

Marla watched Rachel, but said nothing.

"Did *you* see anything unusual?" Rachel turned to the artist, feeling suddenly crazy and alone. She dared not say a word about the two little men who had accompanied them for a moment.

"I can't say I did, although I detected a smell I couldn't quite recognize. I know I've smelled it before," Marla squinted, thinking.

Rachel gasped. She knew that smell. "Frankincense!" she whispered.

Michael put his arm around his sister. "C'mon, let's have some herbal iced tea and relax a little. You're probably just not used to the heat. You have to drink a whole lot more water in this arid climate, Rachel."

Gary ushered the women back into the living room. "I'll get us some drinks, girlfriends."

"I'll finish preparing lunch. Are you all hungry?" Michael asked. Not waiting for an answer he added, "I think some protein is in order."

Rachel sat down on the sofa with Marla. "Gosh, I feel bad. I didn't mean to make such a scene. You must think I'm a bit nuts," she said.

"Oh, don't worry about it. Sometimes our imaginations can play tricks on us when we're tired." Marla was graciously calm.

"I guess you're right. Maybe I was hallucinating from dehydration." Rachel tried to allay her own discomfort, but before she could take a deep breath to calm herself, the library door opened by itself. Rachel startled, alarmed. She looked over at Marla who was fingering the worn cover of her book. The artist seemed oblivious to any disturbance. Looking again, Rachel saw the light go on in the library and the two little men running from the doorway to the other side of the room, obscured from her view.

Strangely unafraid now, Rachel stood up and walked quickly back into the library. She scanned all four walls and book shelves, opened the few built-in cabinets and drawers. She did not find a trace of the little men or anything unusual. Just as she was about to leave, a book fell off one of the shelves when she reached for the light switch. Rachel picked it up and read the title. *A History of Herbal Remedies.* She checked the row of books. Finding nothing else out of place, she put the book back on the shelf.

Feeling suddenly exhausted and bewildered, Rachel returned to the living room and sat down on a green love-seat next to Marla. "So you didn't see the two little men?" But no sooner had she spoken, did she regret her lack of restraint. "You must think I'm out of my mind, huh?"

Marla looked up momentarily at Rachel. "No," she said. But there was something different in Marla's tone. Her voice had changed. It was deeper, penetrating.

Rachel stared at Marla whose face was changing before her eyes as well. Marla's nose, no longer visible, was replaced by a long trunk. Within seconds Marla's whole head was that of an elephant, her body more masculine with a little pot belly. Rachel was stunned for a moment. Then recognition came in a blinding flash. "Ganesh," she uttered under her breath.

"There are entities, toxic energies that feed off the energy of fear, and of those trapped and deluded by the heaviness of fearful energy. They are obstacles to be overcome. You must investigate and discover, dig up the roots with your tools, your light and your memory to dispel them. Your thoughts are powerful." Ganesh's voice reverberated in Rachel's ears.

Suddenly, Rachel felt a fog lifting from before her eyes, from her mind's eye. She tried to grasp what was happening. It felt familiar, as if she had known it forever, it seemed. Something so big, yet just beyond her reach. "I can't," she said. "How can I? I am not equipped to do this by myself. Who am I to try? I am just a woman, a widow, nobody important."

Rachel looked into the fathomless depths of Ganesh's eyes, his serious countenance. At once, she knew her own words were untrue. Claiming to be nobody was a lie born of fear. The full weight of her responsibility vibrated in every cell of her body. Then, like a lightning strike, it all became clear. For one split second she remembered who she was and what she had come to do, what she must do. Then, as if through a mist, she heard another voice.

"Lunch is served!" Gary's soulful voice seeped through Rachel's frequency. She felt a rush of wind in her face. She looked up. Marla was Marla again. Gary carried a tray of sandwiches, and Michael stood close by with a pitcher of iced tea boasting fresh lemon slices.

"C'mon you two," Michael chirped. "Follow us. We're going to eat out by the pool on our new shaded deck. No ghosts or goblins allowed!" he laughed.

"I'm looking forward to seeing you all at my art opening," Marla said when dessert was done. She and Rachel walked into the living room as the guys cleared the table. "It's been great meeting you Rachel. It's funny, you remind me so much of a friend I once had, although she'd be a bit older than you." Marla's deep brown eyes smiled, but Rachel could see something else—a sadness.

CHAPTER 10

Professor Emari

AllSouls College, Pleiades

Indigo and Chartreuse entered the class together and sat close to the front, to be near their favorite teacher, Professor Emari. Soon the rest of the students came drifting in. Viridian watched them from the back of the room where she could observe and evaluate the progress of all the soon to be incarnates. Professor Emari finally arrived, making an entrance in fabulous shades of cerulean blue and purple.

"Good day, students," she began as usual. "Today we will continue your orientation. I realize some of the material may be a little cumbersome for a few of you, so take notes and ask questions. You may want to form study groups, as well." Emari waited a few moments for her students to get settled before beginning her lecture.

"Our lesson today covers the topics of soul groups, masculine and feminine principles, and further repercussions of incarnation," Emari began. "The most common problem thought-based humans encounter is the loss of connection to intuition and memory—universal energies and the foundation of our *Mutable Essence*. As I mentioned, incarnation onto planets such as Gaia 1 have required that *Mutable Essence* be forgotten and supplanted by belief in linear time, as well as the solidity of space and gravity. This of course makes most humans more reliant on instinct and thought, less likely to trust intuition and memory, all the while unaware of the power and nature of thought itself—a paradoxical dilemma. To recap, the loss of memory is a loss of soul history. Humans are afloat in what appears to most as a mystery of life. They often find themselves asking such questions like '*Why am I here? Where did I come from? What is my purpose?*'"

The students laughed aloud.

"Yes," Emari responded. "It seems funny to you, because you are aware of the answers. But that is the point."

She raised a small luminous ball and touched her breastplate. "There are many human cultures and belief systems that encompass the concept of reincarnation. However, there are few who can comprehend all incarnations of souls happening at once in a multi-dimensional universe. Time on Gaia, during incarnation— is linear. Absorbing the concept of soul groups is quite another matter."

Emari walked from the podium to be closer to her students, seeing some of their questions telepathically. "While you understand that you are part of a larger soul system, human acceptance of soul groups is limited. It is to us a simple procedure because we are fluid within the environment at this level. But once the vibration slows and you enter the intricate physicality of the organism, the gravitational environment becomes paramount. That is why often non-human life forms, animals in particular, are highly desirable for souls. Animals have the ability to forgo the time-based consequences of physicality and duality. There are far fewer past, present, or future scenarios, or gender contradictions."

Emari paused, looking around the room "Before we continue further in that vein, the concept of duality cannot be overlooked at each step. And especially as it applies to gender and its applied principles. So let's discuss gender and duality. Who can describe the principles associated with gender? It should have been studied by now." Emari waited.

Silver volunteered, standing up. "For the masculine principle, duality can become an extreme contradiction," Silver answered.

"By interpreting form as a lack of access to reproduction, which is a potential pathway of light afforded to the feminine energy, in most cases—the power of opposites is misconstrued."

"Correct," Emari said. "And what is the result?"

"Twisted by fear-based thought and emotion, seen as deprivation or loss of control, the human male organism finds methods of coping."

"I see you studied," Emari smiled ever so slightly. "Yes, you are correct. Furthermore, where the sense of loss is mitigated by flashes of memory, such as incarnation leaks known as bleed throughs, or opening of multi-dimensional portals due to intentional movement in the magnetic field, a variety of less destructive coping methods become options. This includes engineered anatomical and biochemical changes. However, more often the sense of loss to access and control is thought-based fear, which results in emotional anger, physical force, or domination of the feminine by the masculine. And what is the consequence?"

Indigo stood up to be recognized.

"Indigo, do you have an answer?"

"Yes. The subtle and extreme forms of subjugation mean a lack of equilibrium for the majority. Solidity of thought or belief can produce overpowering restriction resulting in confinement to opposites with no middle path of resolution."

"Right," Emari offered. "It becomes male or female, black or white, right or wrong, present or absent...past, present or future. The latter, the illusion of time, has been the hardest lesson to override for so many incarnating into slower vibration. Thus, we come full circle to the paradox of incarnation filled with unmitigated intransigence often culminating, on a larger scale, as war.

Emari continued. "Some of you, for whom human incarnations on planet Gaia I are almost complete, have chosen to continue incarnating to expedite others' enlightenment, to enhance the vibration of the whole during the shift, rather than taking a break. In spite of your experience, you will still go through all the steps the others do, albeit on an elevated level in this next cycle. How many incarnations in whichever dimensions you choose is up to you entirely. We do suggest you stay within familiar soul groups and not take on more than what is manageable for you, in light of the fragility of the human system. Are there any questions?" Emari waited. She saw a few float into the air.

"We have a guest today that can help answer some of your questions." She nodded to the tall green-shimmering entity standing in the back of the room. "Let me introduce you to Viridian. Many of you will recognize her as your honored mother soul, your Oversoul."

Viridian approached the podium. "Hello dear ones. Congratulations on your impending graduation. You'll soon be joining your human families within the linear time frames you have chosen—all new experiences are yours. You are an addition to my several hundred incarnated souls on Gaia continuing with their goals. Though I have never incarnated on this particular planet, I will demonstrate how it works."

Professor Emari touched her breastplate and third eye. Viridian's energy field opened. A vivid green aura appeared around her and spread out across the room. Viridian herself turned into an orb of green light. She hung mid-air in the center of the high ceiling. From her, four lighted paths appeared, each equal distance from one another, at ninety degree angles. Along each path, a group of human figures walked. Each group encompassed humans of various skin tone, age, gender and size. Each wore clothes of a particular earth-based time, locale and climate. As the students watched, one or two of each group would cross from their own path to join others on a different path. As they did so, they would morph to match the appearance of the group they joined. There was a dominant female human that crossed each path. She seemed to be aware of all of them. Viridian's voice reverberated through the air.

"This is the A-Soul-4. You have just observed Professor Emari refer to her as the woman in distress in a desert landscape. She incarnated originally along path four, as an artist. She learned of soul groups during her meditative creative time, using her heightened senses to dissolve the time-space continuum. But I chose this example because she is moving up—has the most experience. A-Soul 4 will become A-Soul-6 this cycle. Her creative ability will enhance her telepathy. She is already aware of similarities in the physical realm of soul groups through her portrait art. As her consciousness shifts to accept many more of her incarnations, we can appreciate the connections and enhancement of twin souls, soul mates and others in one's soul group."

Viridian continued. "Like you, each soul has a mission, voluntarily accepted and in most cases initiated in the quest for knowledge and expansion of the whole. Twin souls share a common goal. When the goal becomes a heightened imperative to universal truth, twin souls meet—their combined energy expanding into ever greater light. I am a mother soul, the platform from which each group takes off, and comes back as it were. I help guide you and in turn, learn from you."

Slowly the green orb dissolved and the entity that was Viridian stood once again in the back of the room.

Emari stood at the podium. "Thank you, Viridian. You may learn even more from A-Soul-4 as she transcends to higher consciousness." Emari reminded Viridian. "It is imperative that we all understand the strength of human thought, the power that positive energy can exert when used for the benefit of the whole, the highest degree of *Eviray*." Emari smiled inside. She alone knew Viridian was about to embark on a transformational experience, part of a vital step for Gaia's survival and their own.

CHAPTER 11

Rita Kerner

Early October 2004; Pacifica, California

Rita opened the blinds letting the light into her new art studio. She loved the misty colors of the sky just as the sun burned off the gray morning fog. Aries wandered into the studio and climbed up to the window ledge surveying the yard longingly. "Yeah, it's nice out there," Rita said. "Worth the plane trip, huh?" She pet Aries's soft fur and opened the window to let her roam.

Delighted to be settled with Cleo in a small cottage in the hills along the coast, Rita surveyed the studio with its shelves of brushes, palettes, and paints. She adjusted the angle of her easel for the best light. Rummaging through her half-painted canvases, she pulled one from the pile that she was excited about, determined to complete it in the next few weeks. It had been a long time since she had felt like painting in earnest. Her travels had dismantled the mental block of what now seemed like irrational fear.

Rita wiped off the dry canvas with a damp rag to remove the dust from long neglect in storage and the cross-country trip. She dried it, removing any water before applying a thin layer of varnish and turpentine to prepare for the paint. She ran a soft brush over the images of a petite eighteenth century French woman sitting in front of a mirror dressed in turquoise velvet, brocade and white lace. In paler colors, a younger woman, a servant girl stood behind her in the act of brushing her hair. The portraits of each woman glowed with realistic radiance.

Rita squeezed blues, greens, reds, and yellows onto her glass palette and began to paint. Within minutes, she was lost in the colors and textures. In the meditation of her art, Rita felt connected to the women in the painting. And she felt a loving caring relationship between them, more than a woman and her servant might have. What was their story? Rita wondered. Now, she wished she had read the entire book she had given to Noah. Perhaps there would be some clue.

She looked carefully trying to glean a connection. A ripple of memory passed by so quickly, Rita could not grab it, hold it in her mind. But this was not uncommon. Now it was time to take the next step. It was time to know, not question.

Rita closed her eyes keeping the portraits in her mind's eye. She listened into the stillness. She heard the wind, then a bird chirping outside the window. Rita breathed deeply, slowing her breath. Soon she heard two women talking. Rita recognized the language—French. But she could only understand some of the words.

She continued to paint, listening. Suddenly there was another voice. It was a deep droning tone, like an undercurrent. "*Their love must be kept hidden,*" the voice said as if a command. Rita heard the words clearly. She dropped her brush, startled. She had not heard a voice like this since her childhood, when she had willed away the demanding voices that called her name.

She jumped out of her chair and pranced around the studio, shaking her arms to calm down, to dispel the adrenalin she felt coursing through her body. She knew she had just stepped through a doorway. It had been her intent to do so, but now she was unsure she was ready. Could she handle what she was about to discover, to know, had somehow always known?

Rita moved a few feet from the painting with a small mirror in hand and observed the painting from the reverse angle. It was an old masters' technique she'd learned to determine what adjustments to symmetry, shading and perspective were needed. She decided it would be less stressful to work on the details of the walls, the chair and vanity. She would not have to concentrate or contemplate anything else. She would work her way slowly back to whatever and wherever the portraits took her another day. But best laid plans were just that.

Although she tried to delay the inevitable, a presence of something bigger tapped on her shoulder. She breathed away her trepidation and resigned herself to the unknown. "Okay, okay," she said into the air. It was time. She knew there was no point in procrastinating any longer.

She pulled out a blank canvas. "All right," she said, "I am ready to be guided." Rita lit a candle and burned some New Mexican sage, a present from Irene. She put Bach's Brandenburg Concerto 5 in D major into the CD player. Perhaps some of her favorite music would make it less scary, she thought. Not since she had first understood her gift of painting portraits of people she imagined, but who turned out to be real, had she ever heard commands like this. Perhaps she was ready to know the force behind her gift—the reason for it.

Pulling some fast-drying acrylics from a shelf, she squeezed the colors out on a new palette. Then she dipped brushes into the paint and applied one hue after another allowing the images to evolve and transform, colors gliding over the canvas in long strokes. Three figures emerged.

The one in the center of the canvas was clearly a female, although she had blue-green skin. She sat enthroned on a tree stump, near a lake in a deep green forest. Two other beings also seemed to be taking shape, on either side of her, but were less distinct. Both were very tall and thin. Each had an elongated, almost human face. A turquoise and gold head-dress wrapped jet black hair and covered the forehead of the brown-skinned female being. Her blue robes shimmered. The other one, whose skin was the color of milk, was dressed in a long white tunic and did not appear to be either male or female. The top of its elongated head was the shape of a crown with three distinct gold balls.

Rita took out her hair dryer and dried the first layers of acrylics. Then she reached for her oil paints and glazes. Turning up the music, she lost herself, wildly applying more layers of colored glazes and allowing the undertones to bleed through, until she was hypnotized, transported to a place where time did not seem to exist.

Dizzy in her euphoria, she stepped back with her hand-held mirror to see her creation. Emerging from the canvas were three stately ethereal beings. The green woman was crisp and clear, as was the lake and forest where she sat. The tall beings on either side of her seemed to vibrate though, vacillating from clear concise form to vague auric, iridescent features, almost holographic in nature. They appeared and disappeared into the forest trees leaving only a wisp of themselves in lines and cuneiform, as Rita observed her work through the mirror. Suddenly, Rita noticed an image she did not recall painting. Shocked, she spun around and stared, transfixed. In the trees behind the green woman was her own face, a self-portrait in tones of blue and green.

Through the crescendo of music, Rita thought she heard that same baritone voice. She listened intently. The voice was barely audible at first, but gradually grew deeper in tone.

"Fear manifested from thought is one of the heaviest and most powerful forces we know. Fear solidifies matter. In order to shift, the lightness of being must be of greater value and hue...a change in frequency, vibration..."

"In order to shift..." Rita repeated without forethought. She turned off the CD player as if in a trance. *"Just like water,"* Rita heard, *"the vibration of energy transforms into vapor or solidifies into ice—shifting form and identity."* The image of a lake, like the lagoon in her painting, appeared in Rita's mind. "Shifting form and identity," Rita repeated.

"Who are you talking to? Or shouldn't I ask?" said another voice.

Rita felt a sudden wind rush passed her. She opened her eyes to see Cleo standing in the doorway of the studio. Rita's heart beat wildly, flustered by the sudden re-entry into earth time. She did not greet Cleo. She turned away fumbling to clean off her brushes, compose herself.

"You okay, honey? You had the music on kind of loud so I just—what are you painting?" Cleo peered to look at Rita's latest work. "Wow! That's, uh, different. Doesn't look, totally…"

"Human?" Rita finished Cleo's sentence, upset by the loss of her privacy and wary of what Cleo might think of her new endeavor. She felt embarrassed, exposed.

"Well it's beautiful, like a tarot figure kind of—definitely not your ordinary person. Hmm, a green woman?" Cleo observed, not wanting to hurt Rita's feelings. Who was she to criticize Rita's creative process? Besides, she loved Rita's portrait work of real people. "So it's a being from another planet?" She glanced around the room trying to appear nonchalant, although she was a bit disconcerted by this new art form. "What is that writing, those lines?"

"You can see them? Tell me what you see, okay?" Rita asked trying to keep her voice casual.

"Of course. I see a beautiful lake and a forest. A young green woman is sitting on a tree trunk like a queen in a tarot deck holding a spear and a crystal ball. Oh, and I see the lines, like writing of some kind in the trees." Cleo obliged. "It is ethereal looking for sure."

"That's it?" Rita asked.

Cleo looked harder. "Oh," she laughed. "Is that your self-portrait in the trees?" She smiled broadly. "That's so clever. I get it. It's like a fantasy. Is this from a dream or something?" Her voice turned lighthearted.

"Something like that," Rita replied, relieved Cleo did not see the other two extraterrestrials cloaked in symbols, letters and numbers.

Then Cleo noticed the painting of the French women propped up against the far wall. "Oh look at this one! This is the painting you were working on before you closed the gallery. I remember this one. It's fabulous! Was this from the character in the book you gave Noah. What was her name again?"

"Nicolette. You like it? It's pretty intense for me, feeling like I know both the women in this painting, you know." Rita wanted to talk to Cleo, really explain what was happening. "Do you remember when we met, I told you how I came to have the gallery?" she continued. "I had painted a picture of a woman whom I hadn't met yet. When I did meet her, she not only looked like the painting, but she was sure she recognized me—but from another time." Rita waited for Cleo's response.

"Sure, your friend Jane and her mother. You said you all had a past life together. I remember. You and I have that connection too." Cleo winked.

"Yes, Jane, the astrologer and her mother, Mrs. McCarthy. They inspired me to open the gallery and helped me get started. I had made dozens of paintings of people I didn't know, by that time. Once I opened the gallery, as if by magic, all those paintings except a few were sold to people who knew the people in those paintings. I mean, they recognized the portraits of their family members or felt somehow related to a specific painting," Rita reminisced.

"Yes, I know, hon. Your gift is amazing. And?" Cleo knew Rita was leading somewhere.

"Well, I just have a feeling I am not supposed to wait to find out anymore," Rita whispered, sharing a confidence.

"What does that mean?" Cleo sat down on a stool.

"I am not sure how to explain it. Something is happening to me. I feel like I need to explore further, find out the deeper meaning of all this."

"All what?" Cleo looked perplexed.

"This is going to sound crazy, but I think I do have a double out there. Every place I go people recognize me. Just the other day I stopped at the library to apply for a card and the librarian asked me why I would think of applying a second time, after I had just done so!" Rita almost screeched. "I just don't get it. It means something. All these portraits are connected to each other and to me." Rita took a breath. "But I don't know why!"

Cleo was quiet for a moment. "Does this have something to do with that new painting?" she asked, pointing to the glowing green ethereal being on Rita's canvas.

"Yes, I think so." Rita voice quivered. "Since that experience with that man who found our car key in the desert, I have had this feeling that there is something more going on than painting people I don't know—something I don't get yet. Why am I recognized by people I don't know, seen everywhere even when I am not there? Why do I have this gift of painting pictures of real people I have never met? There has to be some reason, some greater significance!"

"So let me get this. You're talking to a picture of the *Green Queen of the Enchanted Forest* to find out?" Cleo said as gently as she could. "Is she talking to you, too?"

"Yeah, yeah, I know. People can talk to God, but if God talks back, you're crazy. I've been down that road already." Rita turned to finish cleaning her brushes. Then on second thought, she decided to pursue the question. "What difference does it make if it's portraits of real people or beings from somewhere else that I channel?" Rita paused. She dared not tell Cleo about the holograms she saw of the other beings, now just appearing as hieroglyphics. "Are you going to leave me?" Rita's voice softened.

"What? Where did that come from?" Cleo stood up and massaged Rita's shoulder. "C'mon now, let's have lunch, honey. I think you need some protein and some air. You look a little dazed," she added. "I'll go make some turkey sandwiches and a salad. Let's take Oliver for a nice long walk to the ocean."

"Okay," Rita shrugged. "I'll be right there."

Cleo left the studio, while Rita covered her paints. She soaked her brushes, then straightened out a pile of art books and magazines on her table. One book fell onto the floor. Rita picked it up and looked at the cover—*Intuition and Creativity; The Art of Marla Cherise Woods.*

Rita's mood suddenly lifted. She smiled. "God works in mysterious ways," she whispered reaching over to her computer. Rita clicked, searching for a possible website of the artist. Finding only an article about her, she scrolled down the page. The article featured a picture of Marla Wood's book and a sample of her sculpture, but no photo of the artist. At the bottom of the page though, was an announcement for a Thanksgiving show at the Aphrodite Gallery in Tubac, Arizona. Rita's heart beat faster. She clicked on a map of Arizona. The closest big city to Tubac was Tucson.

"Should I?" she asked herself. It was a mute question. Her fingers were faster than her better judgment. She clicked on a few airline sites for plane ticket prices to Tucson. Distracted by her spontaneously wild excursion plans, Rita did not hear the phone ring.

In the kitchen, Cleo picked up the receiver after the first ring, holding it between her shoulder and ear before wiping her hands on a dish towel. "Oh, hi Patricia. I'm well. How are you?" Cleo listened. "Sure I'd love to try out for the choir. When is a good time?"

Cleo had met Patricia at her new job at the university. Over lunch one day, Cleo had casually mentioned her desire to sing in a choir, like she had done as a youngster. So Patricia had invited Cleo to sing with her church choir, rehearse for Christmas throughout the fall.

"Okay, so Friday I'll be there at seven to meet everyone. Thanks, see you then." Cleo hung up.

"Be where?" Rita asked, walking into the kitchen and picking a fresh slice of cucumber from the cutting board.

"Oh, just going to sing with my friend Patricia at her church choir." Cleo turned toward the sink and washed the cherry tomatoes. She did not see the look on Rita's face.

CHAPTER 12

The Strega's Daughter

Two Years Later 1420, Outskirts of Padua, Italy

Davina was almost fifteen when Chaim finally allowed her a small desk of her own in the corner of his study. He told no one. It was unheard of to allow a female such privileges of study. But he knew Davina was no common female. She had a gift that he alone knew and understood. How she had come to her gifts he could only assume had been God's will. There was no denying it was divine intervention. He had no other way to explain the sheer brilliance of her knowledge, her ability to know what had taken him so long to learn-- how to manifest cures out of the simplest of plants, how to combine infusions to create potions, how to write and decipher the most complicated languages—cuneiform, Hebrew, Aramaic and Latin—with no prior training or study. She had the gift of sages, the transcendent gifts of a *Kabbalah* master far greater than most. Her ability was often more than he could handle. Chaim feared for her, lest anyone else comprehend the nature of his daughter's divine knowledge.

But what concerned him most these days was the imminent pressure from his family and community for Davina to marry. He had been approached by the Rabbi whose son was an eligible young man. Chaim knew Davina could never live the life of a normal woman, a mother of children, an obedient wife and homemaker. But he didn't know how to prevent such a fate, one he would be more than happy with had she been a normal daughter.

126

For her part, Davina couldn't abstain from study. Like a mathematician, obsessed with measures, combinations and proportions, she invented salves, creams and teas for every ailment brought to her attention. Her writings had grown to be an impressive volume—a manuscript filled with astrological symbols, seasonal planting instruction, a hundred medicinal herbs, drawings of the stars, moon and sun cycles, tubular fixtures and inventions for cleaning water. In her quest for a desk, she had decided to take a chance and reveal her work to Chaim.

"When? How?" His eyes grew wide, his mouth hung open. Astonished, overwhelmed and nearly speechless, Chaim leafed through the pages of her manuscript like a man sleepwalking, stunned senseless by some invisible blinding light.

Davina was overjoyed in spite of the bizarre reaction of her father. "Can I have a desk please, father?" Can I write and draw with you in your study?

Coming out of his stupor and grounding himself, his face turned stern. "You will tell no one, not even your mother, about this manuscript, especially not this invented language," he demanded. "What language is this, Davina?" His face mellowed. He was almost in tears. "What language is this?" he asked again, knowing full well that it was the language of a magician, a sage, an esoteric master.

"My mother and my dreams..." she began.

"Never mind, you can explain it to me at another time. We must find a hiding place for it." He rummaged about his books and papers in his cupboard until he found an old wooden box that he saved for precious ritual pieces. He pulled it out and opened it, removing the silk cloth that held his items. A small wooden cross on a thin cord slipped out from the edge of the cloth. He looked at it as if seeing a ghost. Then he looked at Davina. He had forgotten that he'd taken this from her neck when he'd pulled her from the river, lest Bella see it. Davina was peering into his closet, so she didn't see Chaim grab it from his desk and stuff it back in his bundle.

"Davina, your time with me in my study will be to help me organize my papers, sharpen quills, refill the ink well, you understand?" Since his eyesight was getting worse, he would tell his wife that their daughter was simply a good helper. He didn't think Bella, whose own health had been failing lately, would need to be burdened. She would be none the wiser.

But he underestimated Bella. She was no fool. It was she who had been keeping the secret of Davina's journal. Hadn't Davina found a cure for the itching rash that the women had suffered from at the bathhouse years before? Hadn't the girl figured out how to purify the waters of the bathhouse and cure many of the women using concoctions of plants and herbs that none of them, even in their own healing wisdom, ever thought of or tried? Davina had a gift, Bella knew that. And so did other women of her family. It was not until Bella had been cleaning the house thoroughly in preparation for the holy holidays that she had come across the book, quite by accident tucked far back in a corner under Davina's bed.

Upon opening it, Bella's heart pounded, so frightened had she been. It was not the drawings of small naked women in ritual baths that disturbed her, as embarrassing as that was. Nor was it the pictures of the many variety of plants, most of which she did not recognize. It was the writing. Beautiful in its symmetry, but unmistakably not an alphabet nor language she had ever seen. Bella only knew some Italian and Hebrew. At first, she thought perhaps it was Latin or Greek—but how would Davina know such an alphabet, such language, let alone write so many pages?

For weeks and weeks Bella had worried, not knowing what to do. She could not sleep well and lost her appetite, worrying that her daughter was under some curse or spell. She was afraid to tell Chaim and afraid to tell anyone in her family for fear of what might happen. Soon, she stayed in bed half the day, too distraught and weak to do her daily chores.

Davina was disdressed watching her mother suffer. The more she tried to help Bella, the worse things seemed to get. She prepared soothing teas which Bella refused to drink. One day, Davina sat by her mother's bedside. "Mama, why won't you eat the food and drink the tea I make for you? It will be nourishing for you."

"How is it you come to know what tea and concoctions will heal me?" Bella hissed.

"What do you mean? You know I learned to make poultices, salves and teas when I was very young. You know father taught me about tonics, measurements, how to make oak gall ink. Remember? You also taught me about plants your own grandmother used for women's time." Davina feigned innocence remembering her promise to her father. "I've practiced combinations since the waters turned bad at the bathhouse. I thought you were proud of me, Mama."

"What about the writings and drawings?" Bella whispered.

Davina's dark eyes grew wide.

"I found that book under your bed a month ago, when I was cleaning for the holy days. What is that? Is it some kind of witchcraft?"

Davina was silent, feeling suddenly struck across the face. She had only heard the word *Strega* once, a very long time ago it seemed. "No, it's not, Mama. I'm sorry. I cannot say." Her eyes watered.

"You mean you won't say, don't you? Where did it come from? What does it mean?" Bella's pitch grew higher.

"I promised Father I would not talk about it. Please Mama," Davina cried.

"Your father knows about this?" Bella shrieked hoarsely. She threw off her covers and bolted from bed. "What do you mean you promised him? " Bella shook with anger.

"Please Mama, don't be upset. I only want to help."

"Help? Help what? Play with Evil and get us all killed?" she hissed, sitting back on the bed exhausted from exertion.

Just then Chaim came down from his study, hearing his wife screaming. "What happened Bella? Are you hurting? Let me get Bianca and Lupe to come help Davina take care of you."

"You!" Bella gasped, shaking her fist at her husband. "You knew she was playing with fire and you allowed it? You said nothing? I have almost died of worry not knowing what to do, what to say when I found that book of hers—and you told her not to talk to me, her mother! Have I not cared for her like my own? Am I not entitled to know what is going on in this house?"

Chaim walked over to Bella and tried to calm her. "I'm sorry," he said. "I was trying to protect you—and her." He shook his head. "That was foolish of me," he mumbled.

A year later, 1421

Davina scraped the galls from the oak branch and leaves, combining the tannic acid and ferrous sulfate in proper measure with water and gum arabic. She tempered the ink with egg shells. Satisfied with its acidity, texture and depth of purple-black color, she filled Chaim's two small ink bottles and placed them carefully on his desk. Then she turned her attention to sharpening the new goose quills. She fingered the fine new parchment her father had purchased as well, remembering the rough and rudimentary paper she had fashioned for her own writing.

Her parents had forbidden her to continue her manuscript for a year. Now, Davina was only permitted time in the attic study to help Chaim with his calligraphy since his eyes tired easily. Davina acquiesced to her parents wishes, although her spontaneity and zest for life had suffered because of it. She kept her thoughts, feelings and imagination to herself, never speaking of the manuscript hidden with her father's most sacred books.

In all appearances, the tension in the house had lessened and Bella had begun to recover from her nervous condition, much to the delight of her family, especially her cousins. Bianca and Lupe commented on the reversal of her illness. "Your husband is a good physician, yes?" Some praised Chaim.

"Your Davina is like a miracle worker, isn't she?" others commented, mistrust lacing their gossip. "First, she discovers what is in our water making us sick and finds a cure, and now she cures you! Perhaps she will become a midwife as well," they rattled on.

"A midwife is not a bad thing if her husband approves. We need a young midwife in the community now that our Sarah is getting old," said Lupe, pregnant with her second child.

But a husband was another story. Finding one who would accept Davina's considerable resources of knowledge and willful determination would not be easy. The more time that passed without a suitable mate, the more people would talk. And talk they did.

Finally, Bella took it upon herself to put an end to the gossip. In the fall, as Davina turned sixteen, the Rabbi, his wife and their eligible youngest son paid a call to the family. It was an honor to have them, so Bella and Davina went to great lengths to prepare an extravagant meal of chicken, root vegetables, egg bread with raisins and wine. Davina barely talked at all that evening, only furtive glances at the young man gave any indication she knew he existed. She was in fact mortified.

Bella admonished her afterward. "You couldn't at least pretend to be a little friendly?"

"Mama, I do not want to marry. You and Papa know that, right?"

"I know, I know, but what will become of you? You cannot sit in your room and write books. You are a woman. You must act like one, Davina. People will talk—or worse."

"And what will they say, Mama?"

"They will say something is wrong with you. They will say you are not normal," she paused. They will say you are..."

"What? A witch?" Davina yelled.

Bella began to cry.

"Oh, Mama. I am sorry!" Davina rushed over to her mother and put her arms around her. She towered over Bella, who seemed to be shrinking of late. Davina was just over five feet, voluptuous and strong. With long dark hair, rosy skin and large brown eyes, Davina had turned from a pretty child into a beautiful woman. It made little sense to anyone, besides her parents, why she should remain unmarried. It was this very fact that would bring her mother's warning ever closer to reality.

CHAPTER 13

Nicolette Marchand

Early December 1778, Paris, France

Throughout November the shop had been unusually busy with new customers courtesy of Madame Courtier's distinguished clientele and the upcoming concert of Claude Gustav. Obviously word had spread, Nicolette thought, as she closed up shop one evening. Before she could lock the door, Mademoiselle Amelia appeared.

"Bonjour, Mademoiselle Nicolette." Amelia was out of breath. "Excuse me. I ran halfway to get here before closing time. I wanted to let you know your dress is ready."

"Oh, how wonderful. Merci, Amelia. When shall I come pick it up?"

"We are still open for another hour if you would like to come now. Madame Courtier thought you might like to try it on for any adjustments to be ready for your occasion in two days."

Those two days nearly flew by. Nicolette stood in front of her mirror, glowing.

"I've not seen anything so beautiful in all my days." Jean-Paul wiped tears from his eyes. Nicolette turned from her mirror to see her father standing in the doorway of her bedroom, his face bursting with pride. "Tonight *you* may be the center of attention."

"Is this not the most magnificent dress you have ever seen?" Nicolette exclaimed. She looked back at herself in the glass. The blue velvet hugged her bodice, defining and softening her curves, the satin vibrating against her smooth skin turning her aglow.

"Ahh, the dress is indeed beautiful, but it is you who are radiant in it," Jean-Paul whispered kissing her cheeks one after the other.

Nicolette moved slowly, her pannier under her fine gown, puffing out from her hips. She gathered up her matching shawl, just as there was a knock at the door. She could hear Claude Gustav coughing, trying to catch his breath after the walk up the three flights of stone steps. Nicolette opened the door.

Claude startled, his handkerchief still covering his mouth. When he looked up to see Nicolette smiling at him, his eyes grew wide. "Oh" he exclaimed. "A vision from heaven!" Nicolette blushed ever so slightly.

"And you, why you look so handsome, like a fine gentleman about to make his royal debut." She curtsied, assuming the air of high society. She gave homage to the young man who was about to embark on a journey of grandeur.

"Welcome, Monsieur Gustav," Jean-Paul ushered Claude into the flat. "It is good to see you again. Are you ready for this big night?"

"I have practiced diligently since getting my scores from you. Thank you again. I could not have done it without you, Monsieur Marchand. I only wish I could have invited you to the concert, as well." Claude fidgeted. "The only thing I am not ready for are these clothes," he said, shaking the long lace at his wrist. I guess I won't be joining the aristocracy anytime soon!" He laughed chaffing against his collar.

"Well, you look the part. Once you start playing you'll forget about it," Jean-Paul advised. "Besides, just look over at my daughter and all will be fine, won't it?" Jean-Paul let subtlety fly by the wayside. This time, it was Claude who blushed. Then he cleared his throat.

"We should go," he said turning to Nicolette.

Jean-Paul closed the door behind them and sat down in his overstuffed chair by the window so he could see them climb into the carriage. He sighed with satisfaction. Just then, a vision of his late wife, Violette appeared to him. "Ah, my dear," he heard the words slip from his lips. "Our daughter will be married one day soon to a fine young man, a musician with a future."

He saw Violette in an angelic haze--smiling. As her image faded, Jean-Paul fell into a deep sleep. He dreamed of his youth in the fields of Normandy, herding the sheep and playing with his older sister, while his mother and father tended the fields.

Then his dream shifted and he was in a room with several other people, people he did not know. A tall woman with green eyes and flowing auburn hair came out from behind a door and motioned for him to come with her. He obliged, as he felt he must, and they walked down a long hall. They seemed to be walking very slowly. Jean-Paul looked at the paintings hung along the walls of the hall surprised to see images of his deceased family. There were portraits of his mother, father, sister, grandparents, and cousins as he had known them throughout his life. He stopped at a picture of his mother and father appearing as he remembered them in their old age before death. He longed to see them.

On the street below Jean-Paul's window, Claude's carriage, drawn by two stately black mares, stood in wait when Claude and Nicolette reached the street. Nicolette had looked up at the window to see her father watching her. She smiled and waved at him before she stepped into the carriage. She knew he was as happy and excited for her as she was for the special honor of accompanying Claude to the grand salon.

The carriage rumbled along the cobblestone road before it slowed into the wide circular entrance of a palatial home. Hundreds of gaslights lit up the halls, parlors and ballroom. Gowned women, dignified gentlemen—aristocrats arrived one after the other. Nicolette accepted Claude's gloved hand to exit the carriage and walked up the marble stairs with the members of the nobility. Through the massive gilded doors was a hall elaborately adorned with silk tapestries and glittering crystal chandeliers.

After many introductions, Nicolette and Claude were separated. Without fanfare, Claude took his position by the harpsichord and

Nicolette was escorted to a plush seat in the front row, next to a heavily perfumed elderly woman. The old woman, a Duchess and cousin of the host, made little attempt to hide her disdain when she inquired after Nicolette's title.

"I am the friend of the musician," Nicolette said, which meant of course she was a commoner.

When no further conversation ensued, Nicolette looked over at Claude who caught her eye, smiled and cleared his throat. She watched him sip from the glass of wine on a small table next to him, relieved when he was finally introduced and the concert began. Nicolette was both excited and nervous for him, but within moments all tension left her body.

Claude's long fingers moved gracefully, swiftly over the ivory keys. The music floated like a cloud in and around the audience, mesmerizing its listeners, captivating them in its magical embrace. Lulled by its waves, the Duchess's head drooped until she exuded a soft snore. A loud crescendo halfway through the piece woke her with a start. Nicolette just smiled politely at the old woman's embarrassment.

"Excuse me," the elderly woman whispered, appreciative of Nicolette's poise.

Over the applause of the company at the end of Claude's first opus, the Duchess leaned toward Nicolette, "Your lover plays well, my dear."

Nicolette was shocked by the word *lover*. She did not quite know how to respond. "Oh, we are not...I mean, we're just friends." Even to her own ears, Nicolette's words sounded like an apology. She thought the Duchess would think she was lying. And why not? It would be an obvious assumption. After all, she and Claude were not man and wife. She was not his mistress or an adulterer as neither of them were married nor engaged. Did the old woman think she was a 'loose woman'?

"Monsieur Gustav befriended me and my father, Jean-Paul Marchant, at our bookshop on Rue Haute Feuille, where he purchased some sheet music for this evening's performance," Nicolette explained. "He was kind enough to invite me to the concert by way of thanking my father for the assistance." Nicolette thought that should put an end to the old woman's insinuations.

"Oh, I see," the Duchess responded, less arrogance in her tone. As if trying to make amends she added. "You have a most lovely gown, a very fine choice."

"Merci. Madame Francoise Courtier's niece, Mademoiselle Amelia was kind enough to create it for me," Nicolette boasted. There, Nicolette mused, that should give her some food for thought. She could not wait for the music to resume.

Just then, Claude announced his next musical number and the audience settled into anticipatory silence. It was Brandenburg Concerto 5 in D major, one of Nicolette's favorites, one she had heard him rehearse one afternoon just a week ago.

They had been out walking along the Champs-Elysees and had stopped at a patisserie for some warm rolls. "Why don't you come to the conservatory, where I am staying, and I will play for you. I can offer you a cup of tea." Claude's eyes lit up.

Nicolette loved the idea, but she was unsure. They had been spending a lot of time together. It filled the loneliness she felt, having someone besides her father to talk to, someone with whom to laugh and enjoy walks along the Seine. She found young Claude Jacques Gustav an intense young man, passionate about music and politics. Except for his health, the persistent cough that zapped his stamina after a long walk or kept him sleeping long after dawn, he was kind-hearted and sincere. He might make some woman a fine husband someday, she thought.

Lost in her thoughts, Nicolette was surprised when the music seemed to come to an abrupt end. She heard the demure clapping of the crowd and snapped back into the present. An aristocratic gentleman was shaking Claude's hand and patting him on the back in congratulations of a fine performance. Champagne began to flow into fine crystal glasses. Exotic cheeses, smoked meats, fish, pastries, and chocolates brought out on silver and gold trays enticed the guests. Nicolette had never seen nor tasted such delicacies. She picked out a small raspberry-filled pastry. She scanned the room looking for Claude as she took a small bite.

"A good choice," said a familiar voice. Nicolette turned to see the old Duchess standing next to her by the table, where candelabras cast a bright glow over voluminous bunches of dark red grapes and platters of glazed pastries. The old woman's diamond tiara in her silver hair glittered in the reflection of the candle's glow. Her green eyes, that Nicolette had not noticed before, twinkled. "There is someone I'd like you to meet, my dear," she said, leaning so close that Nicolette could not wait to get away from her heavily perfumed body.

"May I introduce the Baron Pierre Etienne L'ecuyer, a most upstanding supporter of King Louis XVI."

"Merci, Madame. Whom do I have the pleasure of meeting?" the middle-aged Baron asked, taking Nicolette's hand with a bow.

"This is Nicolette Marchand. I think you may know of her father's shop on Rue Haute Fueille, not far from Madame Francoise Courtier's Dress Shop. If I recall, your late wife knew Madame Francoise, the proprietor.

"Ah, yes. A lovely and talented woman. You wear her designs most beautifully, Mademoiselle Nicolette."

"Thank you," Nicolette smiled.

"Mademoiselle is the invited friend of this evening's new musician, Monsieur Claude Jacques Gustav," the old woman added.

Just then, Claude walked over to the three of them. "Congratulations, Monsieur Gustav!" Pierre L'ecuyer shook Claude's delicate hand. Claude winced.

"My hands are a bit tired. You'll excuse my weak handshake." Claude apologized.

"Think nothing of it, my good man. You did a splendid job with such a long performance. You will be the talk of the town come morning."

Claude looked surprised. "Why Merci, Monsieur L'ecuyer. What a great honor it has been."

"It has been a pleasure to meet you both," Pierre said. "I do hope we meet again." He obliged the Duchess who had taken his arm and was determined to solicit him to other guests.

"You played magnificently, Claude." Nicolette gave his arm a squeeze when they had finally climbed back into the carriage and headed home. "Not a flaw in your performance. And you hardly coughed all evening," she added with a wink.

"I could not have done it without you and your father, of course, but especially not without you. And thank you for telling me about using honey for my cough. It really helped. You have been such a good friend to me, Nicolette. You are like a big sister and friend all in one. I am so grateful. It's like I have been blessed."

Nicolette, taken aback, exhaled a nervous laugh. She didn't know whether to be hurt by his lack of romantic interest in her as an attractive woman, or relieved that she would never have to turn down advances from him. She felt grateful though that he appreciated her. If she had to put her feelings toward him into words, she might say their meeting had blessed her life as well. "I know what you mean," she said. "You're like a brother I have never had. A dear gifted brother."

"Merci," Claude whispered. Then he coughed. He wheezed a bit and coughed again. "Would you mind, I dare ask, for the driver to drop me off first at the conservatory. I am so very worn out. Would you be uncomfortable to be taken home without my accompanying you? Do you think your father would be terribly upset with such impropriety?"

Nicolette hesitated, more concerned for Claude's health and Jean-Paul's feelings than her own. "You've had a long arduous evening. I will just tell him you apologize, that you were not feeling well," Nicolette agreed. "I'm sure he will understand, especially if you promise to come by tomorrow for dinner and tell him all about the evening."

"Ah, merci. That I will! Make sure to tell him that I will give him a very detailed account."

Nicolette soon arrived home and climbed the three flights to her flat. She let herself into the darkened parlor, then tiptoed into the kitchen. She lit the oil lamp on the table, careful not to wake Jean-Paul, asleep in his bedroom alcove. Light shone its way to her own bedroom. Undressing quickly, she put on her warm night clothes and carefully hung her precious gown in the closet. She took the combs out of her hair as she walked back to the kitchen to extinguish the lamp. The light was casting a soft glow into the adjacent parlor. Out of the corner of her eye, she saw a figure sitting in the stuffed chair by the window. "Papa?" she whispered recognizing his silhouette. He must have fallen asleep in the chair waiting up for me, she thought.

She walked over to him, careful not to rouse him too suddenly. Jean-Paul's eyes were closed, and she could make out the glimmer of a peaceful smile on his face. Nicolette took a knitted blanket from the side table shelf and covered him. Then she leaned over and gave his forehead a gentle kiss. Despite an unusual pungent odor, it took her a moment to register how icy cold he felt. And another screaming moment to realize that he was not breathing.

CHAPTER 14

Rita Kerner

Week of Thanksgiving 2004, Tucson, Arizona

Tuesday morning, Rita packed the last of her toiletries into her luggage. She didn't know why she felt so uneasy. Maybe it was taking a trip without Cleo. Maybe it was hiding her hunch that Marla C. Woods was her long-lost friend, Marla Remy—her last name changed by marriage. Perhaps it was the fact that she might actually come face to face with Marla in Tucson, after so many years. Or face to face with something more.

She lugged her suitcase into the hall and went into her art studio to view her three most recent paintings. The finished painting of the French woman, she now called *Nicolette and Handmaiden*, hung on the wall. The shapely figure bedecked in a blue velvet dress sat in front of a vanity mirror with her hand-maiden behind her, a brush and tortoiseshell combs in her hands. Rita stared at it. Slivers of memory of lust, upheaval, and loss seeped through her veins.

Across the room near the large window, Rita's newest painting sat drying. The unfinished canvas, glazed in tones of viridian green—the *Green Queen of the Enchanted Forest*, as Cleo called it, sat on her throne made from an old tree stump, surrounded by woods and a lake, all shimmering in moonlight.

Rita placed the green-hued painting in the drying rack. She pulled out the only other painting she had begun. It was a portrait of an ethereal being she had seen only briefly holographically, flanking the green queen. The wise, dark eyes of the portrait seemed lit from within.

"I think you should call this one *Goddess Emari.*" Cleo had offered one day, out of the blue.

The name resonated with Rita too, although she didn't know why. Rita closed her eyes momentarily listening into the deep silence, a process she had learned, in order to enter a place of surrender, a place of knowing, where she could commune telepathically with this wise being. But before she could completely submerge into the sublime, Cleo's voice interrupted Rita's meditation.

"Honey, are you all packed and ready?" She walked over and handed Rita a hot cup of coffee. "I'll miss you, you know."

As if Rita didn't feel guilty enough, she winced. "I'll miss you too, honey." She sipped her coffee, then looked at Cleo. "I'm sorry you're not going with me. It would be fun to spend time with Donna and Sharon together. You sure you won't change your mind? You could do stand-by in a pinch if we can't get a ticket."

Cleo rolled her eyes. "Really? I don't see that happening, hon. Besides, don't worry about it. You know, I've invited my cousin for Thanksgiving and my kids are coming on Friday for the weekend. Her face lit up. "And you'll get to see Noah on your way back—it's all good."

"I know. I'm just sorry we won't be together. I left a card for the kids on the dresser." Rita shrugged. "Will they stay all weekend?"

"That's the plan. Sunday they will go to church with me too."

"Church?" Rita's eyes opened wide.

"Oh, did I forget to mention that my friend Patricia from work invited me to her church on Sunday to meet the choir leader? Remember, I told you that I've been thinking of singing again?"

"Yes, you mentioned you might be singing on Friday evenings." Rita hadn't equated singing with religion. "But, Sunday church service? Really, Cleo? Don't tell me you're getting religious. Are you?" A look of concern spread across her face. Rita stopped herself from saying anything more, knowing there was a line not to cross.

"No, I just want to sing, besides it was a nice invitation, no harm done." But there was a defensive tone in Cleo's voice. They had argued about getting married again with the recent announcement from the Mayor allowing same-sex marriages licenses to be issued. Cleo wanted a real wedding with a minister and all the fixings, not only city hall. Rita wasn't ready for any of it. The institution of marriage was not on her list of must-haves.

Rita recalled Cleo telling her that she'd sung in a church choir as a youngster. As an adult, Cleo's political consciousness and being gay clashed with the strict religious teachings of her youth. "The homophobia was intolerable," Cleo had told Rita once when explaining her lack of interest in celebrating Christmas.

But wouldn't marriage just bring more homophobia, more recriminations in a religious environment. Perhaps not so much within a Unitarian Universalist congregation or in a progressive Reform Temple, Rita considered. Still, the idea that they needed to prove something felt unnecessary. Then again, she thought, being able to visit her partner in case of emergency in a hospital or having joint financial agreements afforded to married couples would certainly be important. Rita remembered having to pretend she was the sister of her former partner to visit her after a surgery, a long time ago.

"You're still envisioning a church wedding, are you?" Rita teased.

"Hey, you're Jewish, and you like all the Christmas hub-bub more than I do, remember?" Cleo noticed Rita's stunned, vacant stare—a protective stance that allowed her to emotionally disappear, but only momentarily.

"Yeah, okay. You're right, I guess." Rita reneged. "I do like the festivity of the Christmas season—but only the decorations and the eggnog!" she laughed. The light turned back on in her eyes. "I guess I'll have to tolerate the songs a while longer, especially if you're singing them." She mimed her disgust with a finger aimed down her throat, then recovered with a sheepish grin. "I don't mind Jingle Bells, though!"

"Very funny," Cleo quipped, giving Rita a playful smack on the butt.

"Okay, okay, I should finish getting ready. Do we have time for breakfast, more coffee?" Teasingly, she kissed Cleo's cheek.

Soon they were kissing goodbye at the airport. "I'll call you when I get there, Babe." Rita dragged her luggage out of the back seat and waved. She gave the sidewalk baggage clerk her ID and luggage. With boarding pass in hand, she went through security with only a minor blip. She'd forgotten to take off her belt with its metal buckle. It was not lost on her that with the new homeland security system in full force, her dyed hair and light skin tone might make it easier for her to get a simple nod. Not so for the African American couple in line behind her, who were pulled off the line for further inspection when their jewelry triggered bells. She'd heard of people missing their plane for the same reason. Rita felt lucky to make it to the gate in time for boarding.

Once the plane was aloft, Rita relaxed a little. She sipped her complimentary ginger ale and took out the book she had brought with her—Marla's book. Removing her blue-framed reading glasses from her carry-on, she settled in to read the foreword.

I began painting in my early years at art school. I fell in love with the colors and textures of the paint itself. Several years later, after an emotionally difficult period of my life, I returned to my ancestral home in France, to heal and devote time to painting. I traveled around both France and Italy for several months luxuriating in the art of the Masters. Then I spent a year in India learning about the art, the food, the spiritual traditions-absorbing as much as I could about such an old culture, one where so many lived in poverty yet had such faith.

Upon my return to Italy in the spring, I happened across an art school in Perugia. I began taking sculpting classes and was sure I had found my artistic goal. I sculpted in clay, plaster, wood and even stone.

During the summer, I was invited to Nice to the home of my cousins. I spent a month living on the beach. Working in sand was a profound experience for me and led me to the medium I would eventually choose.

It was easy to see the figures to be sculpted, buried in the sand— like lovers in a passionate embrace. Wiping away the excess grains of wet sand, they emerged as if they had been lying there a lifetime. The sand was forgiving, moved easily like clay. Clay could be molded, subtracted and added to create form, no mistakes too big or small. Sand, like clay, could be changed. It responded to touch, to the push and pull of hand, the slightest pinch or pat—almost a thought could move it.

But stone was different. Stone was permanent. One chip, one cut, a flinch or flick of a chisel and the shape was forever changed. You could not fudge or ignore an error. It stood there mockingly honest.

I thought about this long and hard. How had Michelangelo sculpted the David so perfectly? More perfect than a living being, not a flaw in his magnificent structure of stone. One could almost see his muscles rippling, feel blood flowing through the veins, his stare into the distance, transfixed forever in a thought-filled glance.

Stone became my medium, a metaphor for what I needed in my life—strength and stability.

"Looks like an interesting book." The passenger next to Rita leaned toward her.

"Uh, yes, it is," Rita mustered a polite response. She hoped that would be the end of it.

"Are you an artist? I noticed the cover. I really like art too." The woman continued.

Rita took a deep breath. At the crossroads of a decision to strike up further conversation with the nosy passenger or find a nice way of extricating herself from one, Rita suddenly recalled a similar incident some years back.

She'd been traveling by train to a writing conference, when a young woman had sat down next to her. Rita had been minding her own business, reading her writing conference brochure, when the young woman demanded her attention with questions about her reading material. It had started the same way.

"Are you a writer?" the young woman had inquired. "I'm a student at NYU. I'm studying women writers and historical anthropology."

Nakisha Washington was not only a student and friendly young woman, though. She was someone with whom Rita had an unexpected connection. After finding out that Rita was an artist who had owned a gallery in Newport, the story evolved. As it turned out, Nakisha's grandmother owned one of Rita's painting. They realized it had been Nakisha's mother, Olivia, who had come into Rita's Rhode Island gallery one Christmas and bought the painting that resembled Nakisha's family's matriarch.

Rita still sent birthday and new year's cards. Rita had just heard from Nakisha recently, she recalled, about her acceptance to graduate school at Yale. The encounter with Nakisha on the train had been more than sheer coincidence.

"Yes," Rita replied now, turning to this inquisitive passenger next to her, "I'm an artist too. I'm always interested in other artists' work." Rita looked at the woman's warm smile, her mature, sculpted face with high cheekbones and copper complexion.

"Hi, I'm Lucy" the woman offered her hand. "I have a small gallery at my home, where I show work of Native American artists like myself, and some other emerging women artists. We have a wonderful community of artists. Perhaps you'd like to visit?"

Rita knew she had made the right decision. "I'm Rita Kerner." She shook Lucy's hand. "Thanks for the invitation. I'm actually going to Tucson to visit friends and see a show at a gallery in Tubac. This is the artist who's having the show, opening Friday evening after Thanksgiving," Rita said, pointing to Marla's name on the book cover.

"Looks inspirational. And what kind of work do you do?"

Lucy inquired.

"I'm a painter, mostly oils." Taking a second to filter her thoughts, Rita continued. "I have a gift, some would say, of being able to paint people whom I've never met, but who inevitably turn out to be people who exist. I mean I don't work from pictures."

"Like a psychic," Lucy said matter-of-factly.

"Uh, yes. Something like that, I guess."

"Oh, I think you're going to love Arizona. There is so much spirituality in the Southwest, so many spiritual people." Lucy smiled. Her dark eyes twinkled.

By the time the plane landed, Rita promised to find her way to Lucy's gallery sometime during her visit. They walked to baggage claim, where Lucy's family awaited her arrival. After cordial introductions, they departed.

Rita finally spotted her suitcase on the luggage carousel. Rolling it out of the terminal, she was greeted by warm weather. Sitting down on the shady sidewalk bench surrounded by her belongings, she scanned the perimeter. Within minutes Donna and Sharon pulled their Honda alongside the curb, honking a swift hello. "Hey girl, you made it! Hope you haven't been waiting long." Sharon jumped out of the car, gave Rita a hug, and flung her suitcase into the back. Rita kissed Donna's cheek through the open front window, then climbed into the back seat. They headed slowly north, out of the airport and into the desert's afternoon heat.

Up ahead, the towering, rust-colored Catalina Mountains kissed huge white nimbus clouds hovering in the azure sky. Saguaros and acacia trees soon replaced stores along Oracle Road as they headed away from downtown toward the foothills. Homes tucked into the hillsides glistened white against the orange sand and purple cactus flowers.

"We're so excited you're here for Thanksgiving," Donna bubbled. "We were invited over to Michael and Gary's place. Michael's sister is in town from the East coast. He wanted us to meet her, but we decided to have Thanksgiving at our place instead and have you meet some of our wonderful women friends." She continued, her enthusiasm unabated in spite of Sharon's attempt to slow her down with a knowing glance. "So we'll stop by to see Michael and Gary on Saturday or maybe go to Marla Wood's art opening together Friday evening. How does that sound?"

"Wow, sounds great. I would love to meet your friends," Rita said. "Is that the same Gary we ran into when I was here last time? The charming gay guy at Tohono Chul Park?"

Donna thought for a moment. "Oh yeah, now I remember. Yes, the same. He and his partner, Michael, live on the west side, pretty far out in the desert. They have a cool house you'll like."

"So how is Cleo? Sorry she couldn't come. Is everything okay with you two?" Sharon finally managed to join the conversation.

"Yes, everything's fine." Rita replied. "She's having Thanksgiving with her family, so I think that was a priority. She hasn't seen them in a while." Rita didn't mention her own ulterior motive that had sparked the trip.

"What about Noah? How's he doing?"

"He broke-up with his girlfriend. It wasn't easy, but I think he's glad to be out of the relationship now." Rita smiled. "My sister sent him a plane ticket, so he could spend Thanksgiving with her and his cousin in Santa Fe. We plan to see each other when we get back, hopefully."

"He's such a great kid. I'm sure he'll find someone new who appreciates him," Sharon consoled.

"Thanks, he is." Rita agreed. "And what about you two? How are things going?"

"Aside from the election you mean? Can you believe a second term?"

"It is pretty unbelievable isn't it?" Rita shook her head. "People are still scared. Maybe next time. Did you hear the speech from that senator from Chicago? What's his name, again?"

"Yeah, he was impressive. Obama, I think," Donna offered.

"To answer your question, though," Sharon redirected, "if we don't read the paper or watch the news too much, we're doing pretty good," Sharon added.

"Yeah, wait until you see what we did to the house." Donna changed the subject as they pulled into the shopping center parking lot to buy some last minute groceries for the impending gala. Donna checked herself in the rear view mirror, brushing her hair back into a short ponytail bound with a clip. "Is it me or is getting really hot, today?"

"It's not just you today, love. I mean you're hot—but it's also eighty-nine degrees." Sharon handed Donna her water bottle. She handed Rita an extra one too.

Thanksgiving Day 2004

Sharon and Donna's big dinner was a celebratory gourmet Thanksgiving feast as touted. Out on the back patio, the twinkling white lights decorating the palm trees cast their reflection in the pool's cool blue water, while Sharon and Donna's friends lit up the evening with conversation and laughter—a joyous tumult over turkey, stuffing, pumpkin pie, and a plethora of alcoholic beverages.

The guests were mostly other couples, a variety of women, some who had lived in the desert a long time, some like Donna and Sharon, who had moved more recently from the East coast or Mid-west, even Canada. Rita enjoyed hearing the "how we met" and "what it was like when" stories. After dessert, Sharon put on a Nora Jones CD. The singer's sultry voice oozed through the balmy night. Sharon wrapped her arm around Donna's back and the two danced a slow romance-filled dance in the moonlight. Rita watched them. She suddenly missed Cleo.

Before turning into bed that night, Rita sat on a lounge chair on the new extension to the house, a screened veranda attached to the guest room. Taking in the cooling night air, she thought how Cleo would have enjoyed this evening. On impulse, Rita picked up her phone and dialed home. She waited as the phone rang once, twice, three times. From her vantage point, Rita could see the moon climb above the mountain ridge. Cleo's smooth voice on the message answered, then a loud beep. Rita hoped Cleo would pick up if she spoke. "Hi Honey," Rita said, "Are you there?" Rita waited. "Cleo?" she said again. No one answered.

In the distance the howl of coyotes sent a chill through Rita's otherwise content repose. Rita rose and went indoors. She changed into her cotton night shirt and climbed into bed. Soon the silence of the desert and the tryptophan-laden meal ushered her into a deep sleep.

In a dream, Rita saw herself as a passenger in a car going down an unfamiliar dirt road. She didn't know who drove the car although it didn't faze her. She was focused on a male figure standing on a low concrete bridge over a little river. The sun was shining and Rita felt happy in spite of not knowing where she was. Suddenly, Rita recognized the old man as the same one who found her key in the desert. Oddly, he was adding bricks and mortar to the bridge railing. He stopped, looked up at her anticipating her next move. In her dream, Rita rolled down her passenger side window and asked him directions. "What's up ahead?" She was looking for something, but did not know what.

"You have all the keys you need. Follow the path past the boulder, into the forest," he said without moving his lips. His eyes shone as if lit from within. Then, just as swiftly, he vanished and in his place stood a woman. It was Lucy, the woman Rita had met on the plane.

"Just follow the path through the forest to the lagoon. You will find what you seek." Lucy smiled.

Rita woke with a start. She looked about the room to get her bearings, recognizing her surroundings slowly. She breathed deeply. What was the dream about? she thought. She reached for the glass of water on her night stand and drank it all. Then she lay back on her pillow and drifted off until morning.

CHAPTER 15

Professor Emari's Class

AllSouls College, Pleiades

"As I was demonstrating," Emari began her next class, "human beings regardless of so-called time frame in which they incarnate on Gaia I are subject to the laws of matter that guide all universes." The room grew dark, then suddenly burst into colorful swirls of light that danced and hummed. They moved about until they formed definitive symbols, spheres, letters and numbers, each with their own tone.

"All matter in all universes is the same and operates the same way. There are no exceptions." Emari's voice was loud and clear. "We are all made of the same matter, same energy, same force. Each civilization and all entities, regardless of contracts for specific circumstances has codes, symbols, signs, letters, language, and tones of infinite variety to decipher the make-up of the universe—some more advanced than others naturally, according to the cycles of expansion and contraction."

The swirls flowed into circular patterns, turning into luminous spheres. Colorful scenes of land, sea, vegetation, animals and human forms appeared within each. Iridescent gold threads moved from one sphere to another against a starry background of dark space.

"Amid the infinite inhabited planets, Gaia is a perfect embryonic petri dish, an ideal place for human soul groups at early levels of development to flourish, due to its ability for rapid energy expansion and the abundance of water."

A giant hologram of interlocking, overlapping spheres each containing building blocks of life, filled the room as Professor Emari pressed her middle eye and breastplate. All the students levitated, floating in and around the images hoping to absorb a visceral impression of form.

Emari continued. "Earth, the blue planet, is a planet with abundant water in this cycle. There is birthed the idea, the thought, the intention, the seed, the egg—the force, the spark and the manifestation. There a multitude of species and organisms thrive—from microscopic life forms to off-planet, non-human entities, that even humans are unaware inhabit the planet. The most prevalent species are viruses, bacteria, algae and other micro-organisms, insects, and vast numbers of sea inhabitants. The largest entity, of course, Gaia herself—her clay, her minerals, her fluids, her molten core are part of her soul's evolutionary path. For now, she is a school where beings are free to practice the illusion and boundaries of free will within their programmed field, as well as experience emotion, thought, senses, physicality, whether human or non-human.

Emari looked over at Viridian who stood as usual in the back of the room. She sent a message telepathically. Soon Viridian came up to the podium and spoke.

"Depending on the incarnation of your group, the signs, symbols, language, culture or other stimuli adapted by, or particular to your species of choice, will be learned over what appears as time, through education, experience or memory." Viridian's voice was melodic. She had the students' attention as hundreds of signs and symbols floated in and out of view above them. "Physicality, and to some extent personality, will be inherited through the genetic code immediately. If incarnating as a human, your infinite memory will be lost as part of your contract initially, as Professor Emari has explained. It is your responsibility in this elevated cycle, my dear ones, to retrieve it."

"Thank you, Viridian." Emari said. "Now, would anyone like to give us a historical summary?"

"I will," Lavender spoke up, while still dancing around the room. "The life cycle of humans was altered, shortened early on during an experimental phase. However, the genetic code to enhance longevity, technological knowledge and consciousness is in process of being re-established."

"Excellent, Lavender." Professor Emari continued. "This advancement is monumental, part of the coming shift which will elevate the entire species to the next level in preparation for Gaia's ascension to Gaia II."

The students glowed with excitement.

Emari moved the energy field once again. All holographic images, and signs and symbols evaporated into a golden mist. "It is of great significance to know that many of you are embarking on a phase of planetary transformation that is unlike anything the humans on Gaia have seen. The response will be confusion initially. As children, for example, recognizing yourself in the form you engender will be uncomfortable. The female body to some will feel odd—to others the male body will feel strange. To others, gender and even name recognition will be disturbing. It's not new to the species, except that elevation of consciousness, memory and awareness will occur, and be restored on a mass scale in what seems moments, as humans experience time."

Emari continued. "As with any cataclysmic event in the universe, when the level of constriction reaches critical mass a balance is sought to stabilize the energy—the middle path. What is being restored in this cycle is what some humans call feminine. But restoring balance is not as humans interpret gender, nor what is expected or anticipated. It is outside most of their understanding. The concept and definition of masculine and feminine principles that are at play here, in weaving closed the split in the fabric— is about restriction and expansion, as we have discussed briefly before. The only way for consciousness to expand dramatically is by exposing what seems impossible, which has only been seen as a limited abnormality, on a grand scale. Gaia I must live on and we must help her. That is certainly why you all chose to be here. A new Earth will evolve organically."

With the wave of Emari's hand, a chart appeared on the ceiling. There were ten green bars in various lengths in the center of many more bars to either side in various hues of red, blue, yellow, orange and violet. "Here is frequency level one—the bars in green. This is like a scale of music, an octave. It's what is available to most of the human species at current evolution, in spite of origins, adjustments and interventions. In this basic frequency there are specific principles: the vibration is slow, therefore gravity is of paramount importance.

On Gaia 1, the acceleration of a body due to gravity is a approximately 9.81 meters per second squared with variances due to topography. This is what the human and non-human animals in this frequency are bound by—it is their physical reality—both visible and auditory. Without the knowledge, desire or belief that vibrational frequency equals physical reality, including gravity, humans rarely see or move beyond level one, except during sleep when the frequency expands to higher levels and thus moves into the fourth dimension. That is part of the program for the majority. But there are exceptions."

Emari wiped her hand across the image and the green bars appeared in 365 shades, one behind the other in a seemingly endless tunnel of light. The shades were barely discernible one from the next.

"Look carefully at the minuscule difference in their value. Each represent the slight shifts in frequency and therefore dimensions that humans experience as *Time*. For our demonstration, think of each as something akin to 365 rotations around Center Star, the sun around which earth revolves.

Other species, other souls can transmutate and move freely, instantaneously along these frequencies, and all others." Suddenly, the image of every other color exploded into view along the same pathway. "Free movement accounts for the ability to be in different places at once or to go back and forth along the curve of the space-time continuum."

Chartreuse's excitement bubbled over into laughter. Everyone looked in the youngest soul's direction. "Mutable Essence!" she exclaimed.

"Very good!" Emari said. She was pleased with her pupil. "Can you explain more?"

"Mutable Essence also encompasses humans' capacity to see entities that are in other dimensions if they can raise their vibration. They can tap into the frequency and cellular memory of their and others' incarnations, by vibrating at a higher frequency and..." she hesitated, "travel back and forth in dream-time."

"Yes, that's right." Emari nodded. "It's Mutable Essence Basics."

"Can humans tap into a particular dimension in other forms, or by other means also?" Chartreuse asked. Emari looked over at Viridian to answer the question. If she could give an example, Emari would assist her in demonstrating.

"Yes," Viridian took her cue. "Not all humans are the same as far as their DNA. Their origins vary, which means their ability to trans-mutate is variable as well. Their ability is tied to planet of origin in addition to their understanding of gravity, electro-magnetic vortexes, vibration and, of course, soul development.

"Place of origin?" questioned Silver. "I thought humans were all from the same humanoid composition with some genetic splicing from the original contact with the Elohim." The whole class burst out laughing as they shape-shifted, each one changing form and color on the spot.

Emari raised her voice to quiet the riot. "Okay, now. There are those just going to Gaia for the first time. Let's be patient and explain fully. Granted it will all be forgotten for awhile, but it is important all groups have the information they need to reach their goal.

She continued. "You are not wrong in your understanding, just incomplete, Silver. Elohim are one of the many who have influenced the evolution of the species we call human beings. But since they are from one dimension out of many, they are only one aspect of the whole. While humans tend to distinguish their origins by skin color, belief in different Gods and religions, geographic location of birth on the planet or commonality of DNA prototypes, most cannot yet distinguish their original origins—the planets from which their ancient ancestors come. Their inability to trans-mutate is in part affected by this lack of knowledge. "

Just then, three tall entities entered the room. Light filled the space around them. They were tall like Emari, but with no discernible gender. Unlike Emari, their were pale, the color of milk. They wore white robes and tunics. The top of their elongated heads appeared as crowns each boasting three small gold globes. The students sat up straighter and shifted back into their colors. Emari welcomed the guests in her traditional non-verbal greeting, touching her chest plate and bowing slightly. Each guest nodded in turn. Emari turned to her students.

"I am delighted to tell you that you will each be going to your seventh cycle groups with help from our friends," she indicated, motioning to the silent guests. One of the tall beings stepped forward.

The beings did not speak, but the students received the name, Nemeh. "Nemeh will take the group incarnating in what are known as the nineteenth, twentieth and twenty-first centuries." Emari stood back as the being, Clories, moved forward to be introduced. Emari continued "Clories will take the group incarnating in the sixteenth, seventeenth and eighteenth centuries." The third guest, Jathrop, moved into the foreground as Emari explained. "Jathrop will be taking the group incarnating into the thirteenth, fourteenth and fifteenth centuries."

The excitement in the room was electric. The students could barely contain themselves, their colors swirling about in abandon.

"Settle down a bit," Emari communicated. "I know you are excited to have gotten your requests confirmed. There are still many choices to be made and groupings to clarify. As I mentioned, you will be given all the instruction you need toward accomplishing your goals." She paused and lowered her voice. "Your incarnations are important. We are all dependent on each one of you to do your part to teach harmony and responsibility to the human species."

Emari thanked the dignitaries for coming, then turned back to her students. "While you will be in your human bodies for what will seem like a long time according to your contract to trust in solidity and time—this will be a slow frequency. You will be back to debrief on your experience in 'no time', of course." The students chuckled. Professor Emari smiled slightly, collected her notes and donned her bright turquoise cape.

She looked at her students. Her eyes grew large and twinkled with the light of a thousand stars. Then, with a sudden flash of white light she evaporated into the star-filled void of her own eyes. Only her deep voice remained: "*Remember, we are all One. Split into an infinite number of souls in the infinite universe, your goal is to use your enhanced memory to educate—so the new human species of an evolved Gaia learn to live in harmony with one another. Gaia herself must and will survive.*"

CHAPTER 16

Nicolette Marchand

Four months later, March 1779, Paris, France

Nicolette wiped the soot and dust from the fireplace mantle in the reading corner of the bookshop. She placed her father's adored clock and candelabra carefully into a wooden crate along with his glass ashtray and pipes. She could not part with them yet. She would store them in their flat above the shop for now— *for now* was all she could think of today. The future was a gray, impenetrable vacuum.

She sat down in her father's beloved reading chair and scanned the shop, now partially emptied of its treasured books and rare manuscripts, at least the ones she'd been able to relinquish and sell to his loyal customers and collectors. Tears welled up in Nicolette's eyes. She whisked them away, determined not to spend her day crying and moping about. There was so much left to do. She must find someone to help her.

She stood up, just as the door opened, the bell's familiar ring piercing the silence.

"Bonjour?" a hoarse voice rang out. Nicolette recognized Claude's raspy greeting and his sudden coughing.

"What are you doing out of your sick bed?" Nicolette admonished, walking to meet him at the front counter. "How did you escape the hospital?" she asked, astonished at his emaciated condition. It had only been a week since she had seen him last. "My dear Claude, you must go back to bed. You are too ill to be..."

"I was worried about you," he interrupted before coughing again.

"I am okay, dear one. I will survive. I so appreciate your concern, but you're in no condition...you must return to the infirmary. Come, we will go together. I'll stay with you for a while, if the nuns will allow me a visit." She ushered him out the door and locked up.

Claude was not strong enough to protest. He was barely strong enough to stand. *Consumption* they called it and it was devouring him. He was dying. "I thought perhaps I could help in some small way," he managed before a coughing jag grabbed him.

"Don't try to talk, Claude. Just breathe so we can get back to the hospital at the church," Nicolette whispered into his ear between his coughing and wheezing. She tucked her arm under one of his and held him around the waist with the other. His frail body leaned into hers with no resistance.

Sister Julianna Bugone, an elderly sweet-faced nun held the door open wide for the two of them to enter the church infirmary. "At first we thought you had fallen out of bed, Monsieur Gustav. Then, we realized you were missing. We could not fathom where you were, how you managed to leave and why, dear man? Come you must get into bed immediately." She shook her head in disapproval. "You must have some hot consommé." She motioned to a young novice carrying a tray with cups of hot broth for the sick patients.

Nicolette tucked the blankets around Claude as a mother would a child. She covered his shivering body up to his chin, raising the pillow behind his head enough so he could sip a spoonful of soup. She could tell its warmth soothed him. Sister Bugone nodded to Nicolette. She was glad to have the help.

After a short time, Claude fell into an uneasy sleep, waking only slightly when his breathing suffered and became irregular. Nicolette put the remainder of his consommé on the adjacent bedstand and stood up. She looked down at Claude with tears in her eyes. She knew she would lose him soon. It was almost too much to bear. She crossed herself and said a quiet prayer. Although she was modest in displaying religious sentiment, it seemed appropriate here, now. Faith was all that was left. Nicolette took a small gold cross from around her neck and folded it into Claude's hand.

Just then, Sister Bugone walked over to Claude's bedside to check on him. She looked up at Nicolette and shook her head. "It won't be too long," she whispered. The Sister moved close to Nicolette, and patted her shoulder. "It's late, dear. Why don't you go home and come back tomorrow."

Nicolette could see compassion in the nun's eyes, hear the kindness in her tone. She agreed and donned her cape and scarf. She knew this might be the last time she would see Claude alive.

Once outside the courtyard, Nicolette walked to Rue Saint-Jacques meandering along with no destination in mind. Grief-stricken once again, she couldn't think of going home just yet. Why had this happened, she thought, that one so talented as Claude should die so young? It seemed so unfair that death should be so random, befalling good and kind men instead of greedy pompous ones. She wiped away tears with her handkerchief and blew her nose.

She walked to the bridge at the Seine. What will become of me now? she thought. She could afford the rent for the flat for only a short time with the sale of the bookstore items left. But a woman alone? Would she end up in the poorhouse—or worse? "Perhaps I must join the convent, become a nun and heal the sick," she said aloud. The thought was not appealing, but perhaps it was the only way. Sister Burgone would be aware of my caring qualities, my faith. She saw how I cared for Claude, she surmised.

Before long, she found her way to Notre Dame Cathedral. In its cold, gray, stone sanctuary she would pray for the answer. Nicolette looked up at the high vaulted ceiling and the stained glass windows, awed by the majestic monument of faith to God. She walked to the front where she lit two candles, one for her father, one for Claude. She covered her head with her scarf then retreated to sit on a pew at the back of the church. She looked up at the image of Jesus in the south rose stained-glass window before bowing her head, closing her eyes, praying to Him. She sat in silent meditation for over an hour.

By the time Nicolette left the Cathedral, the sun was going down. Gas lamps were being lit along the avenue. Nevertheless, she walked slowly toward home, still deep in thought. She didn't notice a carriage drawn by a stately black horse come alongside her until it stopped. She looked up to see the carriage door open. A gentleman clearly of aristocratic stature, waved a dark silver-tipped cane in her direction, as he stepped down into the street.

"Mademoiselle!" he called. "Bonjour, Mademoiselle," he repeated coming toward her. "Are you not Mademoiselle Nicolette Marchand?"

"Why yes, Monsieur..."

"Pierre Etienne L'ecuyer," he said, bowing ever so slightly. We met at the home of Charles Jules, brother of Madame de Brionne. Your friend Monsieur Claude Jacques Gustav, the talented young musician was the guest that evening. Do you recall?"

"Ah, yes, yes, I do recall." Nicolette was surprised he remembered her.

"And how is your friend Claude Gustav?"

Nicolette lowered her eyes, caught off guard by the inquiry. She took a deep breath holding back the urge to weep. "He is dying, I'm afraid. Consumption."

"Oh how awful! I am so sorry to hear that. He is so young, so gifted. I was thinking of inviting..." He stopped mid-sentence seeing the sadness in Nicolette's eyes. "And what of your father and the shop you mentioned?"

At that, Nicolette gasped and burst into tears. She couldn't speak. She covered her face with her hands and then leaned into Pierre L'ecuyer's shoulder, sobbing. He patted her on the back to comfort her as best he knew how.

"My dear, you've had such great loss." He took her shoulders to steady her. A drizzle of rain had begun to fall. "Let's go to a dry place. Come, my carriage is here," he coaxed her. Nicolette did not resist as he helped her into the carriage. He directed the driver to his house. "My cook will prepare some dinner for us and you can have a reprieve from so much grief." He gently placed a fur blanket over her lap.

Nicolette could not remember when she had eaten last. She was in no condition to refuse such a comforting offer. Indeed, she felt grateful, being invited to his grand city mansion. As they approached, she peered out the carriage window to the marble building and statues adorning the fountain and stairs.

Inside, the home was embellished with gold leaf moldings, crystal chandeliers, and dark, polished wood doors. Fine Persian and Italian carpets covered shiny stone floors. A grand entrance, lavish parlor, and dining hall began Nicolette's tour. A marble staircase led to six elaborate guest rooms on the second floor complete with an indoor toilet cared for by L'ecuyer's servants.

After a finely prepared dinner, Nicolette felt less fragile, but overcome with exhaustion. "Merci, Monsieur L'ecuyer for such a delicious meal and for your graciousness. May I ask that your driver take me home?"

"Of course, but it is so late," Pierre said checking his gold pocket watch. "Why don't you stay here for the night," he offered. "As you can see, I have more than enough room for guests." He motioned to the splendor of his home.

"Oh, merci, Monsieur L'ecuyer. What a kind offer, but I couldn't impose." Nicolette was hesitant, confused about his intentions.

"Please, Mademoiselle, you have cared for your family and your friend for so long. Now you deserve to lean a little on someone else, don't you think? Allow me to be of service to you. Please let me show you to your room, just for the night." Pierre took her by the arm and led the way up the marble stairs. Nicolette was too weary to object any further.

"Here, my dear, one of my luxurious guest rooms. You can sleep a restful sleep for the night. No one will disturb you," Pierre promised. "If you like, one of my servants can draw a warm bath for you in the morning before you are on your way. How would that be?" He smiled, kissing the back of her hand graciously.

Nicolette had never used an indoor toilette nor bathed in anything but the bathhouses, except when she was a child living in the countryside where she and her aunt bathed in the river. She had not slept in a soft feather bed since her mother was alive. And never in a four poster bed, or with silk sheets and a gold brocade quilt like the one Pierre showed her now. Nicolette was dazzled. The warmth of the mosaic-studded hearth, its mantle embellished with alabaster cherubs, the oil lit lamps and lead crystal chandeliers, all gave the room a seductive ambiance.

"Oh, it's a beautiful room," she uttered.

Just then a woman servant came into the room holding a dressing gown of pink silk and lace. Over her arm she carried a velvet turquoise robe. She lay them down on the bed and awaited instructions.

"These belonged to my wife. Sadly, she passed a few years ago, before Christmas," Pierre reflected quietly. "She never got to wear these garments."

"My condolences." Nicolette's voice softened. "Thank you for your generosity, Monsieur L'ecuyer. It all looks *tres bien,* wonderful. I will be very comfortable, I can see that."

"Ah," Pierre's eyes lit. He smiled. "Then you accept my invitation. I am very glad." He nodded toward his servant. "Cherise will get you anything further you may need. Have a restful sleep and I will see you in the morning." He kissed Nicolette's hand one last time. "Goodnight, Mademoiselle."

CHAPTER 17

The Strega's Daughter

Early Spring, 1424, Outskirts of Padua, Italy

Sarah, the midwife, sat at her kitchen table on an old wooden bench, her wrinkled hands folded on the table. She looked at Bella who sat across from her in the dim lit room. "I will take Davina under my wing and teach her what I can, although my eyesight is poor these days." Sarah shrugged. "Between you and me, it's a wise decision for your Davina," she confided in Bella. They finished their tea and the honey bread that Bella had brought for this clandestine meeting.

"Her father has taught her some about plants and tonics, so she should be able to learn quickly." Bella touched Sarah's hands. "Thank you, Sarah." Bella did not mention just how much Chaim had taught their daughter, nor about Davina knowing even more than Chaim. "I will bring her to you the day after the Sabbath this week. I have been so worried ever since the day Chaim found her."

"Found her?" Sarah looked puzzled.

"I mean," Bella choked up, suddenly realizing she had almost divulged her and Chaim's long-kept secret. "I mean, since she came to live with us, so undernourished from the home of Chaim's sick cousin."

Sarah nodded. "That is what you told us, Bella. We have all accepted her as one of us, as your adopted daughter. You would not tell me something different, now?"

"No, of course not. She is family."

Sarah nodded. "Good, my dear friend. Then there is nothing more to say. I will train her." She hugged Bella good-bye.

Bella wrapped her shawl around herself and climbed down the stone stairs of the old house. She walked with difficulty up the narrow streets to her own abode. Her back ached from age these days. She, as well as Sarah, were the oldest women in their community, now less populated than it had been for as long as Bella could remember. Times were changing, she thought. At least there were enough young women still having babies. She said a silent prayer that Sarah would not be suspicious of Davina's natural gifts, especially after she had just inadvertently blurted out the truth of Davina's sudden appearance into their lives almost ten years ago. Had she covered-up her mistake sufficiently? Anxiety crept up her spine.

When Bella entered her own kitchen, she found Davina sitting by the hearth tending the evening meal. Davina was drawn and thin. Sadness was taking a toll on her daughter, Bella thought.

Loneliness was the real culprit. Aside from her family, there was no one with whom Davina could share her thoughts, her knowledge, her gifts, lest they think her a witch, or crazy. Some days, Davina herself thought she would go mad, listening to the voices in her head, and to the night visitors that spoke to her still.

But that was about to change.

"Davina, dear one," Bella approached her beloved daughter. "I have wonderful news."

Davina looked up from her kettle of savory vegetable soup. "Mama?"

"Sarah, the midwife, has agreed to train you. You will become a midwife! The women will be able to come to you, now that Sarah is too old. She will look to you for help." Bella's eyes shone brightly for the first time in a long time. She stood up straighter, her pain subsiding from sheer joy. Finally, her daughter would have a place in the community and not be looked upon with disdain or pity. She would be safe from suspicion.

Davina's eyes lit too. "Sarah said she would teach me to birth babies?"

"Yes, she's getting too old now, so you will be the one the women will need. You will not have to worry anymore. You will belong, have a place in the community," Bella boasted.

"I'll be needed," Davina repeated trying out the concept.

"You will be appreciated. You can be special in a good way, a useful way," Bella practically cried, she was so relieved. But the excitement exhausted her. She held her hand to her heart catching her breath and reached for the bench, sitting down hard. "Ah, I have to rest."

Davina, poured her mother a cup of strong anise tea. "Here Mama, drink a little. Rest. It will be better."

She wanted to please her elderly mother. Both her parents were old now and she could see the strain of life taking its toll, especially where she was concerned. She would have to accept her fate and become a midwife. As a woman, there were few choices for her. She was not royalty, after all. She could not become an artist, a physician or a publisher of books. But she could heal people as a midwife, at least the women and babies who would need her services, Davina thought. She would discuss it with her father. And her green lady.

"Thank you, Mama, for helping me." Davina gave Bella a warm embrace.

Bella's heart melted, her eyes watered. A weight lifted from her shoulders. It was settled then, she thought. Wiping away her tears, she stood up. "Let's make a special bread with the dried fruit I have been saving to celebrate for when your father comes home." Bella was already at the cupboard before Davina could respond.

"Let's make it with his favorite honey!" Davina said proudly. She could feel her own appetite returning.

Two days later

"Before you start your training with Sarah," Chaim pulled at his beard, "I think we should study, perhaps go over some of the remedies we have learned as they apply to childbirth."

Davina nodded. "Yes, Father."

"I realize you have other ways of knowing things, my dear daughter. But to stay safe let's do what is expected, so Sarah can teach you in a manner that is suitable for a midwife. I can offer to go over tonics first with you, if you'd like."

"Papa, can I write?"

"Write what? Keep to the way I showed you, Davina, when you are working with the women and children. Can you do that?"

Davina was far away. She was roaming in a forest of enchanted trees and a green lake shimmering in the moonlight. A chant beckoned her to the lake where she stood looking at the plants growing from the forest floor. She could name each one and see the way in which they could be mixed together for healing.

"Davina?" Chaim's voice was deeper, louder.

Davina returned her attention to the study and lowered her eyes.

"Are you going to be able to concentrate, do what is expected of you? You cannot wander in the other realms when you are attending a birth." Chaim looked worried.

"Other realms?" Davina had never heard him use such language. "You know my other realms, Papa?" Davina smiled.

"Not entirely. I know you have the gift of a mystic." Chaim spoke to her more honestly than he ever had. "I've seen your writings. I knew of your gifts from the first time you came to my study years ago. But you were a child, then. So we could hide the musings of a child. Now you are a grown woman." He paused. "We have tried to keep you safe, Davina—for a long time. No one can know of your gifts. You must disguise your ability in practical application. Now you have a chance to do that if you are careful. Do you understand?"

"Yes, Papa," Davina said. "I know you and Mama have cared for me well, especially not treating me like just a mere girl. I *will* take this responsibility very seriously, I promise."

Chaim finally smiled. "Good," he said. "Now let's get to work." He took his own books from a shelf and poured over them, cautious to share only commonly used remedies and tonics for nausea, pain, and bleeding. Davina listened carefully, trying to pretend this was new information that she had to remember.

Her memory and attention were honed when the first call came for her. Her cousin Lupe had suddenly gone into labor with her second child, not due for another month. Lupe was frightened.

Sarah calmed her with soft words and crampbark tea to ease the pain of her contractions. Davina applied cool compresses to her sweating forehead when her cousin's contractions became stronger and more frequent.

In spite of Sarah's soothing demeanor, Davina could see that she was worried. The baby's head was not near the birth canal. It was breach. Sarah didn't want Lupe to push the baby out before she could make an effort to turn the infant—a dangerous feat in itself. If the placenta was displaced, or the cord was around the tiny one's neck, it could be deadly. Sarah oiled Lupe's bulging abdomen and began massaging in circles with just enough pressure to coax the unborn baby to turn. When this did not work, she prepared for another method.

"Davina help me place this pillow under her, so her buttocks are up, then bend her knees, quickly." Davina lifted Lupe onto the pillow. With Lupe's legs apart, Davina could see there was some bleeding. She knew that excessive blood would be disastrous—perhaps a placenta rupture. Lupe screamed as another wave of contractions hit her.

"Lupe, don't push." Sarah demanded. As soon as the contraction subsided Sarah placed a well-oiled hand into the birth canal until she could feel the child's bottom through the partially dilated cervix. Trying to change the child's position was critical yet dangerous at this point, but she had to try. "Davina, massage her abdomen clockwise in a circle," Sarah instructed. Lupe groaned loudly.

Minutes passed. As soon as the next contraction came Sarah removed her hand from Lupe's birth canal. Lupe screamed in pain. "It's too late, we can't change the child's position," Sarah whispered to Davina.

"May I try?" Davina asked. Sarah looked at Davina, speechless, then turned without a response, and walked over to the pitcher and basin to wash her hands.

Davina chanted softly into Lupe's ears and then moved her hands above Lupe's abdomen chanting under her breath. She made letters and symbols just like the ones she had made in her manuscript, only now she made them in the air over Lupe.

Then in a low voice, she chanted another incantation. In her mind's eye she could see the letters and numbers she had observed in Chaim's study. Davina felt suddenly warm all over. Her hands especially grew hot as she moved them in a spiral a few inches above Lupe. Lupe dozed.

When Sarah finished washing, she turned to see Davina moving her arms above Lupe in a strange manner. "What are you doing, Davina?" Sarah asked coming back to Lupe's bedside. She was shocked to see Lupe resting. "Oh, this is not a good sign. No contractions is trouble." She propped Lupe's head up. Lupe opened her eyes.

"I need to push!" Lupe screamed.

Sarah grabbed Davina's arm and pulled her to the edge of the bed so she could assist in the imminent birth. Sarah was sweating, in her nervous attempt to direct Davina through the terrible danger of this breached delivery. But as Lupe began to push, Sarah saw a mop of black hair crowning, emerging—not the infant's bottom or feet. The tiny infant's head, then shoulders, arms, and rest of it's little body came swiftly into Sarah's skilled hands, alive and whole.

Davina eyes sparkled. She grabbed a dry cloth and wiped the child as Sarah instructed, wrapping a blanket around him, and lifting the infant boy onto his mother's body. The baby let out a cry. Lupe cried with joy, holding her first son. "The afterbirth, Davina." Sarah pointed to the cord. "She must push the afterbirth out and you can cut the cord. I will show you how."

The sound of the baby's cries rang out. Lupe's husband waited in the kitchen, relieved to hear the baby wail. He prayed for his wife and new child.

Sarah wiped her brow, her duties completed. Lupe was an experienced mother. And Davina could clean up the room and help care for the child a while.

Sarah congratulated Lupe. She reassured Lupe's husband, then left. But she was more than exhausted from the ordeal. She was shaken. Even with her long years as a midwife, Sarah had never seen a breach turn so suddenly. Turning a breach was a difficult, tedious, and precarious endeavor. She had done it a few times, but not all with success. Sadly, she had lost a few breach babies over the last forty years.

The old midwife walked home, dusk settling around her. Her eyes burned, and her feet hurt. But Sarah's mind ruminated with questions. She knew she had been unsuccessful herself this time and the possibility of Lupe losing this child had been great. How had it been that the child turned as if by magic? What had Davina done? Could it be that Davina had used a spell to create such a result? Were the rumors about Davina true? Sarah suddenly recalled her conversation with Bella. How odd, she remembered, that Bella had used the word *found*. It had always struck Sarah as strange that a little waif of a child should suddenly have appeared from an unheard of distant cousin from a far-away place.

Sarah made herself a cup of tea. She would have to watch Davina for signs of magic craft more closely, she decided.

CHAPTER 18

Rita Kerner

Friday after Thanksgiving 2004, Tucson, Arizona

Rita awoke early on Friday, before everyone else was up. She walked out onto the veranda and watched the clear morning sky turn pink and gold as the rising sun peeked over the mountaintops. The air was cooler than she expected. She closed her robe and surveyed her surroundings. At the edge of the screened veranda a sandy path lined with rocks and small cacti led toward the back of the main house and pool. On a small boulder, she noticed a lizard doing his morning push-ups. Rita laughed. Humor broke her nervousness, anxiety that had woken her at dawn and not allowed her to fall back asleep.

She stretched her arms above her head and bent forward, sideways and backward in slow motion, taking her exercise cue from the lizard, who soon ran down the path. A mother quail scurried by, cooing to the perfect row of eight little ones following close behind her. The air, sweet with the smell of orange and lemon trees, alive with the buzzing of bees busy collecting pollen from cactus flowers and oleander, calmed Rita. The sun rose into full view, warm and inviting. With each breath of balmy, perfumed air she absorbed the palpable sensations of nature's beauty. It suddenly struck her how little time she'd really spent outdoors, living as she had most of her life in cities, at work, in her studio.

Deciding to take advantage of her early rise on such a glorious day, Rita washed up, put on her bathing suit and walked out to the pool. She set her towel down on the patio chair noticing a little sign stuck in the sandy path. *Check pool for snakes before swimming.* Startled, Rita eyes darted from the perimeter into the deep end of the pool. It was not until she felt all was clear that she dove in. The water had cooled overnight. Rita came up for air quickly, shivering. It was only then she noticed something brown moving slightly in the pool's filter alcove. Like a roadrunner swimming for its life, Rita was up the ladder and out of the pool in two seconds, her heart pounding.

"You okay, Rita?" Sharon opened the sliding glass door of the pool house. She'd been getting the pool cleaning supplies ready when she'd heard splashing. "I didn't know you were up yet. What happened?"

"Something in the alcove there," Rita shuddered and pointed.

Sharon walked over to the circular panel covering the filter box, removed it in one swift motion and peered in. "Oh yeah, you're right—a Diamondback. We get them or king snakes and lizards falling into the pool sometimes. They swim into the filter area here for safety. This kind is endangered."

"A rattlesnake?" Rita whispered. She looked on in disbelief as Sharon took a long stick, carefully looped the snake and tossed it gently over the short stone wall into the wild cactus-strewn desert beyond their property.

"There you go, buddy." Sharon said to the snake. Then she turned to Rita. Standing tall in her shorts and T-shirt, hands on hips, she laughed.

"I'm not a city-slicker anymore!"

Rita, still in shock, could only manage a forced smile.

"Hey, you two—coffee's ready!" Donna poked her head out of the back door of the kitchen. "Breakfast on the patio in fifteen minutes, okay?"

"The social director has big plans for us," Sharon laughed. "Rita, you can have a better swim later after I clean the pool. The water will be warmer by then too. And no snakes, I promise!"

"Sounds good," Rita agreed. She wrapped her towel around her shoulders and headed back to her room to dress, still recovering from her first encounter with a real rattlesnake.

"So here's the plan," Donna said, placing the toasted bagels and cream cheese in the center of the patio's glass-topped table. She poured herself more coffee and passed the coffee pot to Rita. "Gary, Michael, and his sister, Rachel, who's in town from the East Coast, will meet us at the art opening this evening." Donna continued. "We can have an early dinner before heading down to Tubac. She turned to Rita. "It's about an hour's drive. So I told them we'd meet there around six." She looked at Sharon. "How's that sound?"

"Okay, I'll get the pool cleaned and take my convertible in for an oil change so we can drive in style later. I filled your car with gas yesterday, so you're good to go today." Sharon, glad to have some time alone, sipped her coffee.

"Great. I'd love to take Rita out to see more of Tucson. And there's someone we both want you to meet—an acquaintance of ours." Donna winked at Sharon. "Actually, she's another artist we know. She has a little gallery at her house.

"We thought you might have some things in common." Sharon said.

"She's a wise woman, a very intuitive healer also." Donna added.

After breakfast, Donna and Rita drove out into the desert, where the homes were few and far between. Down a dusty road, they came to a cluster of small adobe houses at the foothills of the Tucson Mountains.

"It's kind of a cooperative," Donna explained. "It's mostly women our age, all different backgrounds. Everyone has their own place, though. Some have trailers, some casitas. They share a common space, fruit trees and a garden too. Here it is."

They stopped in front of a low-roofed house with a lemon tree and two mesquite trees in the front. A small covered porch provided shade for the woven hammock that swung between the two large wood posts on either side. Bright-striped Mexican blankets draped two bulky chairs on either side of the doorway. Donna smoothed her wind-blown hair, removed her sunglasses and knocked on the wooden front door.

"Oh, hello!" said the dark-haired woman who opened the door, " I am so glad you made it. Welcome! Come in Donna and, uh, aren't you, Rita?"

"Yes, is that you—Lucy, right? "

"You two know each other?" a surprised Donna exclaimed.

"We met on the plane coming here!"

"This is *b'shert,*" Donna proclaimed. "That means, *it was meant to be,*" she said to Lucy.

"Ah, yes. We have a name for it in my Tohono O'odham language and culture too, the meeting of the ancestors," Lucy explained. "Come in, come in, I have made some lemonade for us in the gallery out back. Let me show you some of the wonderful artists whose work is here. She put her arm around Rita's shoulder. "How wonderful you have come," she repeated. She looked directly into Rita's eyes.

Rita was fixated. Lucy's eyes shown with a radiant light that Rita had seen only once before. It was the same intense light she'd seen in the eyes of the angel who had found her lost car key. It crossed Rita's mind that perhaps the desert was in fact, magic.

"Look here," Lucy announced leading Rita and Donna to a small casita. "The theme of most of the art in this space is *water.* In deserts all over the world, native people have always looked for and found water, clean drinking water. Indigenous cultures have prayers and chants for all sources of water, including rain." Lucy explained. "Tucson was not always a desert, though. Once a very long time ago, it was an inland sea. You can still find seashells if you dig in the sand. There are aquifers that run deep under the desert," Lucy pointed to a large painting of a hand-dug well by a Spanish Mission with Indian symbols in the sky above it. Rita wondered why a Catholic Mission would be about water.

Lucy could read her thoughts. "My ancestors used to grow corn in the flood plains of the great river. Before so many people arrived, the Santa Cruz River flowed all year long, not just in monsoon season. Look here." Lucy rummaged through a drawer of a small desk in the corner of the casida's main gallery room. She pulled out a worn photo album. "Here is a picture of the Santa Cruz River in 1912. This was taken before the great flood of 1915."

Rita and Donna looked at the photo. The caption read:

"The Santa Cruz River is about 184 miles long. It begins in the grasslands of the San Rafael Valley east of Patagonia, Arizona. It runs south into Sonora, Mexico, then north again into Arizona passing the early Spanish missions including San Xavier del Bac."

"Look at this painting of the Mission San Xavier del Bac." Lucy pointed to another painting in the room. "The Mission is several miles from here on the Tohono O'odham San Xavier Indian Reservation." Lucy explained. "You see the site is also known in Tohono O'odham language as, *the place where the water appears.*"

Then Lucy looked directly at Rita. "Maybe you should go there," she said in a lower toned voice. She looked deep into Rita's eyes. "You will find answers in sacred places where there is water."

Rita was still smiling when she and Donna got back into the car. "That was amazing. I would love to go to see the Mission one time. Maybe, I'll start to figure out..." Rita paused. "I haven't told you something, Donna. I am nervous about this evening." Rita confided. "I think I know Marla Woods."

"What do mean? You met her on the plane too?" Donna laughed.

"No," Rita smirked. "I think she is someone I knew in college, only her name was Marla Remy, back then."

"How do you figure that?" Donna asked. "What's the problem, even if it's the same person? Did you hate each other or something?"

"Kind of the opposite, I mean..."

Donna looked over at Rita wide-eyed. "Really? You two were an item back then?"

"Not exactly. It's a long story. But it was a painful time. Anyway, I am a bit nervous it may be the same person."

"Look, don't worry. Even if it is, you're both older. It was a long time ago." Donna waved her arm. "Maybe it will be just what you need to heal old wounds. You never know." But Donna had second thoughts. "Did you tell Cleo?"

"Yes, well sort of. No, not really. I just wanted to check it out without it being a '*thing*'. I am trying to put all the pieces of the puzzle together. I feel like I *can't see the forest for the trees.*" Despite the embarrassing cliché, Rita suddenly had goosebumps.

"Okay, my friend. I won't ask. Just be careful, okay."

By the time they got back to the house, Sharon had dinner made—hot dogs and burgers on the grill. It was a perfect easy meal, except for Rita whose stomach was in knots. She forced down one hot dog, thankful for the accompanying beer that calmed her nerves.

After their meal, Rita washed and dressed in white jeans, a blue striped blouse, and her favorite sandals. She took one last look in the mirror running her hands through her auburn hair. She loved the way the color shone in the setting sun's orange light. Feeling more confident knowing she looked good—not too old at any rate, her decision to cover the gray finally felt right.

Later that day, *Aphrodite Gallery,* Tubac, Arizona

Marla stood at the far side of the main gallery room chatting with guests. There were over a few dozen people mulling about admiring her work while partaking in an array of hors d'oeuvres and champagne. Marla turned her head toward the door and glanced at the three woman who had just arrived. She smiled at them nonchalantly, then attempted to extricate herself from conversation with the couple of patrons. When she looked toward the door again, her gaze penetrated Rita's.

Rita's heart pounded. "I don't think Michael and Gary are here yet," she thought she heard Sharon say.

"We can just..." Donna stopped mid-sentence noticing Rita's cheeks getting red. Like a true friend, she motioned to the champagne server. "Three, thanks." She handed the first one to Rita.

Rita took the drink on automatic pilot and downed it watching Marla head toward her. "Oh my God, it is you!" Rita said aloud before she could control herself. She blushed. Marla was as beautiful as she remembered her, even with age—or maybe more so because of it.

Marla smiled. "Rachel?" she asked. "Are you here with Gary and your brother?"

"It's me Rita, from college" she mumbled embarrassed.

"Oh, my God—it *is* you, after all!" She kissed Rita on both cheeks like old times, her French greeting. "*Ma cheri,* how wonderful it is too see you!" she gushed. "What a coincidence! For a moment I thought you were someone else I met recently. But I recognize your wonderful eyes and smile now." She took Rita's hand. "I'm so sorry I did not get back in touch with you after Geraldine gave me your number. I meant to so many times. Oh, but here you are!" She turned momentarily to take a glass of champagne as the server walked by, then back to Rita with a distinctive flamboyant air—her trademark. "We have so much to talk about, *Mon amour*!" She glanced at Donna and Sharon. "And who are your friends, dear one?"

Still flustered, overwhelmed by Marla's bold beauty, Rita introduced Sharon and Donna. Marla gushed over them as well, but Rita thought she noticed something more in Marla's eyes, behind the bravado, the glamour, the famous artist's persona.

"I'm sorry too. I never called you back to say goodbye. I thought you were leaving and I, well..." Rita blurted out.

Marla looked both startled and perplexed.

Rita blushed, embarrassed.

"It's no matter now, Rita." Marla waved her hand, brushing away the past. "We have lived our own paths. We are here now. The past is past. Come." Marla motioned turning her head. "Let me introduce you to my husband. He just arrived from our home in Maine today for the opening." She perused the room. "Oh, Enrico!" she waved and walked toward a handsome, middle-aged gentleman engaged in conversation with a couple about one of Marla's sculptures. Rita managed to swipe another glass of champagne and gulped it down.

"Oh, look! There's Michael and Gary, finally," Donna exclaimed, nodding to the guys. Gary waved to Donna and Sharon, then scanned the room for Marla. Michael noticed Rita.

"Gary had mentioned you looked like my sister, but wow—quite a resemblance! How do you do, I'm Michael." He held out his hand.

"Nice to meet you too. I'm glad to know there's a real person who looks like me out there. So many people tell me I look familiar to them." Rita smiled a champagne smile.

"Hi, you two. We thought you might not be coming," Donna said.

"Aren't we just appropriately late?" Gary chimed. "We do like making an entrance, honey!" he teased.

Sharon laughed. "Where's your sister, Michael? We were all looking forward to meeting her."

"Rachel wasn't feeling well. I think it's just jet lag. She needed some down time. Maybe you could all come over to our house tomorrow?" Michael offered.

"Why don't you," Gary added. "My niece is making a stop to visit us on her way to a conference in California. So we'll have a little welcoming party for everyone! You're all invited and I'm cooking." Gary held up his glass of champagne. "Oh, there's Marla!" he nodded and waved.

"Oh darlings, you all know each other? How perfect!" Marla had Enrico's arm. "This is my old friend Rita from college. And these are her friends..."

"How do you do?" Enrico smiled and offered his hand to Rita first. He seemed a charming man, dressed casually in light colors that accentuated his brown skin and a well-trimmed, graying mustache and beard. Rita thought she saw a knowing glance pass between Gary and Michael.

"You're a sculptor too?" Enrico asked Rita.

"Actually, I mostly paint. I haven't sculpted since college."

"And you remember Gary and Michael?" Marla added. "They're thinking of purchasing *Night Flight*." Marla winked at Gary.

"Why don't you all come with me. I want to show you my new work." She took Gary's arm. "I know you love my intuitive work, but I am transforming. I'm becoming an environmental artist." She strutted into the adjacent gallery room. "It's very avant-guard. I mean it can be disturbing. My theory is if people don't stop polluting the environment, mutations will become the norm."

In the next gallery room, on individual pedestals, were sculptures of fish, birds, and reptiles. They were exquisitely carved in stone, some alabaster, some limestone, some marble. But they all had one thing in common—too many legs or heads or eyes or fins, one more foreboding than the next.

"This is hauntingly beautiful," Rita whispered.

"This is what makes art and especially artists so important. They are the heart and soul of social consciousness." Gary said.

Rita felt hugged. "So true, Gary and thank you for saying that."

They looked at each piece and read the descriptive captions beneath. On the walls juxtaposed to the images of environmental disaster were photographs of elephants in the wild, strong and whole and majestic.

"I'm partial to elephants," Marla said following Rita's gaze. Marla tossed her neck scarf over her shoulder. A gold pendant of Ganesh studded with turquoise and garnet hung from a chain around her neck.

"What a beautiful pendant. It looks familiar—is that possible?" Rita squinted.

"Do you remember when we were in Paris together so many years ago? My grandmother gave it to me on that trip. It was given to her to hand down to her granddaughter, a family tradition started by my great, great-grandmother, Cherise, after the French Revolution. The story goes that it belonged to a woman of nobility for whom she worked. My middle initial, C for Cherise, remember? I was named after her." Marla's eyes twinkled.

CHAPTER 19

Madame Nicolette L'ecuyer

April, 1789, the Estate of The Baron Pierre Etienne L'ecuyer, near Versailles, France

Nicolette waited for her breakfast. She fingered the gold place setting and fine linen napkins, while she stared dreamily out the windows where morning light drenched her flower gardens. Even after eight years since her husband, Pierre L'ecuyer, had bought the country mansion, it still felt strange that she had come to marry into such wealth.

Cherise, her handmaid, interrupted her introspection, pouring the morning consumme. "A buttered roll, Madame?" she asked.

Nicolette noticed there was something different about Cherise's manner today. She seemed to be harboring an inner light, as if something had made her unusually buoyant. There was no sign of the heavy drudgery from daily toil and monotonous labor, the worry about the dire conditions of family members, since the storms and subsequent drought. The sadness of the last few weeks that she had displayed, gone.

"Thank you, Cherise," Nicolette said taking her cup. "Have you had good news?" Perhaps word of her son had come finally after months of waiting for his return from the army.

"Yes, Madame, I've had a letter from my son. He is well and plans to return soon."

"What good news, my dear. I'm so glad for you." Nicolette

felt a tenderness toward her handmaid, who had been in service to her from the beginning. She trusted Cherise like a confidant and often found herself longing for the familiar closeness of her femaleness.

What startled Nicolette the last few weeks was her attraction to Cherise. At first she had thought it was just her own nurturing tendency, the kind she always had when those she cared for fell ill. Since Cherise had begun feeling sad of late, Nicolette had noticed her own desire to comfort her. But in their closeness Nicolette felt a passion rising within her, the kind she had had for her husband once upon a time, when they had courted and were first married.

Monsieur Lecuyer's charming ways had waned long ago, their intimate physical connection a mere handful of times in their marriage had all but disappeared, replaced by politeness and an occasional embrace. Pierre seemed to prefer the company of men and the talk of politics, philosophy, and astronomy. Not a particularly handsome man, it was his height and proud posture that had once proved the saving grace of his commanding stature, his allure. With age, his large features and pouch belly had grown making him a less appealing caricature of his former self.

He had married Nicolette out of compassion for sure, but more so out of a sense of duty to his position, needing someone who could keep his books, write his letters, and run a household of servants especially designed for the social events of his station. Although Nicolette was not born or bred of nobility, the fact that she was from the educated merchant class made her acceptable. That she was a beautiful woman added to Lecuyer's sense of prestige and status.

For Nicolette's part, she had been vulnerable. Overwhelmed by Pierre's charm, and wealth, it was her need for security that won her over to him. With few choices and little money, she had married Pierre out of practicality. It was a common sense decision, she had convinced herself. He needed her writing and organizational experience she had learned at her father's side. She believed she would come to care for Pierre. But their intimacy had been abrupt, without tenderness. Except for the dream of bearing a child, Nicolette was relieved at her husband's waning interest after the first year.

Now Nicolette could smell the sweetness of Cherise's skin as she approached to serve her breakfast, the mild aroma of rose water mixed with body heat. She had refrained from thinking about her feelings for Cherise though, keeping busy with running the household, assisting with her husband's administrative needs— writing letters and invitations to support societal duties and expectations of Pierre's position, in order for him to stay in the good graces of King Louis XVI.

However, today there was a moment of hesitation. Nicolette looked at Cherise's smiling face with new eyes. She noticed the flush of her cheeks, the wisps of dark hair that fell across her forehead, her smooth neck that flowed gently to her ample bosom, her movements more graceful with her lightness of being, her happiness at hearing from her boy, no doubt.

Before she realized, Nicolette caught Cherise gazing back at her with an intensity she'd never seen. Embarrassed, Nicolette looked away. She sipped her consommé trying to control the heat she felt rising in her cheeks, averting her eyes momentarily.

The moment was not lost on Claudine either. A new servant, she was Cherise's young helper assigned to her for training. The poor farm girl, not more than fourteen, followed Cherise around like a shadow observing her every move.

"Nicolette, my dear," Pierre's voice broke the silence.

Nicolette turned to see her husband swagger into the room. He dismissed the maid servants with a brush of hand. He waited for Cherise and Claudine to depart before he spoke again.

"I am going to Versailles shortly. I need you to prepare a letter of my introduction to the Duke and Duchess de Orleans. Also, my dear, the King himself should be inviting us shortly to the upcoming Gala at Versailles, so you will need to order a proper gown in Paris for the occasion," he pronounced, with the same tone with which he gave orders to the servants.

Nicolette nodded.

"Perhaps some of the fine fabric I brought from India would be a fitting tribute and present for her majesty," he pondered aloud. "There must be a necklace left in the collection too." He looked at Nicolette directly. His voice softened. "You might consider wearing the gold elephant brooch I brought you. I'm sure the other guests would admire those jewels of the Orient."

"Of course, *mon cher*. I will visit Madame Courtier's shop in Paris for a proper gown," Nicolette said. She had wanted to go into Paris for some time. She would take Cherise with her.

Pierre did not wait for a further response, but sat down at his dining place and rang his dinner bell. Cherise came in promptly from the kitchen and poured him a cup of tea. She placed a gold trimmed plate of breakfast rolls and a crystal butter dish in front of him.

"Will there be any jam this morning, Monsieur?"

"No, that's all," he said, buttering a roll. Nicolette wiped her mouth with her linen napkin and smiled politely.

"I will get to work immediately on your letter of introduction, my dear," she said excusing herself.

As the sun rose the following day, Pierre dressed for an important Court appearance. He and others had been summoned by the King to discuss raising the needed funds to pay the rising debt. Before Nicolette arose, Pierre had had his breakfast and with letters in hand, climbed into his carriage. He motioned to his driver. The sound of horses hooves drifted into Nicolette's boudoir. With her husband gone, she was alone with the servants. Nicolette breathed a sigh of relief. She would have time for herself and to make plans for her trip to Paris.

Rising from her bed, she first used the chamber pot, then draped her robe about her and walked into the dressing room, anticipating Cherise or Claudine coming with her bath water. Not hearing anything, she peered into the hallway. She was surprised to see Cherise running her hands over a stone bust of Madame du

Barry. It was not the first time Nicolette found Cherise admiring Pierre's collection of art.

"It is lovely. A copy of one of Jean-Baptiste Pigalle's fine works," Nicolette said.

"Oh, Madame, *Je suis tellement désolé.*" Cherise picked up the pitcher of water and bowl she had set on an adjacent small table momentarily.

"You like art, don't you Cherise?" Nicolette asked as Cherise helped her bathe.

"Yes, very much," Cherise said. "I wish..." she blushed and shook her head.

"What do you wish?" Nicolette inquired while Cherise washed her back.

"I wish I had the skill and talent to create such beauty. Oh, it is a very ridiculous thing for me to think." She handed Nicolette a clean towel. "But when I touch the sculptures of the cherubs, the faces, the bodies or study the portraits, I feel like I am in another world." Cherise shook her head. "Oh, pardon, I sound like a foolish old woman."

Nicolette wrapped her silk robe around her. She leaned over to Cherise and kissed each of her cheeks.

"Madame?" Cherise's startled face turned red.

"You are neither old nor foolish. You are an artist at heart, obviously. But you're a woman. We do not have many women as members of the *Academie Royale de Peinture et de Sculpture.* Even women of nobility are not permitted into life drawing classes," Nicolette said. "Besides, until the world changes, even Labille-Guiard and Vigée Le Brun need the admiration and grace of the Court to be successful. Ordinary women don't have a chance."

Cherise's eyes were teary. "Merci, Madame," she whispered.

"Times are changing, Cherise. Maybe someday, everyone will have more opportunity. For now, we shall go to Paris for a trip to buy new clothes! How would you like that?"

Late June, 1789

Pierre L'ecuyer looked disturbed. "Nicolette, my dear. I need you to write a letter to Monsieur Necker, finance minister of the King Louis XVI himself. It should say that…

I, Baron Pierre Etienne L'ecuryer, in reverence to King Louis XVI, am writing to ask an audience with Monsieur Necker to discuss the severe distress I have witnessed in Paris. Word of higher taxes to resolve the debt is proving unattainable and solders in the streets of Paris are heightening tensions. Food shortages are not only affecting the poor. As you are aware the Estates General plan for the Third Estate has already broken with the Church as well as our nobility and is demanding a written constitution. They are calling for an National Assembly."

"Nicolette, please make all the necessary additions, compliments, salutations as appropriate and send it off forthwith. I am going to Versailles to be of service to the Court." Pierre left Nicolette to her duties.

But Nicolette had other ideas. She would write the letter and take it to Paris herself. She knew Suzanne Curchod, wife of Pierre Necker, and their daughter Anne Louis. She had gone with Claude Gustav to arrange a concert at one of Madame Curchod's salons many years ago, before he had become too ill to play. She would ask Cherise to accompany her as she had before. Together they would enjoy the conviviality of Paris again, she thought.

CHAPTER 20

Rachel Rita Padini

Friday After Thanksgiving 2004, Tucson, Arizona

Friday morning, Rachel awoke early to the aroma of brewing French roast coffee.

"Great, you're up!" Michael gave his sister a good morning hug when she appeared in the kitchen in her robe. "We have a fabulous day planned for you. Gary and I want to show you around the area before the art opening this evening. There are some great sights, if you're up for some adventures."

"Sure, sounds like fun," Rachel said pouring her cup of coffee and indulging in one of Gary's freshly made cranberry muffins. "Where will we go?" She was determined to be a normal tourist—no hallucinations today she prayed.

"Okay, so I thought we would go up to Mount Lemmon. It's an amazing view." Michael bubbled like a kid anticipating his favorite candy.

"Besides that, Michael loves to stop at Summerhaven." Gary winked at his beloved.

"Summerhaven?" Rachel asked.

About nine thousand feet up Mount Lemmon in the Santa Catalina Range is a small town cafe known for its pie." Gary explained.

"Wow, that's a long way to go for pie. But I bet the views are magnificent."

"Oh, amazing!" Michael added. "And maybe we can stop at the Mission San Xavier del Bac afterward, on the way to the gallery opening." He could see the question forming in his sister's head just by the expression on her face.

"It's a Spanish Catholic Mission on the Tohono O'odham Indian Reservation. It's an historical place, Sis—the oldest European structure in Arizona. I'm not a fan of imperialism, but it's famous for its Spanish Colonial architecture, built by Franciscans originally. I thought you might appreciate it since you liked the historical museum work."

"It all sounds wonderful." Rachel was overwhelmed. "You guys are something. I really appreciate all the fuss you're making on my account."

By mid-morning Gary's Toyota, carrying the three happy adventurers, climbed the steep road up to Mount Lemmon. "Breathtaking!" Rachel exclaimed looking out at the panorama from her backseat vantage point. Mountains jutted up from an ancient sea floor nine thousand feet below. When they finally reached their destination at Summerhaven, they found a half inch of snow covered the trails between the pine trees. The pie shop had outdoor heaters on for tourists eating mouthfuls of the delicious berry pie at small tables on the deck. Rachel breathed in the crisp mountain air and looked up at the sky. It was a deeper blue than she had ever seen it.

"You see, Sis. You can swim in the valley and ski in the mountains all on the same day."

"It is beautiful," Rachel agreed.

As planned, after blueberry pie with whipped cream, they headed down the mountain and south to the Mission. From Highway 19, the Mission stood out from the surrounding desert. The "*white dove of the desert*" as it was known, glittered in the sun. They drove onto the Tohono O'odham Reservation turning into the dusty parking lot, then walked up to the impressive church. Between two tall, white towers on either side of the entrance, the building boasted a terra cotta wall of stone filled with symbols, statues and carvings of deities, saints and priests. The iconary told the history of the Jesuits and Franciscans, the Spaniards who had invaded the land for "*God, Gold and Glory*" according to the historical pamphlet given to visitors at the entrance. "*The Spanish had come to bring Christianity to the Native population,*" it said.

Michael grimaced as he read the brochure changing the words as he read. "Never mind that the Spaniards were not invited by—*the Native population who had lived on the land they called "Wa:k" for over a thousand years, farming the fertile flood plains of the Santa Cruz River that flowed eleven months a year. It was not easy to set up the Mission with opposition from the more warring Apache tribes—*who tried like hell to get rid of the invaders" he ad-libbed, "*who succeeded in the destruction of the first Mission in 1770. The Mission was rebuilt in 1789.*"

"I'm sorry" Michael said. "I should not put in my two cents. There's a lot of history here and well, maybe since you both relate more to Christianity than I do, obviously, I should just be quiet before I offend someone," he reflected.

"Hey, not on my account, Boyfriend. I get imperialism. But, we brought your sister here to see some history of Arizona. And by the way, you remember I'm a Black Baptist turned atheist, married to a Jewish man, right? Don't get me started..."

"Hey, you two, I'll just enjoy the beautiful architecture and sculpture," Rachel said, walking into the main chamber of the church. It was dark inside in comparison to the bright light of the afternoon sun. Only small windows near the high ceiling cast light in the narrow entrance where old wood pews stood in perfect rows. Every wall was covered in imagery which extended up to the high vaulted ceilings. In some cases the ceilings were no longer painted, due to weather and an earthquake in the 1800's that had caused extensive damage to one side of the building leaving it at the mercy of the elements, so it said in the brochure.

The main rotunda of the church was built in the shape of a cross, the bulk of sculpture reaching from floor to ceiling with Christ on the cross at the center of the main altar. On either side, the walls were covered in old, darkened with age, story paintings—Jesus and the apostles at the last supper, Franciscan priests and symbolism of church doctrine.

The further Rachel walked into the church, the more uneasy she felt. As she viewed the towering sculpted and painted walls filled with depictions of centuries old stories, a woman approached Rachel and touched her arm. Rachel jumped.

"Oh, I'm sorry, dear. I thought perhaps I could explain some of the imagery to you and your friends. Look over there. That is a sculpture of Saint Francis Xavier. If you wish to light some candles and receive blessings..." Michael and Gary walked closer to hear her. "I work here as a docent, but I'm not beginning another tour for a short time. I noticed you looked a little perplexed."

Rachel felt dizzy. The musty smell of the old walls and iconary had made her eyes burn. She felt claustrophobic. "Thank you," she said. "I'm just feeling a bit, uh... I just need some air."

Before she could say more she thought she heard someone screaming. She gasped as a monk-like figure dressed in black walked toward her, his face hidden by a black pointed hood reminiscent of white or red hoods worn by the modern Klan. Only his eyes showed through his hood. He sprayed her with a fowl smelling liquid and spoke to her in what she thought might be a combination of Latin and Spanish. Then, Rachel noticed a heavy rope in his hand. She smelled smoke. Her heart pounded. Out of the corner of her eye she saw the glow of lit candles. Terrified, Rachel forced herself to focus on them and yelled Michael's name.

Suddenly Michael grabbed her arm. "Rachel! Sis, what's wrong?" He looked at her startled to see the color draining from her face. She was pale as a ghost.

Gary came over to aid them. "What happened?" he muttered looking at Rachel. "Oh, girl you better have some water, quick." Gary offered his water bottle.

Michael gave Rachel a drink and took her arm. The docent stood nearby.

"She can sit in a pew awhile," the woman said. "Sometimes people are very moved by the great power of the church icons. I could tell you more about them, if you like."

"Thanks," Michael said, mustering control over an impulse to say something inappropriate. "I think we'll just head outside to see more of the architecture."

Outside, the air and light steadied Rachel. "Whew, that was pretty intense," she whispered. But she could not say what had happened. It was a vision for sure, but also a feeling that had overcome her. A sense of doom, of panic. She could feel something sinister slither under her skin, feel it in her bones, in her very soul, but she could not explain it.

"How about we walk up the hill over there. You can see the mountains all around and the flood plain from there." Michael suggested. " There's a little carved out grotto with the Sculpture of the Lady of Guadalupe there—I think more to your liking, Sis."

"Oh, that sounds good. Yes, the Virgin Mary and Madonna images do calm me. The sun feels so good too. Would you mind if I go myself, guys? I just need to clear my head."

"Sure, Sis, if you want to. We'll walk around here—meet you at the car in a while. Take this bottle of water though. Dehydration can sneak up on you in the desert."

Rachel took her time up the incline of the hill next to the Mission. A path circled around the hill midway up. Rocks and boulders covered the summit with a tall white cross protruding from the very top. Only courageous climbers and young people dared traverse the jagged rocks. Rita walked counter-clockwise on the path breathing in the clean air and absorbing the reassuring sunshine. Halfway around, she helped a young mother and child who were having trouble climbing the last few feet down from the rocks.

As Rachel got close to the grotto, she passed a middle-aged couple first and then an older light-skinned gentleman with a balding head and a gray beard. The couple looked like tourists on holiday, with tanned skin, overdressed for the weather, the woman carrying a camera and the man, a map. She overheard them speaking in French.

The solitary old man, in worn jeans and a somewhat tattered white shirt, walked with a wood cane. Rachel wondered how he had climbed the embankment, noticing the man's gnarled fingers were wrapped around the top of the cane partially covering a brass elephant head, his thumb resting on the upturned trunk. A kindred spirit, she thought. Rachel smiled at him as she passed.

He didn't acknowledge her, seeming lost in his own thoughts and talking to himself. He shook his head a few times muttering something over and over. It sounded to Rachel like he was saying, "but it was a woman." Since he had not made an attempt to engage her, Rachel decided to ignore him, in case he should be just a poor old guy with a bit of dementia. She found it a bit easier to dismiss the presence of all three people the second time circling the mound. A calm meditative sense of peace came over her as she gazed out at the mountain ranges in the distance and imagined what the land had been like when the native population had flourished and the Santa Cruz River flowed in what now was only a semi-fertile, dry flood plain.

On Rachel's final trip around the path, the old man unexpectedly stopped and stared at her. "May I talk to you?" he said. "I need to tell you something."

Rachel stopped. "Me?" she asked, looking around for the couple or anyone else.

"We cannot go to Mars, you know," he declared, as simply as if he were saying, "*Nice weather today, isn't it?*"

Rita smiled. "Thank you," she said, hoping that would be the end of it. *Dementia,* she thought. She put one foot forward to continue her walk. She was ready to continue down the hill to meet the guys and enjoy the air-conditioned ride home.

"No," he insisted. "I am supposed to tell you. They told me to tell you—that you would tell everyone." He shook his head.

"I almost died, you see. I went to heaven and I am Catholic, you know," he continued like he was confiding in a trusted old friend. "You see, I was expecting St. Peter. I waited for him. But he never came!" The old man was near tears it seemed, his eyes watering.

Poor thing, Rachel thought. She hoped the couple might return or Gary and Michael might come looking for her.

"I'm so sorry," she said. "I understand. I'm Catholic too," she uttered, not knowing if she really was Catholic anymore or why she would say so.

"Ah, that is why I am telling you. It was a woman—a woman at the Gates. Not St. Peter. It was a woman!" He raised his voice an octave. "I don't know why! Why?"

"I see," Rachel said, not sure what more to say or do.

"No," he said again. "It's not just that. She said it was not my time yet. I had to come back and tell you—we can't go to Mars! She said, *'go back and tell them three things.'*" The old man held up three crooked fingers of his left hand. His eyes grew big. "She said, *'tell humans they have to educate themselves, take responsibly and learn to live in harmony,'*" he exclaimed, leaning his golden elephant-head cane against his thigh. Using his right hand to point each of the three extended fingers to demonstrate one—*educate*, two—*take responsibility*, three—*live in harmony*. "Earth is our home. We can't go to Mars." He put his head down and closed his eyes. Rachel saw tears at the corner of his eyes. "It was a woman," he moaned, bewildered.

Rachel stood still not knowing how to react. She almost burst out laughing, but compassion overrode her impulse. Perhaps she should point out the grotto to him with the statue of the Madonna honoring the vision of the Virgin of Guadeloupe at Vorurhes. But before she could compose herself long enough to respond, the old man looked up, glanced at her like nothing had happened, and walked away.

"How was it?" Michael asked when they reunited with Rachel. "Meditative, huh?"

"Did you see an older man leave? An old bald guy with a cane?" Rachel asked.

"No, Gary and I were in the car with the air-conditioning on for the last ten minutes." Michael looked at Gary. "We saw a mom and her kid and a couple—a man and a woman a while ago. Why? What happened?"

Rachel couldn't find the energy to explain. She was exhausted.

"You, okay, Rachel? It can be an intense experience." Gary offered.

"Have some more water, Sis. We have some almonds too. We'll go home, wash up, rest. We can have a bite before we head down to Tubac for the art show. How does that sound?"

Rachel took a deep breath. "Sure, sounds great." She tried to sound convincing, but the constant apparitions were diminishing her optimism, to say nothing of her sense of sanity. In spite of the walking in the clean air and sunshine, she could not shake a sense of doom, a sinister feeling. Suddenly, she remembered how much she had resisted the stories of the church after first converting. The constant superstition of Joseph's sisters, cousins, mother, and grandmother. She had felt that same darkness enveloping them, steeped in biblical stories of good and evil, righteousness and sin, permeated by fear. But it was more than that, she thought—something darker, deeper, older. Something she could feel in her very cells.

"Oh, turn off here," Gary's voice interrupted Rachel's trance. "Let's see if Lucy is at home. I think Rachel would like meeting her, don't you?"

"Actually yes, good idea, "Michael said taking the next exit. "Rachel, a slight detour—we want you to meet a friend of ours who has a little gallery at her place. She's a healer also."

They drove up to Lucy's place and got out of the car. "Doesn't look like she's home," Michael said knocking on the door. They waited. Rachel noticed a little gallery sign on one of the front windows. It was written in another language. Gary pointed to it.

Uchu no mugen no chikara ga kori kotte
makoto no daiwa no miyo ga nari natta...

"It's a Hopi water blessing. Her gallery is having a show about the sacredness of water, cleaning the waters of this land and all of earth. It's a very spiritual show."

"Maybe we'll get a chance to come back when she's home, before you leave, Rachel," Michael shrugged.

"Okay, sounds good, but I hate to say this, you guys," Rachel paused. "I'm not sure I'm up for any more activity today. I think I need a rain check on the art exhibit tonight. I'm sorry."

Gary and Michael looked at each other, communication passing silently between them. "All right, well, Gary can go. I can stay home with you, Rachel."

"Oh no, I won't hear of it. You both go." Rachel protested. "I'll be fine. I just need to rest a bit. So much excitement. I have been kind of hibernating since Joseph passed, except for the moving business, you know, so this is really my first excursion outside my comfort zone, as they say. I'm just a bit overwhelmed is all. And maybe just a little jet-lagged still," Rachel confessed. She turned to her brother. "You've both been looking forward to the opening—please go. Besides, you guys have such an amazing collection of books. I can settle in and be comfortable with a good read." Her smile was convincing.

"Okay, Sis. We won't stay too late, then."

Later, when Rachel had the house to herself, she changed into her sweats, stretched, and exhaled away the tension in her shoulders. Looking through the wine rack in the kitchen, she pulled out a bottle of Pinot Noir, her favorite. She opened it and left the wine to breathe, while she meandered into the library, turning on the light with a slight apprehension. But all seemed perfectly normal—just shelves of books.

Rachel pulled one at random from the book shelf closest to the door. It was titled *A History of Healing Herbs*. She shrugged off a fleeting sliver of memory, then flipped through the pages of the leather-bound book, its yellowed pages and botanical ink renderings looked like a rare book treasure. Intrigued, she tucked it under her arm and went back into the kitchen.

The bottle of Pinot Noir beckoned. She walked out onto the deck with a glass of comfort in hand. The sky was turning a deep turquoise. Rachel sat down at the patio table and sipped her wine, looking out at the last pink and gold swirls of a sunset. Suddenly, out of the corner of her eye she noticed lights in the sky. She looked directly in the direction of what appeared to be some sort of writing, symbols made up of bright white light, like the stars. She would later describe them as crop circles in the sky. Rachel stood up quickly—half-fearful, half-mesmerized, knocking over the remaining wine in her glass. "Oh damn!" she said automatically patting the liquid dry with a napkin.

When she looked up again, though, she could not believe her eyes. She gasped, holding her hand to her heart. "Oh, my God!" she said. That was all she could utter. In the clear azure sky, high above the mountains in the not so far distance, appeared a planet exactly in the image of the Earth, looming, like a giant hologram in the remaining daylight, ten times bigger than the moon. The planet looked solid, then faded as its molecules seemed to quiver like a mirage.

Rachel could not remember how long she'd stood transfixed, when she awoke later in the guest-room bed overcome by a great thirst, her hair, clothes and a coverlet disheveled. The almost empty bottle of wine was next to her on the nightstand, the book lay open to a page about planting season for Italian herbs. She tried to piece together the events of the last few hours, but could not. Had it just all been a dream? What did it mean?

"I must be losing my mind" she said aloud picking up the bottle. "Did I drink all this wine?" This is what it must feel like to be going crazy, she thought. Perhaps, she should consider seeing a doctor before it was too late. She headed to the bathroom to relieve herself and get a drink of water. The house was dark and quiet. Michael and Gary were not home yet. She was glad. She would eat something and watch TV.

It was a good plan. She felt calmer after a meal of Thanksgiving dinner leftovers, tryptophan taking the edge off her anxiety. She topped it off with a piece of pumpkin pie and some milk. Feeling full, she turned on the small TV in her bedroom, glad to find *Boston Legal,* a show familiar to her. Halfway through it, she dozed.

In the space between consciousness and sleep, she found herself in a classroom. What seemed to be a green light cast an aura around her, turning her skin light green. She looked out from the back of a classroom where she observed the teacher at the front podium—a tall, iridescent dark-skinned figure, waving her arm in a wide arc, creating pictures in the air as she spoke.

CHAPTER 21
The Strega's Daughter

Early Winter 1424, Outskirts of Padua, Italy

Davina watched Sarah, her mentor, carefully administer the wine with valerian root, Sarah's pain remedy, to soothe Eva's labor pains. Eva was a petite, frail girl of nineteen, the wife of the cantor, Jacob ben Chazan. It was a risky birth for any woman whose husband was over six feet tall, but for Eva even more so. She had been in labor for eighteen hours, when Davina had arrived to help Sarah.

Still suspicious of Davina, Sarah made a plan to keep a watchful eye on her protégé. First, she would make sure Davina knew she was being watched. Then Sarah would act as if she trusted her, turn away pretending to be distracted by her own preparations for the birth. Meanwhile, Sarah listened surreptitiously for any incantations, peering sideways to notice any unusual hand and arm movements, facial distortions, or amulets that Davina might resort to in her craft.

Davina, thinking Sarah just strange due to her old age, paid no attention to her idiosyncrasies and sideways glances. She concentrated on the birthing mother, taking special care to notice any changes to Eva's breathing, secretions, and the heartbeat of mother and soon to be born baby.

Eva moaned with each contraction. This was her first birth. The baby was bound to be big, maybe even too big, given the father's size. Davina had not yet been present at any stillbirth or death, but she knew how dangerous childbirth was. She said a silent prayer in Hebrew as Chaim had taught her. Then, she placed her hand on Eva's swollen belly and closed her eyes. She waited for a vision. Soon she was able to see, in her mind's eye, the position of the infant in the vaginal canal, head down. This was good.

Sarah looked at Davina with disdain. Why were her eyes closed, her hand on Eva's stomach. What was she thinking, praying?

Sarah came along side Eva and helped Davina lift her onto the birthing chair, so the pregnant woman was leaning back, her legs parted. Sarah moved her draped skirts and reached between her legs to feel if there was a bulge of the cervix yet from the infant's head. Sarah looked at Davina and shook her head. No progress was not a good sign. Sarah began to sweat. She had delivered dead babies in her long years as a midwife. She had not been able to save every mother, either. But it had been a long time since she had lost one.

"Davina," she motioned her helper to the wash basin in the corner that was stacked with towels and rags. "We may have to pull the baby out. Pray to God we will not have to do anything worse," she said. Then she returned to Eva and rubbed oil on her vulva. "Over there, Davina," Sarah motioned with a turn of her head and her eyes. Take those implements from my satchel."

Davina reached into the satchel under the table and pulled out a pair of spoon-shaped tongs and iron spring scissors. Davina's eyes opened wide. What was she supposed to do with these?

Just then, Eva let out a blood-curdling scream. The two mid-wives came quickly before Eva almost slipped off the chair. Eva began pleading for God to let her die.

The two women boosted Eva up, holding her under each arm. "I think we will need Bianca or Lupe also, to help keep her calm enough. And more wine for the pain." Sarah said as she rubbed oil on Eva's perineum. Davina could see the fear in Sarah's eyes.

"I've got her. I can hold her while you go for help." Davina whispered. "She turned to Eva, and began to sing a child's lullaby that Bella had sung to her when she had had nightmares many years ago.

Sarah, acknowledging the common children's song, wiped her hands on her apron and hurried out of the room.

As soon as Sarah was out of earshot, Davina's song turned into a chant. As her melodic voice soothed Eva between contractions, the young mother closed her eyes. Davina now concentrated all her energy on the infant. She stroked Eva's belly and sang to the infant, envisioning the child smiling, running, playing joyfully. Soon the green lady hovered beside Davina in a soft mist. Symbols, letters and numbers appeared and vibrated in the air, changing color and shape until they formed a perfect sphere. The slow beating of drums, and the soft notes of a flute accompanied images of a forest filled with exotic plants, wild flowers and a lake of clear green water.

Davina reached into her apron pocket for a potion she had made last evening, sealed tight in a small corked bottle. Her green angel had prepared her for this birth in a dream and her mother Francesca had guided the measures and mixtures.

She opened the cork with her teeth and carefully poured the contents into Eva's mouth. In a dreamy state, Eva sipped without hesitation, licking the sweet liquid off her lips without opening her eyes. When Davina heard Sarah coming, she quickly dropped the empty bottle and cork back into her apron. She resumed the position of holding Eva as she had before. Eva slept.

"What is wrong?" Sarah ran toward them, with Bianca in tow. "What has happened?" Sarah checked to see that Eva was breathing and picked up her skirts to check her progress. "My God! Hurry! She motioned to Davina for pillows and towels, and instructed Bianca to hold onto Eva. Just then Eva gasped and opened her eyes. Then she screamed.

"I need to GO! Poohing, I'm poohing!" she cried, tears streaming down her face.

"You are fine, Eva. Push, push the baby out!" Sarah yelled, shocked. "Push again," she urged Eva.

Eva pushed hard once, twice, the third time her face grimacing in pain.

Sarah's skillful hands delivered the head, then the shoulders. Out came the big baby boy. Sarah turned him over to release the fluid from his mouth and the infant howled. Bianca came with towels to wipe the infant. Sarah laid the child at Eva's breast, then motioned to Davina. " When I deliver the afterbirth, you will cut the cord with those scissors."

A few days later

What was a joyful occasion for Eva, her new baby and her family, did not turn out as such for Sarah. She had detected remnants of some strange substance on Eva's breath, tiny droplets on her chest when she had laid the baby to suckle. Beyond that fact, she knew there was some magic that had taken place. In spite of the gratitude the family had expressed, Sarah was more frightened than ever. She could not prove what she knew—that Eva was not going to deliver that big child alive or even live through the birth. She had birthed too many babies to have made such an error in judgment. Sarah decided she must talk to Bella. Who else could she confide in? Who else would know the truth?

"Come in, Sarah." Bella welcomed her friend with open arms. I am so grateful to you. Davina told me of the wonderful news for Eva and her family. I'm sorry she's not home to see you too. She went to visit Lupe. Chaim is out as well, but we are both so thankful for your teaching Davina. It is a blessing." Bella was surprised to see the frown on Sarah's face.

"What is it, my dear friend? Has something happened to the new baby or Eva?"

"No," Sarah replied. "They're doing well, so far, thank God." She was quiet for a moment.

"We are old friends, Bella, no?"

"Of course, Sarah."

"We have seen bitter times, we Jews. Only our faith and love for God and one another keeps us together, surviving, no? We have seen much hardship and death at the hands of those that hate us, have we not?"

"Sarah, tell me what is bothering you so?" Bella was concerned for her old friend. Maybe her age was starting to affect her ability to think clearly. "Let me make you some soup."

"I don' t need soup, Bella, I need the truth," she said, her voice more commanding than normal. "Who is Davina? Where did she come from—the truth! Is she a *strega*?"

Bella gasped. She raised from her seat as best she could on her old legs, her joints aching. She held her hand to her heart. "I don't know what to say." Her eyes filled with tears. "She is my adopted daughter, Sarah," she uttered. "Please..."

"She is performing *magic*. It is dangerous." Sarah spoke in a steady calm voice, not giving in to Bella's tears. "Tell me the truth."

Bella wiped her eyes with the ends of her apron. Her hands were still caked with flour which smudged her cheeks. She sat down again. "Please, Sarah, you must not do this. Please, do not tell a soul, Sarah." she whispered like she was praying. "We saved Davina's life," Bella said. "Chaim found her floating in the river, almost dead. We don't know any more. No one came looking for her. It took months to bring her back to life, to heal her. Chaim said she was a gift from God, after our Benjamin..." Bella wept.

Sarah just stared wide-eyed at Bella. "God in heaven. You kidnapped a child? She could be a Christian, a gypsy—anything."

"Yes," Bella murmured. "Even a Jew like us."

Sarah was speechless. "She could be a strega's daughter!" she implored. She got up from the kitchen bench. "I must go, now."

"She is not doing spells, Sarah." Bella reached for Sarah's arm. "Chaim says she knows his studies, knows Hebrew, knew it before he taught her. He believes she is blessed with intelligence beyond her years. She's not a witch, Sarah." Bella pleaded.

Sarah turned to leave.

"If Davina were a boy," Bella's voice angered, "she would make a fine physician. She is cursed because she is a girl? You cast her as a witch, because she is too smart? Has she not become a practicing Jew? Has she not been a blessing?"

Sarah shook her head. Then she closed the door behind her and walked out into the cold gray day. Her heart hurt. Her mind reeled, overwhelmed. She must do something, she thought. But what?

The small community of Jews had its own Rabbinic counsel where men like Avraham Dayan, Chaim's good friend, could pass judgment, resolve conflicts, and make binding decisions for the community. Perhaps she could speak privately with Avraham, if he would be willing to hear an old woman.

But this thought did not dispel the knot of anxiety in her stomach. If the Church authorities found out that Jews had been harboring a child of possible Christian birth, it would not take long to have all the Jews expelled from town or worse, given the harsh treatment they had endured in the past. If their synagogue's Rabbi or judge knew of a witch in their midst, what might happen? Would they all be at risk? The community did not have the luxury of Rome or Florence with their larger congregations, more organized rules, leverage of trade. Sarah was more than worried.

So was Bella. She wrung her hands and paced back and forth in the kitchen. If Sarah went to the authorities, she and Chaim might be arrested and thrown in jail.

What would become of them and the rest of the community? What would happen to Davina? Was it worse to harbor a witch or to be seen as kidnapping a child? Neither was the truth, but who would believe them? Bella was desperate to think of a solution. No matter which way she tried to determine the best decision, find the least terrifying outcome, the more anxious she became. Her heart pounded in her chest. Then everything went black.

Chaim walked slowly home from the synagogue. He was pleased with the accolades he had received from his friends, especially Eva's father who credited Davina with helping Eva birth his healthy new grandson. Chaim climbed the stone steps and opened the door. Usually the aroma of dinner met him. But not today. Bella lay on the cold kitchen floor, a head wound seeping blood.

CHAPTER 22

Madame Nicolette L'ecuyer

September 1789, The Estate of the late Baron Pierre Etienne
L'ecuyer, near Versailles, France

Once it was over, everything had changed. The world had turned upside down. Nicolette had received word of Pierre's disappearance, the attack and ransacking of their home. She had been anxious to return to find him, to escape from Paris after the bloodbath. She had taken her carriage herself, no driver or servants to be found. Her handmaid, Cherise, had been missing since the day the Bastille had fallen, having left their Paris accommodations on Rue Dauphine to purchase some vegetables at the open market. She had not returned. Nicolette had waited as long as she could for Cherise to accompany her home, but to no avail.

After weeks of chaos, Nicolette finally reached her once grand house only to find nothing remained of her life. There was only an empty shell. The life that had saved her, that had changed her into a woman of nobility over the many years since her father's death and Gustav's passing were all gone. Her husband dead, her home in ruins, Nicolette had no one to turn to, nowhere to go.

But she could not mourn. No tears would come. Freezing like the coming winter winds, she was numb. She moved in a trance to the front door. She looked down without emotion at the blood stains on the stone steps where they had dragged away her husband's body. She walked through the large front door onto the marble hallway floor, her footsteps echoing along the once tapes-try-adorned walls up to the gilded vaulted ceiling.

Like a sleepwalker, she entered the gray kitchen. Its cold metal pots and kettles hung empty over the hearth. Beyond an arched doorway and down a few steps, the servants' quarters beckoned. She floated toward the stairs as if drawn by magnetic force pulling her to the room where her beloved Cherise had slept. The door creaked opened as Nicolette leaned her frail body against it.

The bed, still unmade, was empty like the rest of the house. Nicolette caught herself, dizzy and swooning, leaning against the dresser, knocking a small vase that remained to the hard floor. The sound of breaking glass barely registered. But her eyes transfixed on the dresser. There a familiar hairbrush and comb was left untouched as if nothing had happened, as if Cherise would return any moment to finish combing and braiding her own dark locks. Setting out to the kitchen to prepare the morning meal, she'd return when the sun rose to change into her serving clothes. Cherise would come wake her with a soft touch. Their intimacy evoked in the combing of Nicolette's hair. When their eyes met over the morning consomme poured carefully into porcelain cups and rolls served with freshly churned butter, an inconspicuous smile would curl the corners of her mouth reminding Nicolette of their stolen embrace, their kiss.

Nicolette bent down and picked up pieces of the broken glass vase. She felt no pain. Only the sight of her bright red blood broke through the wall of disbelief and denial. She gasped like she had been holding her breath for days. Tears flowed down her burning cheeks. The whole world had gone mad and with it everything she loved, every reason for living had perished.

"Madame," a soft voice pierced Nicolette's silent shock.

She looked toward the voice to see Claudine, the young servant girl, standing in the doorway. She was thin, drawn and unkempt, her clothes threadbare. But her eyes shown with the tenderness of youth, of optimism. "Madame," Claudine repeated waiting for Nicolette to acknowledge her, as she had been trained. Even though hell had descended to earth, she held fast to her station, so indoctrinated had she been by her elders.

"Oh, my dear, Claudine, you are alive!" Nicolette reached for her and held her to her breast like she was a young child. "How have you managed? Are you hurt? Where have you been hiding?" Questions tumbled from Nicolette's throat.

"Madame," Claudine replied, "I have returned to my family in Loire Valley not far from here. But we have little food and few belongings. I came along to see if there might be any provisions, even pots or pans that we might..." She lowered her head.

"It's not stealing if no one lives here anymore, especially if you would otherwise starve. All our lives have been ravaged by politics and greed. You are a French citizen, are you not? Do you not deserve to eat?" Nicolette's defiance erupted on behalf of the poor girl. "A revolution has come, Claudine. Perhaps now we shall all come to our senses!"

Claudine's eyes shone brighter, but she said nothing at first. Then she noticed the blood on Nicolette's hand. "Madame L'ecuyer, you are bleeding!"

"Ah, yes. It's just a cut."

Claudine rushed to tear a scrap of fabric from what remained of a curtain and tightly wrap it around the wound.

"Merci, ma cherie." Nicolette scanned the room once again. "I'm devastated too, my dear." Nicolette's voice was gentle now. "I have lost so much."

"Cherise has gone back to Champagne to be with her son," Claudine offered.

Nicolette's eyes grew wide. "She's alive?" she exclaimed.

"Yes, Madame. She told me if I ever saw you again to tell you, she had to go. She took some of your things for safe keeping— your private letters, your diary and the jeweled elephant brooch your husband brought you back from India," Claudine confided.

"Oh, oh, how wonderful!" Nicolette beamed, joyous the first time in months.

"She said she didn't know if you were dead or alive and she wanted—you are not angry?"

"No, not at all. I will find her now." Nicolette began to plan her next steps, renewed. She reached in her bosom and pulled out an assignat worth four hundred livre. "Here, *ma cherie,* take this to your family. I know it's not worth much and with the drought food is scarce, but perhaps it will help a bit. While I am here take some provisions, whatever you can find from the kitchen. Can you ride?"

"Ride, Madame?"

"Yes, a horse. Can you ride a horse?"

"Why yes, Madame. I learned as a child on the farm, when we had one. Why?"

"You are less likely to be accosted by soldiers if you ride, especially at night. I will give you one of my horses. I don't need two or a carriage. I will ride, as well. We can find whatever is left of reins and saddles in the stables."

Together, Nicolette and Claudine removed the horses' carriage harnesses and brought the mares to the stable to prepare them for their journey. They set their gathered provisions and belongings firmly in place behind the saddles. Nicolette took off her bulky pannier, letting her skirts flow freely along the natural curve of hips. When nightfall arrived, they straddled their mares, a leg in each stirrup to ride unhindered by convention. With no planning or provisions for night travel, they were lucky to have a waxing moon shining through the glen.

They rode for a short time before Claudine pulled her horse up short. Nicolette slowed and turned back to meet Claudine. "This is where I turn to head home," she said in a hushed voice. "Merci, Madame. It has been so kind of you to help me. I can find my way on foot from here, if you want to take the horse."

"No, Claudine, you keep her. Your family can use her now." Nicolette was grateful Claudine had returned to the estate when she did, a miraculous coincidence that had changed everything. "Go safely, dear one. And thank you for telling me about Cherise."

"May God bless you, Madame." Claudine whispered, pulling gently on the reins.

Nicolette moved slowly along the road north for a few minutes glancing up at the night sky full of stars. Then, reining the mare east, she dug her heals gently into her hide, until she could feel the smooth gate of her canter.

Twenty-one years later, 1810, Paris

Cherise lay in bed laboring to breathe. Her white hair flowed onto the embroidered pillowcase in fine strands like goose down. She heard the hubbub of women at the market stalls on the street below as she rested in her son and daughter-in-law's small Paris flat on Rue de Fleurus. Her son had brought her to live with him, his wife and daughter only recently, since Cherise was too old and ill to care for herself.

Her son had been promoted, in the aftermath of Napoleon's victory against Austria. Now, he was preparing for one of Paris' grand military parades. She would hear all about it when he returned this evening, she thought. Today, she was in the care of her granddaughter, Michelle Pauline.

Cherise smelled the soup her granddaughter had left for her on the night table. But she was not hungry. Instead, Cherise rolled to one side with effort to open the night table drawer. She fumbled through it until she came upon a small wooden box. Grasping it tightly, she pulled it toward her chest, and held it like a lost child. Then peering downward, she opened the box. Her withered hands fingered the jeweled broach inside. Memories long forgotten flooded through her mind. She had forbidden herself to remember for a long time, in part out of guilt for violating her faith, but more so for protecting herself from the grief of loss.

"Grand-mere!" Cherise heard the young woman's sudden reappearance. "What are you doing? You will fall out of bed!" Michelle's concerned voice raised an octave. She gently helped Cherise back toward the center of the bed. "What have you got there, Grand-mere?"

Cherise's eyes watered. "It is a brooch," she whispered. It belonged to someone I cared about, a long time ago."

Michelle Pauline examined the brooch, turning it in all directions to see the fine gold elephant figure embedded with ruby and turquoise stones.

"I want you to have it, my dear granddaughter," Cherise said.

Michelle Pauline was wide-eyed, looking for a moment even younger than the pubescent girl of twelve that she was. "I will treasure it always," she exclaimed. "Is it an elephant, Grand-mere?"

"It's an elephant God from India, my dear. Please promise me..." Cherise paused to catch her breath, "you will pass it on to your daughter when you have one and she to her daughter, like a sacred heirloom for our family. That would make me happy," Cherise said. She closed her eyes, seeing Nicolette standing before her smiling.

"She opened her eyes again. "See there," Cherise pointed a frail finger toward her wardrobe. "There is a journal there."

Michelle Pauline took the box down from the top of the wardrobe and opened it.

"What are these Grand-mere?" She waited for Cherise to speak.

"These are for you because you like to write. There is a woman here in Paris. Her daughter is a writer." Cherise coughed. "Her name is Anne Louise, daughter of Suzanne Churot. Anne is a fine writer. She can teach you. Tell her...tell her...I knew her mother's friend, Nicolette L'ecuyer." Cherise closed her eyes again remembering Nicolette taking her along on a visit to Madame Churot and young daughter in Paris years ago.

Michelle leafed through the exquisitely crafted handwritten pages. "What shall I do with these grand-mere?" she asked.

Cherise looked at her grandchild's sweet face. Her blue eyes shone with the innocence of youth. "They are the beginning of a wonderful story," she whispered. "A story about a little bookshop here in Paris, once upon a time."

CHAPTER 23

Professor Emari's class

AllSouls College, Pleiades

Viridian had the strangest sensation as Professor Emari wrapped up her lecture. A kaleidoscope of images and a fleeting sense of density made her feel unusually weighty, almost awkward. She was more conscious of temperature, perceptions of the beating, pulsing of fluid. An impression of a major shift in vibration startled her. Unidentifiable objects entered her awareness absorbing her attention, creating an unfamiliar reaction. Then for an instant, she found herself in a strange yet beautiful environment, surrounded by tall green vegetation and a green lagoon. Moonlight glittered through branches and leaves.

Emari's voice filtered through Viridian's fleeting vision, catapulting her back to the classroom. "The way in which free will operates is solely based on thought. While you set your destiny as a soul of the infinite to follow goals for elevated consciousness and experiences in the physical aspect, your thoughts can override the program to a greater or lesser extent through soul spitting, or for that matter, organic factors like health or environmental issues.

"The health of the species is influenced by interdependence on the natural world—other living organisms, hygiene, sustenance, water intake, temperature, as well as thoughts. This also includes the obvious planetary changes of the earth itself and most importantly, negative effects caused by the species."

Emari checked the level of attention among her students. She decided a visual was in order. She touched her breastplate and opened up a hologram depicting the evolution of the human brain from its primordial features to the last imposed genetic modification. "Human brains have a dual function and history of development as we discussed—an instinctual brain and a reasoning conscious brain. While this brain is affected by nutrients, chemicals, and electromagnetic energy, the latter making it capable of dimensional transformation, it is prone to storytelling, both positive and negative scenarios. The stories represent beliefs, based on memory, a distortion of memory, primitive science, and lack of understanding of universal law, history, place of origin and soul consciousness. Religion is an example of storytelling on a mass level." Emari paused. "Any questions, so far?"

"What is religion?" Silver asked. "I mean, can you explain how it works?"

"That's a good question." Emari looked directly at Silver. "Remember what we discussed about fear? Fear of the unknown is a powerful force in humans. In this present cycle, before the program was modified and the implementation of knowledge advanced, understanding of cause and effect was lacking. The use of storytelling supplemented for the unknown. Based on observation, on a three-dimensional plane, it explained natural phenomena. The appearance of entities from other dimensions and planets was also inexplicable. Both God-apparent beings and the natural world influenced the development of stories of good and evil. Duality being a universal law, humans were at the same time unaware of their expanding capabilities after the last cycle of extinction. So a two-fold cause and effect brought about the growth of religions.

"When more advanced entities and avatars incarnated to assist humans, their superior knowledge and abilities alleviated the fear. Humans began to pray to a larger source guided by these beings who seemed to have more understanding of the great unknown and in some case became like gods themselves. The development of stories of good and evil evolved from these thoughts—conversely, remember that thoughts are energy that manifests in the physical world of humans. Do you see?"

Emari paused knowing this was not a complete description, but would suffice until her students completed their classes in cosmology, biology, quantum physics and math.

"So do all humans believe in a religion?" Chartreuse inquired.

"Yes and no. It is dependent in this cycle on so-called past, present and future—and culture. By and large, most humans have had a belief system, a story-system that diminishes their level of fear or satisfies their speculation, awe, or superstition about the universe. Some do not. For a very few, stories are not necessary—they are able to remember where they come from. These are highly evolved conscious beings who have incarnated into linear time hundreds of times or more.

"However, for those of you incarnating in any earthly culture," Emari explained, "you must realize that on Gaia I, religion plays a dual and monumental role, both positive and negative. Although an illusion, in its positive form it can resemble *Eviray*, by promoting community, common ground, relief from fear-based thoughts, and espousing unconditional love and peace. In its negative aspect it is an extension of territorial rivalry and promotes prejudice, greed, cruelty and war."

Emari could see the questions forming in each of her students. The room vibrated with intensity. Now they were certainly paying attention.

"So to answer your questions. The reason the negative aspect is capable of destruction is that humans have not developed the soul consciousness to realize that one belief system is not superior to another. They all offer positive and negative aspects. Again a dualistic issue. The reptilian instinctual brain is territorial, remember?"

Emari sent a beam of light to the holographic diagram of the basal ganglia, a structure derived from the floor of the forebrain during development. "It acts, at first glance, as a survival mechanism like we have discussed in previous lectures. This protective fear factor is also the first element in providing a basis for the story brain in the development of hate and aggression produced by thoughts and manifestation of domination, control and power. The lack of soul-consciousness, memory loss of universal law and ignorance of the time-space continuum, ultimately enables self-destruction of earthly inhabitants and the planet itself. Some of the problem lies in the engineering of *Eviray* which was incomplete in this cycle—a flaw causing the imbalance. We did not anticipate to see it accelerate in such rapid progression," Emari added reluctantly.

"Nevertheless, fear factors that result in death of a body are not contradictory if it is part of experiences incorporated into incarnation contracts, a more predominant choice for inexperienced souls incarnating as males on Gaia. Part of this imbalance is chemical meaning hormonal, but not so across the board. Cultural and religious stories are influences. It is noteworthy to observe that for Gaia I, many souls contracting for participation in war move through reincarnation cycles quickly, choosing missions as animals, or human females rapidly."

Emari elaborated, "In souls incarnating into a female body the chemical components ignited by fear tend to maintain their instinctual element longer. Ever vigilant and therefore highly observant, females' focus or aggression is like all higher animal species, in defense of their offspring. From the outset in this cycle, and generally speaking, the female human's conscious brain is more capable, has more intuitive capabilities and capacities for higher consciousness."

Emari checked her notes and concluded. "I will take further inquiries tomorrow. Although keep in mind, as I mentioned, we have changed the program, and your group will be among the first en mass to incarnate with your memory enhanced, regardless of chosen gender or multi-gender options. You won't initially remember, but your DNA, electro-chemical brain circuits will be altered so that while the instinctual brain will protect you, your intuitive capacity, memory, and longevity will operate to override impulses toward negativity and violence. The reason for this will become clear very shortly."

Emari wrapped her cape around herself and evaporated. Her voice, softened by a golden light that permeated every corner, reverberated in the air. "Your opportunity to elevate Gaia in her shift to the next dimension has begun. Congratulations to you all!"

Emari's seeds of enlightenment had been planted. The counsel's wisdom would prevail.

Later at Emari's home

Professor Emari went home and rested. She would have to adjust her last lesson. It was always the hardest one to teach. Its paradox was heart-wrenching, often producing much resistance especially from recently re-entering students who still clung to the memories of free will and visceral senses. Accepting the inevitability of evolutionary change was not easy for those who had spent so many incarnations as organic humans or animals on Gaia. But evolution did not have to mean the extinction of the human species. And even an illusion had power if used correctly for the common good.

Creating her own image spheres, Emari rose to her full ten feet height. She looked out over the landscape from a large picture window of her home, a dwelling built into the mountain cliffs. There was still a strong emotional component, a pull of her own time on Gaia left in her memory codes that she felt most strongly when creating the natural landscape. A sense of contentment and peace washed over her watching the red and purple shadows roll over the land as darkness descended.

Soon others would join her for the evening council meeting, where she could discuss the planned lessons for her class. There was so much at stake with the new incarnates at such a precarious juncture. She could not hide the truth. They would have to face it head on and not waiver in their commitment, in spite of the paradox and the uncertainty of the mission before them. Up until now, the levity and excitement birthed by coming events bolstered her students. But even an understanding of the physical pain and emotional agony inherent in incarnation, would be nothing to the shock of self-discovery yet to be revealed.

Emari had been through it many times. It never got any easier. She knew how it would go. Luckily, some would hold out for free will and choice despite all facts to the contrary. They were the everlasting rebel souls, the archetype of mother warriors, mother bears—the genetic survival coding of the female aspect. The incarnated females of every species were always the strongest willed protectors. Conversely, the female humans were also the most gullible, optimistic and easily manipulated by the entity of fear—the terror of destruction of themselves and their young, and some genetically coded to experience more empathy and compassion. It mattered not the quantity of incarnations in male form. The DNA and hormones of any naturally reproducing species was engineered for survival with protection of their young paramount.

That was how it had come to pass that Emari and the others had changed sides against the plan, one that ignored those inspired by the consciousness of compassion. She would work closely with the ones who exhibited the same spirit and understanding. They were used to being together. They'd been together for millennium, from the early days on Gaia —among the ancient ones on the planet. They'd been through shifts of earth poles, ice ages, changes in consciousness, war and peace, advanced technology and multi-dimensional evolution. Now as a clandestine band of council members, they met ostensibly to discuss the next generation of incarnations, as was demanded of their position.

But with the rift in the fabric of free will, they had overridden the codes designed to keep their movement on its projected course toward homogenization. They themselves had become the mother warriors, taking back the roots of the mother heart to shift the paradigm to a more humane dynamic. They collectively believed the evolutionary plan had gone too far. The advent of animosity among increasingly sophisticated trans-humans, the trade in human eggs, organs and DNA with the goal of completely annihilating the human species, as well as ending earth-bound incarnation cycles was becoming more objectionable to them by the nanosecond.

It did not matter the good intentions of those who argued for a peaceful species devoid of a fearful, warring and destructive nature. Those that had argued for that strategy had themselves become more violent and tyrannical. "Power corrupts absolutely" seemed to be a universal theme.

Before she could think through her ideas further, the council members arrived. Emari offered her guests some fruit from her garden, as they sat down on the pillows spread out on the floor in her main room. Soon they linked minds and began their discourse. It was clear they were of one mind. They would not circumvent discussion of other entities, trans-humans, and robotic species in lessons for the soon to be incarnates, even though it was not in the program to discuss the possibility of these encounters with the students.

Emari and her council knew that those incarnating into the cycle seven, from the twentieth century linear time frame onward, would become the target of the robotic movement, and so would have an opportunity to change the course of the program—but only if they were forewarned, only if they had the information hard-wired into their memory banks prior to their incarnation. This was the biggest dilemma—how to do it surreptitiously, tap into their soon to be human ability for compassion that they'd be in jeopardy of forgoing in the name of science and progress, in the name of longevity.

The genes associated with elongated life span had been turned off on purpose in the genetic manipulation, Emari had already explained to her students. It was no accident that the quest for a *fountain of youth* had been an obsessive goal in humans. Humans had cellular memory of longer lives in their ancient past, even written into their religious books and beliefs. The slow atrophy of the genetic code meant the shortening of lives generation after generation.

Emari would demonstrate the fact that there were many solutions. But it was precarious convincing those whose goals were malleable. Those with the need for power over the natural world, over human reproduction and who had access to tools of war also controlled the technology to build non-human robots on a mass scale. Power enticed those harboring delusional desires, fantasies and illusions about self-worth. In short, for incarnated souls whose mission had been forgotten, whose memory of universal truth dismissed, whose connection to soul source broken—the evolution of the trans-humans would be a forgone conclusion.

But human beings had a choice. "Of course," Emari said aloud to the council. "The answer is in the paradox of free will! Don't you see? Because the illusion of free will still exists in the twenty-first century, seventh cycle, the plan could be stopped or at least altered.

"It would take the feminine principle, incarnated souls flooding into the nineteenth, twentieth and twenty-first century dimension seven, whose mission it would be to stop the destruction of the planet, to spread empathy, compassion, harmony, and tolerance. It would take the feminine aspect to reach consciousness, to understand their collective power to save Gaia I, take responsibility to understand soul development, to educate the *Starseed* children and follow them, as well, to prevent human extinction and the influx of cyborgs."

"Yes," they all agreed. An understanding would be needed of the energy of money and the selling of lab-created human body tissue, deceptively disguised in the compassionate act of bio-medical donor transfers, and technology-generated science.

Emari elaborated. "While transmitting advanced technology to humans was of paramount importance over this cycle, it should not have been accomplished without upgrading the capacity for tolerance and compassion through a genetic infusion of *Eviray*. It leaves the door open for those in other dimensions and on the planet already making plans for a future in linear time, that doesn't include more advanced humans."

They all knew that temporary disruption in the dimension of slower vibrational energy would have less effect in the higher dimensions. But even the partial destruction of inhabited planets in any dimension was not a positive outcome for souls, regardless of form. There was a limit to the energy of fear and toxicity that could be put into the universe without some undesirable, even dire consequences. It would be the new *Starseed* children who would begin their mission now, embodied and emboldened with the power of *Eviray*.

"I have chosen an Oversoul to assist us in our plan," Emari announced. "I know it is uncommon, but these are momentous issues. I think she is just the one for this task."

Chapter 24

The Strega's Daughter

The Same Winter Day, 1424, Outskirts of Padua, Italy

Chaim carried Bella into bed and bandaged her head wound. She was weak from loss of blood, but it was her heart that had taken the shock. Her breathing was erratic. She mumbled and cried as Chaim tried to find out what had happened and console her at the same time. "Where is Davina, Bella? I will have her make you some warm broth."

Davina returned home only a few minutes later. "What has happened to Mama?" She looked at Chaim.

"She must have fainted and hit her head. I found her on the floor. I've dressed the wound and bandaged it, but she is badly bruised," he confided in his daughter.

"Is it her heart, Papa?"

Chaim just shook his head and shrugged. "We'll wait and see. I will stay with her."

"I can prepare the rest of the bread and take it to market tomorrow by myself. Even if she feels better by then, she should probably rest another day, yes?"

"Yes, a good idea." Chaim patted Davina's shoulder. "Get her some chicken broth left from the Sabbath, now."

Davina worked late into the evening to finish baking. By morning she was still tired, but determined to take the baked goods to market. The fish monger, cheese maker, and others whose stands were next to Bella's were friends and would help her if she needed help. Usually she and Bella were together on market day.

Today though, Davina felt uneasy. She should be able to go to market herself, she thought, but she had a sense of foreboding, nevertheless. As she carried the sack of breads down the stairs, she was worried about Bella. Then a thought of Sarah, accompanied by a nagging feeling, like something she had forgotten, struck her. Had there been a strange look on Sarah's face the day of Eva's delivery? Had Sarah noticed her incantations? Davina shook off the image. Perhaps it was only her imagination.

By the time she got to market, Davina had shrugged off her misgivings. She greeted her neighbors, then set the cloth out over the table, piling the loaves in neat rows in the middle. She divided the smaller rolls in two baskets on either side, like she had done hundreds of times before.

Just as women and children came to buy bread, a huge commotion of voices, horses and a cart drawn by oxen appeared in the market. People gaped and gasped, women whispered to one another. Children hid behind their parents. Davina looked up to see the town authorities, men in official uniform on horseback and two clergy coming toward her. A monk drove the cart.

"Are you Davina, the midwife?" one of them asked. Davina nodded.

"You are under arrest. Come with us."

Before Davina could comprehend what was happening, one of the tall uniformed men tied her wrists together with a thick rope. He grabbed her arm, pushing her into the cart. Davina struggled to free herself, screaming for help. Several of Davina's neighbors protested, but to no avail. Shoved into the cart, Davina's ankles were then tied together, so she could no longer stand. She cried out again to her friends in the market." Avaham, Rosa—help me!"

Then, she saw Sarah standing a few feet away, staring at her. She wore neither a frown nor a smile, just a look of somber satisfaction.

From the open window in his study, Chaim heard Lupe and her sisters yelling. He came into the kitchen just as they barged into the house, hysterical.

"Where is Bella?" they asked. Lupe looked white as a ghost. "They have taken Davina!" she howled at Chaim.

"Who has taken Davina? What do you mean?" Chaim was alarmed. "Bella is resting. She's had a fall. Lupe, what has happened?"

"The church authorities took her away. They claimed she is a *strega*—that she's been practicing magic, that she may be a gypsy or even a Christian! Where would anyone get such ideas and make such accusations, such rumors?"

Chaim shook his head. "I don't know," he said. But he had an idea. "Lupe, stay here. Don't talk to anyone. I will take care of this," he said, forcefully ushering her sisters out the door.

Chaim went into Bella's room. "I must go find Davina," he said. "I think something has happened with Sarah." Bella tried to raise her head from the pillow, but she felt dizzy. She began to cry.

"It is my fault. It's all my fault," she wailed.

"Hush, my Bella. Nothing is your fault."

"Yes, I told Sarah," Bella confessed, weeping. "She was sure Davina had used some magic. She wanted the truth. She was upset. I thought if I told her, if she didn't tell anyone, if I explained that you saved Davina's life." Bella put her hands over her face and sobbed.

Chaim was silent. He put his hand on her cheek. Bella was burning with fever. "It will be okay. I will go explain to the authorities." Chaim stood up and went to his study. From his shelf he pulled a special box. In it was Davina's notebook. He leafed through it looking at the anatomical, botanical and astrological symbols and drawings. He shook his head. Then he tied the book up with twine. He put on his heavy overcoat and tucked the book safely underneath it, close to his chest.

Chaim wasted no time. He left to find Davina. "Stay with Bella. I will return soon," he said to Lupe, before hurrying toward the monastery at the far edge of the village.

At the door of the monastery three monks stood talking to the head priest. They were about to enter when they saw Chaim. "What are you doing here?" one of them asked sharply.

Chaim approached with trepidation. "I have come to ask for leniency for my daughter. I have something of hers to offer in exchange for her freedom, her life."

The group of clergy looked at Chaim with disdain. "Your daughter? She has performed magic, curses and spells. She will be tried by the court," they declared.

Chaim took the book from beneath his coat. "I would like to barter this book of her pictures of ordinary herbs and the constellations for her freedom. She wrote these pages before she even knew how to write a real language. See for yourself. It's just scribbling and pictures from a child's imagination. She is an innocent girl, my daughter, not a witch."

The priest took the notebook and looked at it. When he came to the pictures of tiny nude women in pools of water, Davina depictions of cleaning the ritual baths, he slammed the book shut. "You had best seek council with your people. This book does not look like the work of an innocent." The priest tucked the notebook under his arm. "There is evidence that this girl was found abandoned, her birthplace unknown. Her fate is yet to be decided." He waved his arm. "Go home old Jew, lest we arrest you for kidnapping next." He and the others turned and walked into the building, taking the journal with them. Chaim stood alone in the cold. A light rain had begun to fall.

Chaim walked home bewildered, bereft. He walked along the river's edge not far from where he had once found Davina. Suddenly, he had an idea. He stood up straight and walked briskly home.

Bella was still feverish, although Lupe assured him that she had administered the remedy Chaim had left for her. Chaim covered Bella with another blanket and went to his study again.

This time, he took out his own studies. He turned yellowed pages until he came to the very page that Davina had discovered when she was a young child, bringing her new Papa some bread and honey. They were his coveted notes on a rare, ancient commentary on *Sefer Yetzirah*.

Now, he stared at the Hebrew letters a long time, when unexpectedly he heard the faint melody of Davina's chant. Suddenly, the letters began to move on the page. They vibrated and changed from letters to numbers and back again, just as they had when Davina had moved her small fingers over them. Before he could realize what was happening, he was standing inside the walls of a dark prison. Behind the barred door he could see Davina, sitting on a stone bench, her legs in chains. Then just as quickly, the image vanished and Chaim was back in his study.

Davina shivered in the chill and damp of the cellar prison. She rocked back and forth out of habit, tears streaming down her face. She prayed against all odds that someone would come. And to her great surprise Chaim appeared just outside the cell.

"Papa?" Davina whispered. "Are you here, Papa? "She could see him through a fog-like mist.

Back in his study, Chaim stood still, silent, not knowing if he was in fact solidly there again or not. Feeling his body whole, his desk and other objects, he became agitated and disheartened. He must discover a way to make the transition permanent, he thought. He took a rare bottle of wine from his drawer and a goblet. Chilled from the dampness, he put on a dry tunic and wool scarf. He closed the window with its wooden shutters and a heavy drape. Then he lit a candle. At his desk, he would study all night.

In her cell, Davina squinted as the first sliver of dawn peeked through the cracks of the door. She had slept in fits and starts waking from nightmares, cold and hunger. She chanted and prayed between bouts of exhaustion and terror. She heard the scurrying of rats more than once and the faint sound of clanking metal. "Please Papa, come for me," she cried to herself. She prayed for help from the green lady, her mother and her cousins.

Only a man in a hooded black robe came. He brought her something that looked like a soupy porridge and left without saying a word. Davina was too hungry to think about what it might be or if they were trying to poison her. She devoured the gruel, slurping it down. When she looked up, she was shocked to see Chaim standing in her cell. "Papa!" She jumped up and ran to him forgetting the chains around her ankles. Chaim caught her before she hit the hard dirt floor.

"Shh, Davina, be very quiet."

"How did you get in here, Papa?" she whispered.

"You must listen, Davina. We are going to leave here. Do you remember your chants?" Chaim pulled his esoteric pages from his pocket.

"Remember?"

"Yes, Papa! You figured it out?"

"You must leave, Davina. You cannot come back to this realm, my daughter. You must be brave, do you understand?"

Davina had heard words like these before. "Yes, father. But what about you, Papa? And Mama?"

"Don't worry about us, daughter. It's you who must continue on your journey now. Hurry. Here," he instructed,"hold these papers in your hands and repeat after me. Then chant. Don't stop chanting until you are solidly in another place—safe."

The clanking of metal and men's voices sounded close by. Chaim sat Davina back on her cell bench and hid, camouflaged against the cell door wall. A figure in black robes with a pointed black hood stood momentarily looking through the grate in the cell door. Davina smelled smoke. Then he disappeared.

Chaim moved quickly toward his daughter. They began to chant in low voices, over and over. Davina saw images in her mind of a woman standing near a bridge with Chaim. They were near a forest. Soon the images evaporated. But Davina could feel the air begin to vibrate. She opened her eyes for a moment. Ribbons of vibrant color, blues, greens and purples swirled around her. Letters and numbers, lit up like stars, floated in the flow of energy. Her feet left the ground. As if she were as light as a feather, a wind blew Davina across the cell. A high pitched tone droned louder and louder. Then, suddenly all was quiet. Everything around her disappeared. She was suspended in a soft pink mist.

Davina floated. Moments later, she found herself in a strange world. She was in a small room. Narrow windows near the ceiling let in sunlight. There was a ball on the ceiling glowing, illuminating the gleaming walls of smooth white tiles. In front of her were several objects she did not recognize. They were basins of some kind. One had water in it and looked similar to a woman's laboring chair. The other was empty with two shiny silver knobs and a spout. The room had familiar scents, ones that overlapped each other, Davina surmised. At first, she smelled the aroma of flowers. But when she sniffed harder, her eyes opened wide. "An outhouse!" she exclaimed.

At that, she suddenly felt gravity, the weight of her body solidly standing on a hard floor. She looked down at herself, a middle-aged body dressed in odd unfamiliar clothes. She was someone entirely different. She felt a jangle of nerves. Instinctively, she closed her eyes, breathed deeply and relaxed her mind. Soon, she felt composed, calm. When she opened her eyes, everything seemed normal again.

Perhaps I was just having one of those strange hallucinations again, she thought. She turned on the faucet and washed her hands. Looking in the mirror, she ran her hands through her short auburn hair. "I look okay for a forty-eight year old," she said to her reflection.

She stepped out of the bathroom and joined the other two women already at a booth in the quaint diner.

"And what will *you* be drinking today?" said the waitress, looking at the straggler arriving at the table. She took her pad from her green apron.

For a split second, the expectation that the waitress would speak in Italian or Hebrew, crossed her mind—but she didn't know why. "I'll have hot tea with lemon, please," she replied in perfect English.

The waitress wrote on her pad and smiled. "I overheard you gals talking about heading to the forest," she said handing them menus. "Best be careful—hibernation season's only beginning. And the bridge is being repaired, too."

CHAPTER 25

Rachel Rita Padini

Saturday After Thanksgiving 2004, *Tucson, Arizona*

Donna, Sharon and Rita drove along North Silverbell Road until they saw a house tucked into the hills that had three round-domed roofs.

"That's it," Donna pointed.

"Isn't it unusual architecture? They found this place in good condition even though it was built in the 60's. They've been renovating. Wait until you see the inside," Sharon said as they parked and walked up the path to the front door.

"Welcome!" Michael opened the front door before they had a chance to knock. "You made it! And right on time. Come in, my friends. We're so happy you're here. I was just prepping lunch for everyone. Of course, I am just the sous chef," he deflected. "Gary's the master. He'll be back any minute. He's picking up his niece at the airport."

"Is your sister here? Is she feeling better?" Rita inquired, not seeing a woman around. She was anxious to finally meet her look-alike.

"Oh, yes, thanks. She's here. She got a call from her daughter in England. She'll join us as soon as she's done. Rachel's so excited to meet you too. We haven't stopped telling her that she has a double." Michael laughed, moving as he spoke. "C'mon, let me show you around." They walked toward the kitchen.

"Wait 'till you see this," Donna declared.

"Wow!" Rita's eyes lit up. "Love the mural. Is that supposed to be Atlantis under the sea?"

"Oh that's right. You must be an artist!" Michael laughed. "Gary told me you paint. Not everyone gets this mural at first. We love it, though. Come this way, I'll show you our new patio and the pool," he said, walking them past a dining room stacked with construction materials, furniture awaiting assembly and picture frames of all sizes, before heading outside.

The tour ended back in the air-conditioned house soon after. Michael motioned to the living room where two white leather sofas were positioned across from each other. Along with a deep green velveteen love seat, the three couches formed a U shape atop a white area rug with a round oak coffee table in the center. Plants and paintings adorned the room and soft curtains on the windows let in the afternoon light, creating a serene ambiance. Against the only bare wall a large TV was propped against a table, looking out of place.

"Sit, relax. What can I offer you to drink? Water, lemonade, soda? We'll have wine with lunch," Michael offered.

Just then Rachel appeared. Rita saw the resemblance immediately.

So did Rachel. "Wow! So you're my famous doppleganger!" Rachel's gleeful voice rang out. "Michael and Gary have not stopped talking about you since they saw you at the art show. Now, I can see why!"

"It's pretty amazing," Rita said startled. "Kind of strange too, like twins separated at birth almost, except a bit of an age difference it seems. The two women shook hands. "Good to finally meet you."

"What year were you born, if you don't mind my asking?" Rachel inquired.

"1947, and you?"

"1956."

"Ah, so no mix-up at the hospital," Rita retorted. They all laughed breaking the tension.

"It's really something, especially seeing you side by side. Almost like seeing double." Sharon added.

"Well, maybe we are just twin souls," Rita offered.

"Twin souls?" Rachel asked. "Is that like soul-mates?"

"Not exactly—at least I don't think so. More like a mirror than a match, but part of the same soul group, with the same Oversoul." Rita thought she had steered too far into esoteric territory. If Cleo were there, Rita imagined, she'd be giving her a look of disapproval.

"That's Rita," Donna laughed. "Tell them what you've been up to the last many years."

"Yes, I'd really like to know more. I have been experiencing so many strange..." Rachel was interrupted by the front door's bell, the sound of wind chimes.

"Hold that thought," Michael said, handing Rachel a tray of lemonade-filled glasses.

He went to the door just as Gary opened it with his niece in tow. "Hi, everyone!" He set the young woman's luggage down and ushered her into the house. "This is my niece, Nakisha."

"Nakisha? Nakisha is that you? I don't believe it." Rita exclaimed getting up from her seat. "It's me, Rita Kerner."

"You know her too?" Donna shook her head. "C'mon really?"

Gary and Michael looked at each other in surprise.

"Rita, of course, how are you? What are you doing here?" Nakisha gave Rita a hug. Then she looked over at Rachel. "Is this your sister? You look alike."

"Okay, girlfriends," Gary raised his voice over the hubbub. "We all are having a moment here." He feigned a faint. "Just what is going on, I mean? We have two look-a-likes and one of them knows my favorite artist, and my niece! It's *six degrees of separation* right in our living room!" He was incredulous. "We need to serve the wine now."

"I'm on it,' Michael was already setting wine glasses on the granite kitchen counter. "So, let's hear the stories," he chimed in, opening two bottles of Merlot.

Nakisha settled down on the love seat next to Rita. "I met Rita on a train in Penn Station when I was going to visit Olivia, my mother, in Boston for Christmas. I was at NYU then." Nakisha smiled at Rita.

"Must have been pretty memorable—that was six years ago," Gary said.

"Oh, it was!" Nakisha's eyes twinkled. "Uncle Gary, do you remember my mom talking about the painting she bought at that gallery in Rhode Island—the one that turned out to be a portrait of our great grandmother, Bertha?"

"Sure do. She was flipping out about it." Gary's eyes grew large. "Oh! *She's* the artist? Rita, you're the artist?"

Rita nodded. "Small world department. Guilty as charged," she laughed.

"So, how did you know Gary and Nakisha's relative, Bertha?" Rachel asked.

Sharon and Donna chuckled. "Rita is a psychic artist. She makes pictures of people she has never met."

Rachel squinted thinking over the concept. "A psychic artist?" she questioned. I could use a psychic just about now, she thought.

Always unsure of how to explain or how much she should reveal, Rita took a deep breath. "Well, I seem to have a gift for creating portraits of people who I've never met and who often have passed over—are dead, that is." She paused waiting for a reaction.

"That's amazing. How does that happen?" Michael asked. He was not skeptical, just curious. Gary had told him stories of his great aunt in New Orleans who would play esoteric games with the kids when they visited her. She would stand in the kitchen holding a crystal ball in her hand and have the children run down the hall to the parlor, only to find her standing there with the crystal ball hovering before her.

Michael had his own experiences of meeting people with mystical gifts and unusual stories. There was the time on the plane to Puerto Rico when a passenger had befriended Gary and him and invited them to his home on the south side of the island. He'd told them a story about when he was a boy, how the evening activity had been hanging off the fishing boat dock with his friends, watching flying saucers come in and out of the water.

Rita sensed that Michael's curiosity was sincere. Rachel too appeared enthralled, sitting at the edge of her seat, her eyes riveted on Rita.

"Well, it started when I was young. I loved to draw and character's faces would always appear to me in my imagination. They seemed to have some kind of story, I felt. They were compelling. Now I'll paint a portrait that appears in my mind, only I know from experience that sooner or later I'm going to run into someone who recognizes him or her. I have been doing this for many years, so the people who have bought my work have told me so many stories of their loved ones. In some cases, they are also related to me from a past life it seems."

Rita stopped. Perhaps her last statement was a just a little too much, she thought.

"Oh girlfriend, I believe we've had past lives too, "Gary said. Michael nodded.

"Of course, it's a common belief in India—among Hindus," Rachel said, fingering the small gold elephant pendant at her neck. She hadn't delved into it before, but it suddenly dawned on her that perhaps it was something she should consider.

Nakisha was beaming as she took out a photo of her family. "Look," she offered, "I brought Uncle Gary this picture of my mom and me. Look where we're standing." She passed the photo of her mom, Gary's sister, standing in their dining room in Boston, with Rita's painting of their family's matriarch, Bertha, on the wall behind them.

"So it's true," Sharon laughed, "you do know everyone!"

"Well," Rita said, "not quite, but I'm sure glad to have met Nakisha. She put an arm around Nakisha's shoulder. "So what are you working on in graduate school, Nakisha? You mentioned environmental science in your card."

"Oh, well, originally I was thinking of doing my dissertation on the history and impact of religious and cultural beliefs on the institutionalized persecution of women healers and midwives."

"Wow! That's fabulous!" Rita's eyes lit up.

"Impressive," Donna said.

"My niece is a feminist, don't you know," Gary raised his glass to toast her. Michael followed his lead.

"Tell us more," Rita encouraged. She looked over at Rachel, Donna and Sharon who were sitting on the adjacent couch. Only Rachel was not smiling.

"I thought I would stick to more of an African cultural path with some concentration on the practice of Vordon, which became known in white slave owner's vernacular as VooDoo..."

"Oh, yeah—Gary told me about that," Michael added. "It's so insidious when you realize the racism behind the language so many people, or should I say white people, take for granted."

"Yeah, that's the point. Historically, Vordon's origin was a mix of spiritual belief, mysticism and herbology practiced as a healing art by women predominantly, along with midwifery." Nakisha's expression, her stance took on a professional air. Rita could see a future professor in her.

"But then the strangest thing happened." Nakisha's face lit up. "I came across a rare manuscript in my research, called the *Voynish Manuscript*. I found it at the rare book library at Yale. I had to wear white gloves to look at it with the librarian. It was discovered a hundred years ago in an old bookshop, by a man named Voynish. Turns out, no one knows for sure who created it or in what language it's written. It was carbon dated to the 15th century, around the early 1400's." Nakisha was animated. "It had hundreds of pictures of plants and concoctions for cleaning water, making medicines or tonics for healing women. There were dozens of pictures of naked women in pools of water, taking baths and..." Nakisha stopped talking, suddenly staring at Rachel sitting across from her

Silent tears were streaming down Rachel's face. Lost in a waking dream of love and loss, she saw a woman place a cross around her neck and hug her close. "Don't cry my child, you must be brave" a voice echoed.

"Are you okay?" Nakisha looked at Rachel and then turned to her uncle and Michael for validation and help.

"Hey, Sis," Michael stood up. "Why don't we get some fresh air." He took her hand and guided her out to the deck, grabbing some tissues from the box on the counter. "What's going on Rachel? Are you in some kind of trouble, emotionally?" He handed her the tissues.

Rachel wiped her eyes and then blew her nose. "I don't know," she mumbled, then cleared her throat. "I seem to be hallucinating. I keep having what appear to be memories, like flashbacks. The odd thing is they involve people and places that feel familiar, but who I consciously don't know or..." she paused. "Or just don't remember. But I have a strong emotional reaction in spite of not knowing. Does that make sense?"

"Well, I'm not sure. Maybe a therapist might have a better idea." he said.

Rachel rolled her eyes. "Oh, great! Not down that road again. Between the years of therapy after Giovanni died, and therapy after Joseph's passing, I've had enough to last a lifetime. But, you know, this feels like something different."

Michael didn't think his sister might like his next thought, however it was worth passing by her. "I have another idea," he offered. "Maybe you meeting face to face with your look-alike, Rita, means something. She's a psychic artist, a medium. She was just talking about how she paints portraits of people's ancestors." Michael took a breath. Maybe it's past life thing," he offered. "I know it's far-fetched, but how often do you meet a doppelganger?"

Rachel squinted. "Really?" She touched the small gold cross she wore today, hanging from a gold chain around her neck. "You haven't been out in the desert sun too long without enough water, have you, Michael?" She smiled at her loving brother.

CHAPTER 26

Professor Emari

AllSouls College, Pleiades

"For our final session before you each move forward to your assignments, one element that by now may be apparent to everyone, but one I harp on because it is of paramount importance, " Emari paused. "And that is the influences impacting all soul's evolution and trajectory from actions and subsequent events whether past, present and future, so to speak, of course. In other words while all time is a loop, all time is happening at the same time. It is also in constant motion. What changes consciousness in one stage of development loops both forward and back to change the course of history and future events in innumerable dimensions." Emari was quiet, waiting for the nods and smiles of recognition— or not.

"An example," she continued. opening her visual frame of reference "is an artist creating a work. There is an idea, the thought prior to manifestation. Then there is the medium—the clay, the transformation and final work all interacting and intersecting. We can see the process at any moment in its development as the artist's mind creates the image before it is executed, before the clay is touched, before the paint is applied." A triple image appeared above her students of a small human girl digging clay along a riverbed and creating a poultice, a woman painting a portrait, and a man mixing mortar to add bricks to a bridge. "Each is working at materializing a thought from consciousness—an idea into substance, into reality —birthing something into their three dimensional world that did not exist before their thought of it. This of course is manifestation."

Emari flipped through her notes. "Manifestation is merely one aspect of my focus, however. It is the cause and effect relationship of manifestation across dimensions that I am after here. But let's continue with simple manifestation as an element of changing one's reality before we look at the ripple effect."

She looked over at Viridian who stood in her usual spot at the back of the room. "Let's say Oversoul Viridian were to incarnate on earth in the seventh cycle human time, year 2004, as it is known by many earth cultures, although not all. Depending, of course, on origin and understanding of origin, 2004 is also year 5764 for some and year 4641 for other humans. But I digress—Oversoul Viridian has several hundreds of incarnated human souls in numerous soul groups on Gaia throughout several dimensional cycles."

Viridian shifted in her spot, slightly unnerved by the thought of incarnating—something she had never done, something Oversouls did not usually do.

Emari continued, "And let's say, she made herself visible, became manifest to a select few of her incarnated souls so they could not only see her, but also hear her in linear time. This would undoubtedly cause a shift in perception and consciousness for those entities regardless of their level of enlightenment at this stage, would it not?" Emari could see her students' anticipation building. She had awoken some who had dozed off.

"How would this change them? How would it change their understanding of Gaia itself, Universal Law, truth, responsibility?" Her voice trailed off. "And what repercussions, reverberations would it produce in the dimensions on every other plane in which these same souls were in fact living past and future lives— in fact, on the very energy of the planet and the course of its history itself? Do you see the significance?"

Viridian was turning shades of blue and purple, uncommon colors for her, ones that shifted her own consciousness at the suggestion of incarnating. A vision of earth appeared to her in form, swirling in space. Then in warp speed she was hurling through a tunnel of light and sound, compacted into a tiny ball of energy. Suddenly, the tunnel opened into a vast space where the sweetest sound of music was all around her and she just floated, ever so slowly along a ribbon of light.

The next thing Viridian knew, she was in solid form hovering in the light of a shining globe in a dark sky—moonbeams glistened on her green skin, and in the green waters of a large lagoon at the edge of the woods, below her. She bent down and peered into what appeared to be a forest of short trees. No sooner had she done so, than her physicality shrank until she was beneath the forest trees which then towered over her. Viridian looked around finding a tree stump to sit on, exhausted from the experience. She dozed. When she awoke she was back in Professor Emari's classroom. Eyes wide open, startled—she breathed a sigh of relief. But she knew the dye was cast.

"Let us look more closely," Emari said. "What has the appearance of extraordinary visitations had on third and fourth cycle humans, for example? Aside from the necessary interplanetary council's genetic adjustments to the species at large, what repercussions ensued? Anyone?"

Indigo indicated a desire to answer. "The relationship of these visitations to development of theories and stories about them?"

"Correct," Emari's image gallery showed in pictorial succession—books, architecture, inventions, customs, climate, wars and technology evolving from such encounters and interpretation of them. And what is predominant, as we have discussed in prior lessons, is the formation of religions to explain phenomenon. In the case of human evolution, enhanced by benevolent interference or not, the outcome or future possibilities change or are altered in direct response to growth of consciousness and understanding of universal principles. So too, for the so-called past, because there is no actual linear time—something that is difficult for all but a relative handful of humans to comprehend."

Chartreuse was eager to discuss the examples further. "Can we follow one soul in his/her various dimensions to see the impact?"

A picture of a human teen-age girl opened in the holographic field. "This young female human is contemplating sex with a young male just a little older. In the moment it took for her thought to become a positive response to his interest, she split in two energetically. Watch." In the first image the girl moved toward the boy to allow herself to be consumed in the act of mating which would impregnate her, and the other energy body chose a negative response and walked away. "This is soul-splitting." Emari demonstrated,"a path of free will you will be on as well."

Emari added, "The dualistic nature of goal setting and free will allow for innumerable possibilities, each and every one moving toward the same goal ultimately. In this case the young woman who will have the baby and marry her mate as a result will continue to assume she is the sole individual of that identity, just as the other energy body will focus on her goal and assume she is the sole identity. The point is each will have an impact on the change in the consciousness of everyone they come in contact with, in each dimension they inhabit as they move toward their identical goal."

The images of the human evaporated. Emari messaged Viridian, who obliged, turning herself into a green orb.

"Here is Oversoul, Viridian." Emari tapped her breastplate to enlarge the image. Viridian, now a glowing green sphere appeared above the class. "Do you see the threads coming from her? These threads attach to the soul groups." Instantly, bright pink orbs dangled from each thread. In each one, were a few dozen white light spheres.

"These light bodies spheres are each individual souls, like you, who travel together in groups. If and when they meet after incarnating there will be an instant rapport of closeness or distance depending on their plan. Once incarnated they are capable of splitting any time or many times during their life. Free will allows for this splitting aspect. However, in cases of trauma, the soul can automatically split. In some extreme cases it is possible for a completely new soul to "walk in" to a dying body. A soul can also "walk in" to another dimension as we have seen previously. This is already within the contracts of both souls." Emari paused, taking a scan of the students' reactions. It appeared they understood, so she continued.

"Split souls will impact each other on an energetic level regardless of their lack of awareness of one another. Exceptions to their awareness will be during dream-time or in cases of old souls whose elevated trance meditation and understanding of *Mutable Essence* allows them to enter other realities.

"Furthermore, twin souls, soul mates and other forms of connection among members of a soul group are also subject to a common goal and to splitting. Each plays a role in the final mission or goal, but the paths toward it are all different. It is the impact of evolving consciousness in each soul that enters the space-time continuum of universal consciousness."

"Thank you, Viridian." Emari said.

Viridian returned to observation mode, while the Professor drew an earthly mature oak tree in the center of the room, with a wave of her hand. "The roots of this tree give rise to its trunk and branches." Emari offered. "All parts are operating as a whole, each part influencing the other in constant motion. The life force of *Eviray* —each part depends on all the parts. It's universal consciousness in action."

Emari knew the information had been a lot for her students to absorb. As a young soul herself once, she thought it might alleviate the seriousness of her lecture to imbue the weighty lessons with humor. She entertained sharing one of her rare pearls. It might be a way for her to express the love and tenderness she felt toward her fledglings, but didn't always convey.

She put on her cape, removed all the holograms and lowered the lights till the room was bathed in a soft pink glow. The sound of a lute playing a ballad filled the air. She could feel the healing calm energy the music evoked.

"Once upon a time," she began, "There was an old soul that was about to incarnate for the last time in the third dimension— on earth. For a lark he decided to be a trickster, to use a play of words as his tools and a play itself, as his vehicle. He embarked on a life of writing plays, teaching humanity that "all the world's a theater and each one of them merely actors in a play..."

CHAPTER 27

Rita Kerner

Sunday After Thanksgiving 2004, Pacifica, California

Rita looked out the window of the plane at the puffy cumu-lonimbus clouds obscuring the view of the Pacific coastline and mountains below. *Magic,* she thought, how she should meet a twin soul and her old heartthrob, Marla, all at once on the same trip. Always trying to find meaning in such coincidences, Rita decided it was time for another painting. The wheels of her mind were turning. When she got home, she would paint more portraits, ask her ethereal images for guidance. Then she thought of Cleo.

Her first instinct was to protect Cleo. On second thought, was it that she was protecting herself from Cleo's disdain and fear about the esoteric path Rita found herself on again? Exploring past lives in small doses was one thing, but delving into soul groups, multi-dimensions and extraterrestrials had not been in the plan for marital bliss. She knew it unsettled Cleo to be confronted with things beyond the earthly dimension of here and now. Aside from dabbling with Tarot cards, Cleo was meat and potatoes. Gravity and the solid security of *what you see is what you get*, was her truth. The exception being Cleo's relationship to traditional angelic stories and a commonly known God, one that she had grown up with and still believed in, to some extent.

It was an old dilemma in some ways. Being in a long-term relationship, a marriage in it's own way even if not considered legal by others, was often confusing. Sometimes, it was downright hard to maintain some autonomy that would not threaten the other person's identity, sense of normalcy and trust. Rita always had a sense that she had to keep some of her thoughts and feelings to herself, in case she might upset the equilibrium of their harmony. They were a good match in so many ways, their common love of travel, similar movies, food—their respect for each others' parental concerns. Even their shared political outlook jived. But now Rita felt a rumbling of nervousness as she headed home and the plane approached the airport. She didn't know what she would tell Cleo.

The *fasten seat belt* symbol blinked on above her. Soon the plane landed in San Francisco without incident in spite of the fog. Rita's uneasiness evaporated though, when she saw Cleo getting out of the car at the arrival curb to greet her. She gave Cleo a big hug, "I'm so happy to see you, Babe," Rita smiled.

Cleo kissed Rita's cheek in return. "Me too. How was your trip? How come you decided not to stop and see Noah? I was surprised you were coming back before that." Rita threw her suitcase in the back seat, climbed into the passenger seat. Oliver tried jumping into the front seat, so excited to see Rita. "Good boy, sit," she commanded.

"Noah's coming up to see us soon. Besides, he had to go back to work after his trip to Santa Fe. I hope you don't mind, I invited Nakisha to visit too in a week, after her conference at UC Santa Cruz."

"Nakisha?" Cleo asked, navigating out of the airport, heading home.

"You know, that young woman who I've kept in touch with over the years from the East Coast." Rita paused. "Nakisha turns out to be the niece of a friend of Sharon and Donna's! They have these friends, a great gay couple, Gary and Michael, who invited us to their phenomenal house." Rita was animated. "And who should show up there, but Nakisha, who turns out to be Gary's sister's daughter. She'll be attending a conference in Santa Cruz and I asked Noah if he would drive her up afterward for a short visit." Rita suddenly stopped. "God, I hope you don't mind." Rita looked sheepish. "I'm sorry, I should have asked you, first. I was just so excited."

Cleo was quiet for a moment. "That would've been nice, but I guess it will be okay. How long?"

"Just a few days—the weekend," Rita answered.

"This coming weekend? I made plans with my cousin Kelly to go to the women's craft fair in the city. Thought you might like to go also."

"Oh! Well, maybe if they want to also. We'll see. Tell me about you," Rita changed the subject. "How was your time with your kids?"

"Good." Cleo said, still digesting Rita's news. "We had fun catching up. School's going well. They're happy. We all got an opportunity to go to church together and sing—that felt like old times." Cleo smiled. "After church, Patricia took us all to Alioto's Restaurant on Fisherman's Wharf."

"Nice! Who's Patricia?"

"You know, my friend who invited me to church for choir rehearsal for Christmas. You met her when she picked me up."

"Oh, yeah," Rita said reflecting on that brief encounter. "Is she gay?"

"No," Cleo replied with a tone of annoyance in her voice. "But she knows I am. She has other gay friends."

Now it was Rita who took a moment to think. She tried to control her anxiety. Why am I feeling so insecure? she thought, berating herself for thinking the worst. She's allowed her autonomy. I have nothing to worry about. Cleo loves me—she wants to marry me. Rita repeated the mantra in her mind.

"Sorry," Rita apologized. "I'm happy you and the kids had such a great time." Rita smoothed Cleo's ruffled feathers. "Maybe I can come to hear you sing in the choir at Christmas—whatda ya say?"

Cleo snorted. "If you behave," she snicked.

"Okay, I deserve that." Rita laughed relieved that the tension was broken. She decided to wait another day to tell Cleo about her twin soul, Rachel.

The following day, Rita woke early, walked Oliver, and had coffee with Cleo before her work day began. "Have a good day, honey," she kissed Cleo goodbye.

"You too, Babe. What are you going to do today?"

"Paint," Rita replied. "Maybe get things ready in the guest room."

Rita had taken off a few more days from work before the onslaught of Christmas and Hanukkah crafts sessions that awaited her at her new school art programs. She was anxious to use the time to start another painting.

She fed Oliver and Aries then walked into her studio. She squeezed red, yellow, burnt sienna, and white paint onto a fresh palette. Warm colors to start, she thought. She pulled out a clean white canvas. Expecting another ethereal being to flow from her brush, she was surprised to see a little girl's face take form. She was a child who looked about nine or ten, with big brown eyes and dark hair. She was carrying a big basket of plants and flowers. Rita squeezed blue, green and violet onto her palette. Taking shape in the picture was an animal in the upper left corner—a light brown and white cow as it turned out and nearby, a woman in an apron holding a ceramic jar. The painting was not like any Rita had ever painted before. It was more like a dream. Rita stood back and laughed.

"I am becoming a female Chagall!" she exclaimed.

Rita was more than pleased. She had always wanted to break away from her traditional, old masters' style portrait painting. She had experimented with cubism at a friend's suggestion long ago, but could never let go of control long enough to embrace abstraction. Too much art school training, she figured. Now without thought, this new painting was showing the signs of fluidity, like a visual stream of consciousness. She dipped her brush in yellow then a bit of red, mixing a luscious orange for a setting sun.

At first, all the colors and tones were joyful, but soon there appeared a darker element at the edges of the painting—whirling waters and what almost appeared as a soldier, bloodied and brooding. There were trees and a river where a dock and raft appeared. Rita painted whatever images emerged, not understanding from where her imagination drew such pictures. But she knew, as she had known for a long time, that the story would evolve just as it always did, if not from her own guidance than from an observer's. Someone would come along who knew these characters, like they had when Rita owned her gallery. Patrons had stopped in *kvelling* over pictures they assured her were the spitting images of their long-lost uncle or aunt or grandmother.

Lost in colors and shapes, Rita didn't want to answer the phone when it rang a few minutes later. But Cleo was at work, so Rita picked it up on the fourth ring. "Hello?"

Rita was expecting to hear from Noah or Nakisha. "Oh, how are you Rachel?" she exclaimed.

Rachel's voice was hesitant. "I'm well, thanks. Hope you had a good trip back."

"Yes, after an amazing time meeting you and everyone. What are your plans now? Are you staying in Arizona a while?"

"Actually, that's why I'm calling." Rachel paused. "I was wondering if we might get together before I head back East. I'd really like to spend more time with you—come to California for a few days. Do you think you might be open to that idea?"

Rita thought for a moment. She knew it was important, not only for Rachel, but for herself as well. Rachel was a missing link somhow.

"Sure, that would be great." Rita said thinking quickly. "I'm expecting Nakisha and my son up in a few days. I think there's room for one more, if you don't mind sharing a room with Nakisha." Then Rita remembered Cleo. "Oh, Rachel, let me get back to you, though. I'm sure it will be fine, but I do have to pass it by my partner. You understand."

"Nakisha is family. That's no problem. And of course I understand. What is your partner's name again?" Rachel asked.

"It's Cleo. And it will probably be fine, but we do check in with each other. I'll call you back tomorrow, how's that?" Rita asked.

"That would be great. You know, meeting you has been eye-opening for me. I have so many questions."

"I think we have a lot to talk about too." Rita agreed. When she hung up the phone she looked over at her new painting. The little girl's eyes had caught the sunlight streaming in the studio window. They were gleaming.

Cleo noticed the painting when she got home from work. "Now that's cool! It's an amazing difference in style, but I like it. Who's the child?"

"Not sure yet." Rita reflected. "Cleo, can we talk?" Rita asked.

"What's up?" Cleo squinted. "I'm kind of drained from work." She walked into the kitchen. Rita followed.

"How was your day? You seem tense," Rita rubbed Cleo's shoulders. Cleo didn't respond to Rita's touch. *Can we talk* was usually an exhausting proposition.

"Okay, the normal routine of client needs. I'm just tired." She put the kettle on for tea.

"I didn't really finish telling you about my trip." Rita's tentative tone caught Cleo's attention.

"What do you mean?"

"Remember that artist, Marla Woods?" Rita paused, waiting for a look of recognition in Cleo's eyes. "I met her at an art opening in Arizona."

Cleo turned around and looked at Rita. "You made a plan to meet her? Is that why you wanted to go to Tucson for Thanksgiving?"

"Well, yes to see her show." Rita replied. "And because Donna and Sharon invited us. Turns out Marla Cherise Woods is my college friend Marla Remy—Woods is her married name. She remembered me. I met her husband also."

Cleo was quiet. "So you couldn't tell me you had an ulterior motive?" she finally asked.

"Look honey, I didn't know if it would be the same person," Rita explained. "I didn't want you to be upset. I just wanted to know—have some kind of closure. I always felt guilty for not saying goodbye when she left to get married."

"Okay, well…How was it? Did you get closure?"

"It was strange, but good. After all these years she didn't care that I hadn't said good-bye or anything. She even apologized for not calling me back after Geraldine got my number."

"Well, it's good you can let that go now, right?" Cleo moved closer to Rita. Her shoulders relaxed. She smiled. "I guess our relationship still needs work."

"Yeah. I'm sorry. I wanted to tell you." Rita paused. She decided to brave the rest. "So, for the sake of being more open, I have more to tell you."

Cleo braced herself.

"I met someone who looks like me." Rita blurted out. "She's the sister of one of Sharon and Donna's friends I told you about. Her name is Rachel Padini."

Cleo waited for the punch line. "So?"

"So, don't you see? I met my double, my twin soul—my doppelganger! She looks just like me. All the time people say I look familiar and so…"

"Really, you're kidding, right?" Cleo laughed. "You think someone who looks like you is a twin soul? That all the time people think you look familiar it's because of this Rachel person? Are you kidding?"

Rita didn't know whether to be embarrassed or angry. "Soul groups, don't you see? She is part of my soul group." Rita tried to explain. "Remember when you met your friend Patricia, you felt an affinity instantly because her expressions reminded you of your cousin, Kelly. People have similarities in looks, expressions, attributes, especially in soul groups."

"Okay, Babe, I get past life connections. But this is getting a little weird. Between your ET's and now doubles and groups of look-a-likes, c'mon." Cleo smirked. "What's happening? Are you okay?" Cleo's expression turned to concern.

"Okay, wait until you meet her. You'll see what..."

"Meet her?" Cleo exclaimed. "What do mean meet her?"

"I mean I wanted to invite her this coming weekend when Nakisha's coming—Rachel's brother's boyfriend is Nakisha's uncle." Rita added.

Cleo looked hard at Rita. "Really? That's a lot to follow. You invited everyone the same time—this coming weekend?" She threw her hands up in frustration. "Okay—too bad about the women's crafts fair in the city. Oh, well," Cleo shrugged. She walked over and looked in the pot on the stove where vegetarian chili was cooking. She stirred the beans, poured herself a cup of tea, then walked into the living room. She clicked the remote.

"Gee I'm sorry. Guess we're both in demand." Rita tried to put a light spin on it. "Maybe we can all go to the craft fair, what do you think?"

"Okay." Cleo's didn't look at Rita. She didn't make an effort to lower the volume on the the TV news either, which screeched, *"Cyber Monday is off to a good start with retail stores reporting record sales."* Cleo put her tea on the coffee table, switched channels and plopped down on the couch. Soon Oliver and Aries joined her.

Rita thought better of pursuing the issue further for now. Knowing Cleo, Rita decided to give her time to mull. She lowered the flame on stove and went to check the day's mail on the hall table. She rifled through the few bills then came across a lavender envelope addressed to her. She looked at the return address. *M. C. Woods, 4585 Bayview Drive, Bar Harbor, Maine.* Rita walked into the study and opened the envelope. The sweet aroma of *Jean Nate* perfume drifted into the air.

CHAPTER 28

Viridian

First December Weekend 2004, *Northern California*

Rita prepared a green salad and added parsley to her freshly made chicken soup, while Cleo prepared cheese sandwiches for grilling later, when their guests would be arriving for lunch.

"I'm going to hang a few of my recent paintings in the studio, so I can show Noah, Nakisha, and Rachel. You think Kelly might like to see them too?"

"Sure, she likes your work. Then we'll eat and go to the craft fair, okay?" Cleo thought for a moment. "You might want to hold off on hanging the extraterrestrial ones, you know."

Rita gave Cleo a look of indignation. Then she laughed. "Yeah, Noah might get wigged out."

"Actually, I was thinking of time constraints. Once you start explaining your process and theories of evolution, we can be here all afternoon." Cleo gave Rita a good-natured slap on the back-side. She was in a good mood today.

"Yeah, yeah very funny." Rita walked toward the studio. Oliver followed her.

Taking a scan of her art space, she straightened up the clutter on her desk and hammered some hooks along the bare white wall opposite the windows, judging dimensions needed for hanging her paintings, by eye alone. She hung *Nicolette and Handmaid* on the left. Next to it she hung the newest painting of the young girl, her more abstract work she'd named *Dreams of Childhood.* Rita thought for a moment. There was space for one more painting on the right.

The *Green Queen in the Enchanted Forest* painting was too big to hang. Rita left it leaning against the wall. She turned it around, so only the back of the canvas was visible, in case it should offend someone. She debated about hanging the smaller work of the tall dark-skinned otherworldly figure, named *Emari,* but decided to put it back in the drying rack. Then, she flipped through her unfinished works. She still needed something suitable to balance the wall display.

Looking through her closet, Rita came across a painting she had started a long time ago, one that had caused her unexplained anxiety. She looked at it aghast now, then laughed aloud. Oliver, who had curled up in the corner picked up his head. She gave him a tussle. "What do you think?" she asked him. He cocked his head. "It looks like Cleo's friend Patricia, doesn't it?" She took it out and hung it on the last hook. Wow, she thought, will Cleo be surprised.

It wasn't long before company arrived. Nakisha and Noah seemed to be getting along exceptionally well, to Rita's delight. Cousin Kelly was her jolly self, rosy skin with freckles, red hair and all. She seemed to have a knack of keeping everyone, especially Cleo, in a good mood.

Once Rachel arrived everyone was excited.

"It's uncanny," Cleo admitted. "The resemblance is amazing, especially since there is an age difference."

"Can I take a picture of my two moms," Noah joked.

"Maybe someone had an affair we don't know about!" Kelly chuckled, taking a camera from her backpack.

Nakisha put one arm around Rachel's shoulder and one around Rita's for another photo. "They are doppelgangers," she announced. Rachel and Rita laughed.

After lunch Rita invited everyone into the studio for a quick viewing of her art, as she'd promised Cleo. Noah loved seeing his mom's paintings. "I want this one!" he said pointing to the painting of Nicolette. Isn't that the one you thought was a character from the book you gave me, from Pops? It's awesome—very old masters' style!"

Nakisha was drawn to the painting of the young dark-haired girl.

"What's the story behind this one?" she asked. "Looks like the style of Chagall. I love it."

"Yeah," Kelly declared, "I love that one too!"

Only Rachel and Cleo didn't look so enthralled. Rachel's eyes were watering as she stared at the middle painting of the young girl. Cleo's mouth hung open, astonished by the painting that looked like Patricia.

"That looks just like Patricia," Cleo finally uttered, it dawning on her that she had seen Rita start this painting in Rhode Island, before Cleo had ever met Patricia. "Geez!" she managed. "How the heck did you do that?"

Rita smiled a knowing smile at Cleo as she walked over to Rachel. "Everything okay?" she asked.

Rachel's eyes were glued to the middle painting. But she was far away. She was at the water's edge where an old man was lifting her wet and cold from a creek. She was with a woman caring for a cow, then another woman baking bread. Then she was holding a newborn baby. The next second she was in a prison cell, her legs tied in chains. Rachel looked at Rita not seeing her.

"You like this painting?" Rita said, seeing if she could get a rise out of her new friend, her twin soul.

Rachel finally took a breath. She focused on Rita. "Oh, this painting is so powerful. It's like I know the whole story of this child. I see all these parts of her life. I can't explain it," her voice trailed off.

"It happens," Rita said comforting Rachel. "People see themselves and ones they know in the work." She patted Rachel's shoulder. "It's startling, shocking even, but it's a good thing. It's most likely related to a past life for you."

Rachel nodded. "I guess." She was dubious, afraid.

"My mom's been painting weird stuff since I was in high school." Noah petted Oliver as he spoke. "She had a gallery opening and all these people came and swore that they recognized their dead relatives. I didn't invite too many of my friends over to my house when I was a teenager, if you know what I mean!"

Everyone laughed. Even Rachel managed a smile. Rita winked at Noah, thankful for his good humor. Just then Kelly reached over to the big canvas propped against the wall. She peered at it from above then turned it around in one swift move. "Hey, look at this one!"

They all stared. Cleo frowned. "Okay, time to go now. We don't want to miss too much of the craft fair." She took Kelly's arm.

"I recognize this place!" said Kelly. "Yeah, this is cool. It looks like the old growth forest up in Mendocino. I've been there," she boasted. "Didn't see any little green men, or green women who resemble a Tarot card like this *Queen of the Forest*, but it was an amazing place! If you've never been to an old growth forest, you should definitely go!" She looked at Rachel and Nakisha. "You guys are from back East, right?"

Cleo nudged Kelly. "Okay, another day we can all go. Let's get to the city now." Cleo rolled her eyes in Rita's direction.

"We can talk about the paintings again later. We should get going," Rita agreed. But Kelly's comment struck a chord. Rita knew that Kelly was right. They must find an old growth forest near a lagoon. Hadn't Lucy, the artist she'd met on the plane and visited at her studio—made mention of that too? Hadn't she said to *go to a sacred place where there is water*? What could be more sacred than an old growth forest near a lagoon? She looked at Rachel and Nakisha. The three of them needed answers. There was a reason they were all here, she thought.

The following day, after Sunday breakfast, Noah straightened up the couch where he'd slept, then took Oliver for a walk. "I'm going to head home, Mom. I have a busy work week coming up." He hugged Rita and said his goodbyes to Cleo, Rachel and Kelly. He and Nakisha made plans to keep in touch.

Rita had convinced Rachel and Nakiska to accompany her on an adventure—a day trip north to the forest in Mendocino. They'd agreed since they had to leave the following day. Nakisha had to be back at school and Rachel had plans for a Christmas reunion with her daughter, son-in-law and Michael to organize, and moving decisions looming large.

Cleo and Kelly opted for the beach with Oliver, but not until Kelly had given the threesome directions north to the old growth forest. Before long, Rita, Nakisha, and Rachel were traveling on 101 across the Golden Gate Bridge and beyond. After almost three hours, they were nearing their destination.

"Do you mind stopping at the next place we see for a bathroom," Rachel asked.

"Sure," Rita looked at the gas gauge. Plenty of gas left, so she could just keep an eye out for a restaurant. They had packed water, snacks, jackets, scarves, and a camera. "I could go for a cup of coffee, when we see a place," she said.

They didn't have to go too much further before their exit from the freeway came into view. A few miles along a small road, a diner appeared. It looked like something out of the 50's, but it was clean and aside from the aluminum siding, it was detailed in an inviting bright green and white. Only a few cars were parked in front. "This looks good." Rita drove into the parking lot.

Rachel went to the ladies' room, while Nakisha and Rita sat down in a booth. "What will you gals have?" asked a plump, middle-aged waitress with blond hair. She pulled a pad from her green apron. She looked from Rita to Nakisha. "You all from the city?"

Rita and Nakisha gave each other a knowing look, used to similar refrains based on ethnicity. "I'll have a coffee. Do you have half and half?"

The waitress nodded. "And you?" she asked Nakisha.

"Just a Cola, please." Nakisha didn't bother to give the waitress a second glance.

Rachel returned from the bathroom and squeezed next to Nakisha. "May I have hot tea with lemon?" she requested.

"You two are twins, huh? You ordering any food?"

"No, thanks," Rachel said.

The waitress grumbled, taking the pile of menus they hadn't touched.

Rita opened a map she'd brought in from the car to review. "Only another thirty minutes, looks like." Just then the waitress reappeared with their drinks and the bill.

"You gals going to the old growth forest? The bridge may still be under repair," she advised. "You know some bears are only in partial hibernation, so I'd be careful if I were you," she added.

"Thanks,"Rita said. She sipped her coffee. When the waitress left she turned to the others. "I think we'll be okay. I just think we are supposed to be there." Rachel and Nakisha were not reassured, but after paying the bill, they got back in the car and drove on.

Soon, they came to the fork in the road where a small stone bridge spanned a shallow river. Rita noticed someone on the bridge. It was a Black man with white hair. He had a pail and trowel and seemed to be applying mortar to the bridge.

Rachel noticed someone too. He was an elderly white man with a scraggly gray beard. He was looking over the side of the bridge to the river below.

Nakisha also saw someone walking along the edge of the narrow cement sidewalk next to the bridge. It was an old woman who resembled a photo she had of her great-grandmother Bertha.

Rita pulled the car slowly alongside the bridge and stopped. She saw the man from the desert standing there near the open passenger-side window. She heard him speak although his lips did not move. *"You will find what you need to know there. Do not be afraid. Follow the path beyond the boulder until you see her."*

Nakisha sat in the front seat passenger-side as the car pulled near to Bertha. Her family's beloved matriarch smiled. "*Your real work begins here, my dear one. Follow the path into the woods and you will see your destiny.*"

Rachel sat in the back seat. She rolled down her window when the car pulled close to the old bearded man. Chaim's voice was low. He spoke in Hebrew which Rachel seemed to understand in spite of only hearing the language at Passover, when her father was alive. "*You will know what you need to know now. Follow the path into the woods and you will remember who you are.*"

The next moment Rita was parking the car in a small outcropping of flat land at the end of a dirt road. A forest surrounded them on three sides. "This must be it." Rachel whispered.

Although bewildered, they all agreed. They exited the car slowly anticipating they knew not what. The meeting on the bridge had been so unexpected. Had it really happened or were they having a collective hallucination? Rita thought for a moment. But she knew better by now. She took her backpack from the trunk and slammed it shut. The sound reverberated in the quiet of this remote place.

Rachel also wondered if she had made a mistake. What were the chances of really seeing an old man on the bridge? Maybe she was dehydrated again, she thought. But she knew she was not.

As for Nakisha, she was used to hearing her great-grandmother's voice in her head. Now, she was excited about actually seeing her on the bridge. Maybe the stories her Uncle Gary told her about his family in New Orleans were not just made up tales.

Together the three women walked in front of the parked car, where a small incline of rocks and dirt marked an end to the road. They climbed up the embankment. Except for their footsteps crunching on dried twigs and dead leaves, there was only a faint sound of redwood needles rustling in the breeze. They did not even hear the chirping of birds. The enormity of silence was only matched by the majesty of the trees.

A small path led into a dense, dark forest. Nobody spoke at first. But adrenalin began pumping.

"I'm not sure about this," Rachel said finally.

"Yeah, I know. In reality, walking into a forest by ourselves doesn't seem like the wisest thing to do." Rita said, stopping to take out a compass from her backpack. She checked her new cell phone, something Cleo had persuaded her to try in case of an emergency. Seeing no bars, no reception, she put it back in her pack. "I do have my camping knife with me, and matches if we get lost." Rita said attempting to reassure Rachel and Nakisha—and herself.

"That's not very comforting," Nakisha snorted a laugh. "A bear or mountain lion won't sit back and wait while we gather sticks for a fire."

"Or God forbid, start a forest fire." Rachel added.

"Well, I know—in this dimension, we might be at risk," Rita began. Rachel and Nakisha looked at each other, then back at Rita.

"Ya think?" they both laughed.

"Look," Rita tried to explain. "We have to suspend our steadfast belief in our own reality for now. Just trust that once we begin, it'll be okay. We have been led here, remember? That is real also," she said, even though she was not totally convinced now, faced with the very real wilderness.

They were silent for a moment. Nakisha wasn't convinced either.

"What I know is that *fear solidifies matter*." Rita said turning to Nakisha and Rachel. She did not know where that thought came from, but it rang true. Hadn't she heard it somewhere before? *"Like water,"* Rita said without thinking *"transforms into vapor or solidifies into ice—shifting form and identity."*

Rachel squinted. "What are you trying to tell us?"

"It's about the power of thought and vibration. It's like what I do when I'm painting. It's about transformation—water has life force, the ability to react, not only to temperature, but to thought." Rita continued. "All matter has the ability to change form—think of solid ground, even roads. In an earthquake, they can move like waves in the ocean, like liquid. Vibration is the key, you see?"

"Yes, I think so," Nakisha said. "I guess I never put my scientific knowledge in that frame, before."

Rachel's eyes sparkled. She knew what Rita explained was a feeling she had experienced. Being calm, meditating, chanting were things she had been drawn to in prayer most of her life. Suddenly, she saw herself in a small room with stone walls. She saw an old man sitting hunched over some papers. She looked at his reading material and saw numbers and letters dancing on the page. When she touched them they turned to colors as she moved them about. Then automatically Rachel began to chant.

The next instant, Rachel was back in the woods with Rita and Nakisha. But the chanting was still coming from her own throat. "*Om Mani Padme Hum,*" She chanted over and over. The air itself seemed changed, vibrating and glowing. Cradled by the lullaby of sound, they all fell into its rhythm, repeating Rachel's words until they were in sync. She had no idea where the chant had come from, but it was as familiar to her as the prayers she had learned in church, " *The Lord is my Shepard...*the prayers of her mother and father, *"Baruch atah Adonai eloheinu melech ha-alom..."* Then more chants came.

> "*Om Asato Maa Sad-Gamaya... Tamaso Maa Jyotir-Gamaya... Mrtyor-Maa Amrtam Gamaya... Om Shaantih Shaantih Shaantih...*
>
> *Uchu no mugen no chikara ga kori kotte makoto no daiwa no miyo ga nari natta..."*

The chants changed, going from one language to the next, over and over.

When the three opened their eyes again, they were astonished to find themselves deep in the forest near a group of massive red-wood trees. The giant trees stood in an imperfect circle, collectively towering over a soft hollow of ground at their base, filled with rust-colored dry redwood needles, small cones and twigs. The women moved in unison toward the middle, a force drawing them to the center of this circular grove. As they approached, Rachel sensed something. She reached out signaling to the others. Hovering at the edge, they hesitated.

Rita and Nakisha felt it too. Like the smell of danger—fear, caution was coming from the trees themselves. The trees seemed alive and afraid of them, like an animal might be.

Humbled by the depth of feeling, Rita's instinct was to compassionately comfort them. She softened her gaze and slowed her steps. She spoke to the trees in a calm voice like speaking to a child.

"Don't be afraid. We love you," she whispered sensing something had happened here. She looked closely, inspecting each tree. She could see the burnt bark, the scars. Had someone caused them harm on purpose—had someone set them on fire? Had something traumatic taken place here, been witnessed here ?

Just then Rachel heard singing. But she wasn't singing or chanting herself. It was an echo, coming from what seemed like the tree tops, from the high branches. Offering solace, she moved into the circle and opened her arms wide. Looking up into the tall tree limbs she sang back to them, the majestic ones, tears flowing down her cheeks.

Rita and Nakisha followed her into the circle. Rita put a loving hand on one of the trees. She heard an audible sigh of relief, as clear as day. Nakisha heard it too. She put her arms out, hugging one of the massive trees.

After a long silent meditation in the grove, Rachel walked toward the edge of the circle. "I think we should head back. It's getting dark."

Rita pulled her watch from her back pack. "Wow, we've been here a while. It's almost five o'clock."

Awe-inspired by their exploration and with a sense of wonder at their sacred experience, the three woman began their journey back. Or so they thought. They followed what they believed to be the path back to the road, to the car.

"This doesn't look familiar." Nakisha was the first to notice. "Look, there's water over there."

The three moved carefully through the ferns beneath some young redwoods. A lake opened up to view. The sky was turning a deep turquoise and a full moon was rising, casting diamonds on the water. Rachel recognized the plants growing along the edge of the water. "Wow, this is beautiful," she said, a sense of both wonder and fear taking hold of her. "But I think we better get out of here before nightfall."

"Let's retrace our steps back to the grove of singing trees." Nakisha offered. "We can look for the path we originally came on from there."

They didn't have to walk very far to come to what resembled the grove. But it was not the grove of singing redwoods. Beyond a large boulder, a thicket of old oaks sprung up before them. A light emanated through the dusk from the center of the trees.

"Something, someone is over there..." Nakisha's voice was barely audible.

They moved closer and peered through the thick mane of tree trunks. A green light cast shadows along the spines of trees and branches. A smattering of what seemed like glitter illuminated the branches above the light. They moved closer. Then they saw her.

A woman-like figure with viridian green skin sat in the middle of the forest on a tall moss-covered tree stump. She was adorned in sheer fabric and a large cape of what appeared to be green velvet with gold trim. She held a crystal-topped spear in one hand and a clear glowing orb of light in the other. On her head was an unusual three pointed crown each point ending in a small golden sphere.

None of them breathed. Entranced, their entire bodies vibrated. They felt light, as if a breath of wind could blow them away.

Instead a sudden breeze blew them to Her. She seemed almost human, familiar to each of them—someone they knew, but could not place from where. It was a feeling of home, of belonging, of overwhelming peace. It was as if they had been holding their breath a lifetime, when finally She spoke. It was not a language any of them knew, but each understood Her nevertheless.

"Souls of my soul, we are one," they heard, although they did not see Her mouth move. Rachel reached forward to touch Her hand, to see if She was real. Rachel could not tell if it was a figment of her imagination. It was like touching air.

"Viridian," Rita said, somehow knowing Her name. Rita's eyes gleamed recognizing her painting, *Green Queen of the Enchanted Forest,* come to life. She remembered the words she had heard while painting. *"Shift into the lightness of being."* Suddenly, Rita floated above the forest floor. She looked down at the trees from above. She could see the surrounding mountains and a lake moving further away as she drifted toward the clouds. Before long, she was out in space in the quiet darkness among the stars, attached to a small silver thread--the only connection between herself and earth. She felt both at peace and ecstatic at the same time. She heard drums and chanting even though she could not see anyone. But oddly she did not feel alone or afraid. Rita felt at peace and happy. All of the sudden she was laughing. "It's all a joke," she said aloud. Then she began to sing herself. *"Row, row, row, your boat gently down the stream. Merrily, merrily, merrily, merrily—life is but a dream."*

Rachel looked into the green woman's crystal clear Orb. An image of a young girl materialized. She was emaciated and wet, being carried in an old man's arms. Rachel watched as if seeing a movie—the child was patted dry, wrapped in blankets, comforted by an old woman and given hot broth. The images sped up a thousand fold, until she could not consciously absorb it all. Yet she knew her cells were triggered, remembering every nuance and detail of that life and every other life she had lived, every being she had once been. The movie stopped abruptly and Rachel found herself at the back of a room glowing in green light. A tall dark-skinned androgynous figure stood at a lectern speaking, disseminating images from her third eye and breastplate into the room above a gathering of what she sensed were her students.

Nakisha meanwhile stared transfixed, seeing her own reflection in the glorious green being's eyes, feeling exalted to be privy to the miracle unfolding before her. She saw herself walking down a path filled with people from every culture, place, and time. Soon, she was standing in front of the great pyramid at Giza. Then she was in a great lecture hall, speaking to a huge audience of dignitaries from different countries. A screen on the ceiling emanated pictures of experimental environmental scenarios for cleaning the world's oceans, lakes and rivers. She heard chanting. *"Uchu no mugen no chikara ga kori kotte makoto no daiwa no miyo ga nari natta."* In what seemed like seconds, she was back in the forest staring into the orb.

Viridian brought each one back to Her. She held her glowing ball close to each of them, until they could see the image of a very tall being in turquoise and gold. Waving her arms, ribbons of color and light enveloped them as she telepathically communicated. "Your Oversoul is here to give you back memory, to fine tune your celestial birthright to its full potential. Your responsibility is to help birth the shift in evolution to bring about a new world of peace and harmony..."

Then the image evaporated as quickly as it had appeared. But long enough for Rita to recognize *Emari*, the ethereal extraterrestrial being in her painting.

Viridian stood up and waved her crystal spear drawing symbols in the air. The forest disappeared and it its place was a land of death and destruction. The three women spun around terrified. There was nothing in sight but dead trees, animals and a blackened sky. The lake had a dark oily sheen.

Telepathically Viridian beckoned them to chant. She raised her clear crystal orb toward the sky and bright green light emanated in all directions as far as the eye could see. The women chanted over and over, louder and louder until every minute cell in their bodies was electrified with energy, pulsing and vibrating. Their feet left the ground and they floated, their very molecules disintegrating into the air.

Then just as quickly they were standing again in the beautiful vibrant forest. Everything was as it had been, except Viridian was only a shadow—her face appearing huge beyond the tree trunks, then disappearing altogether. All that remained were glittering remnants of the hieroglyphics that she had drawn with her septor. Within moments they too evaporated.

The next thing they knew, they were back at the diner. Rita and Nakisha sat in a booth. They looked around disoriented, as if waking from a dream. "I think I need some more Cola." Nakisha said looking down at a half eaten sandwich, she did not remember ordering.

Just then Rachel returned from the bathroom. "Sorry I took so long," she said. "I was feeling so strange, like I didn't recognize myself, like I was someone else almost," she said shaking her head. "I'm fine now. And hungry, still. I could go for a piece of pie with my cup of tea."

"Me too! Maybe some pie ala mode!" Rita's eyes shone.

"Yeah," Nakisha agreed.

"Couldn't help overhearing you gals' plans for hiking to the old growth forest." The waitress interrupted, returning to see if they needed anything more. "I would be careful which road you take after the bridge. There are bears and mountain lions up in some of those remote areas—some bears won't be hibernating yet." The waitress smiled at them, her previous cool demeanor replaced by warmth. "Will you be having any dessert, ladies?"

Rita laughed, trying to get her head around the time warp. "Didn't you mention about the bridge and bears once already?"

The waitress smiled again. Her eyes twinkled as she took out the receipt pad from her green apron. Cherry pie or apple, gals?"

she asked as if she could read their minds. They each ordered a piece of pie. The waitress finished up the tab and placed it on the table.

"How much will I owe?" Nakisha asked taking out her wallet.

Rachel looked down at the tab then at up at Rita and Nakisha. A grin spread across Rachel's face. "Check out the receipt," she chuckled.

The two looked down at the diner's name on the printed tab. **New Earth Diner** in dark green letters stared back. The receipt listed the food and drinks they had ordered, but no charges.

"It's on the house!" the waitress declared with a big smile, appearing instantaneously with slices of pie. She picked up the menus. "Some elderly folks were in a while ago--two men and a woman. They said you'd be coming in," she winkled. "You're here to save the planet, right?"

Source Note and Author's Note

Souls of Viridian, while fiction, has within it some information that is factual. I am referring to the reference of *The Voynich Manuscript* which is a real document. According to Yale University Library website it was...*discovered in Europe in 1912 and named after the Polish-American antiquarian bookseller, Wilfred M. Voynich, who purchased the manuscript from the Jesuit College at Frascati near Rome. In 1969, the codex was given to Yale University's Beinecke Rare Book & Manuscript Library by H. P. Kraus, who had purchased it from the estate of Ethel Voynich, Wilfred Voynich's widow.* *

The Voynich Manuscript is estimated to have been written in the 15th century. In 2018, a publisher in Spain received permission to make copies for publication. To date however, no one has deciphered the language in which the manuscript is written, although many scholars and decoders have tried, including international teams of language experts.

Although I am not a scholar, I downloaded the manuscript a few years ago and studied it, finding it, solely by the many drawings alone, to be a women's herbal. I perceived it to be the work of someone who knew and lived by seasonal changes, planting cycles and astrological implications, among other things. Not only that, I thought I recognized the cleansing rituals depicted in the manuscript as similar to what is known as *Mikvote*— women's ritual bathing, historically done after menses by religious Jewish women. I am not alone in this assumption. In 2018, others, particularly male scholars, have conceived of this manuscript as written by a Jewish physician (which would have been a man, since women were not allowed to be called *physicians,* just midwives—no matter their knowledge.)

While the language of the manuscript remains perhaps a combination of languages yet to be decoded, I have used my knowledge of history, specifically the horrific treatment of women healers in medieval Europe, specifically the 13th to 15th century, as well as the pervasiven antisemitism of the time, to contribute a feminist perspective to the prevailing theories, in creating this fictitious story.

---

*https://beinecke.library.yale.edu/collections/highlights/voynich-manuscript

About the Author

Ayin Weaver was born in New York City and began her career as a fine artist and medical illustrator. After twenty years in the art field, she became an educator, devoting much of her energy to developing a language arts curriculum using art and storytelling as a basis for teaching writing and reading to students with learning disabilities.

Spirituality and a life-long commitment to issues of human rights, peace, and environmental protection influence her personal writing and art. Using her love of history and storytelling, she creates characters who challenge the fear that promotes prejudice, while championing civil rights for women, minorities and the LGBT community.

Ms. Weaver lives in California, where she teaches art, and writes fiction and poetry. She is a member of the International Women's Writing Guild, and Redwood Writers, a chapter of California Writer's Club. *Souls of Viridian* is her second novel. Her first novel, *Bleed Through,* was published in 2013. Both are available on amazon.com.